CUT THROAT

SHARON SALA

THORNDIKE
CHIVERS

This Large Print edition is published by Thorndike Press, Waterville, Maine, USA and by BBC Audiobooks Ltd, Bath, England.
Thorndike Press, a part of Gale, Cengage Learning.

The text of this Large Print edition is unabridged.
Other aspects of the book may vary from the original edition.
Set in 16 pt. Plantin.
Printed on permanent paper.

LIBRARY OF CONGRESS CATALOGING-IN-PUBLICATION DATA

Sala, Sharon.
  Cut throat / by Sharon Sala.
    p. cm. — (Thorndike Press large print basic)
  Sequel to: Nine lives.
  ISBN-13: 978-1-4104-0556-2 (alk. paper)
  ISBN-10: 1-4104-0556-7 (alk. paper)
  1. Women bounty hunters — Fiction. 2. Revenge — Fiction.
  3. Mexico — Fiction. 4. Large type books. I. Title.
  PS3569.A4565C87 2008
  813'.54—dc22   2007049231

BRITISH LIBRARY CATALOGUING-IN-PUBLICATION DATA AVAILABLE
Published in 2008 in the U.S. by arrangement with Harlequin Books S.A.
Published in 2008 in the U.K. by arrangement with Harlequin Enterprises II B.V.
U.K. Hardcover: 978 1 405 64502 7 (Chivers Large Print)
U.K. Softcover: 978 1 405 64503 4 (Camden Large Print)

Printed in the United States of America
1 2 3 4 5 6 7 12 11 10 09 08

At this writing, it is almost the end of 2006, and my mother, at age eighty-six, is still with me. We are together again, under one roof as we first began, only the roles have been reversed.

Today I care for her, and I can say with wholehearted honesty that it is my blessing to be able to do so.

She taught me everything I know in this life that is good and right. She is always behind me, backing up my decisions, comforting me as I meet each test life dumps at my feet.

I am one of the blessed ones, and I know it.

I never had a moment of doubt in my life that she didn't love me, or that she would somehow let me down.

It is through her faith that I have grown to be the woman I am today — a woman centered in life, a woman confident that, no matter what, I will survive what life gives me and, in the end, overcome.

It is with great honor that I dedicate this book about strong women to the strongest woman in my life — my mother, my friend.

To Iris Shero Smith.

PROLOGUE

Nuevo Laredo, Mexico

Gunfire echoed through the empty rooms of the abandoned house, making it seem as if a dozen shooters were involved, not just the two men who were exchanging fire in what had once been a luxurious den.

Suddenly a bullet slammed through an old, rusty barrel near the brick wall of the fire place, igniting the few inches of gas still inside. Bounty hunter Wilson McKay saw the flash of ignition a second before the room went up in flames. He was on his feet and running when the blast from the explosion threw him out the door and onto his knees. He got up quickly and kept on running.

Solomon Tutuola was already ducking for cover when the room exploded. The force of the explosion threw him through a pair of windows at the south end of the house and out onto the ground.

One moment he and Mark Presley had been in a run-and-gun fight with some tall, spiky-haired guy with an earring in his ear, and the next thing he knew, the house in which they had been hiding went up in smoke.

For a few seconds Tutuola lay face up outside, staring into the sun, all but immobile from the force of the blast. He drew a shallow breath, then another and another. Suddenly a white-hot shaft of searing pain brought him to a sitting position as shock subsided and agony took its place. Groaning and shaking from the shock waves, he rolled over onto his hands and knees, and began crawling away from the burning house, dodging fiery debris, convinced that the skin was melting off his face. He passed out about a hundred yards from the house, unaware that Mark Presley, the man he'd chauffeured into Mexico, had been captured and the two bounty hunters who'd come after him were long gone.

When Solomon came to, hours later, it was late afternoon and he was in more misery than he'd ever felt in his life. He heard the soft sounds of a four-legged animal trotting around his head, then his feet. He opened his eyes, horrified to find a coyote nosing at his heels, while a trio of buzzards circled overhead.

The roar that came out of his throat sent the coyote packing. Solomon staggered to his feet, then turned around, staring first at the smoldering embers of the hacienda, then down at his hands. Blisters had formed on the burns, then burst, mixing with the dirt on which he'd been lying. His entire body was shaking from the intensity of his pain. It wasn't until he tried to blink that he realized he couldn't see out of his left eye, and when he lifted his fingers to that side of his face, he screamed.

"Son of a bitch!"

The flesh that came away at his touch was blackened and bloody, and there was a part of his head that was completely devoid of hair. As best he could tell, the entire left side of his face and head had been seriously burned. He needed to get to a doctor, and fast. If he didn't die from the pain, he was damn sure going to die from infection.

Cursing and screaming with every step he took, Solomon made it to his car. The keys were still in the ignition, and Mark Presley's luggage — a large duffle bag and a wheeled overnighter — was still on the backseat.

Without wasting time wondering what had happened to Mark, he started the car and headed for Nuevo Laredo.

By nightfall, he was in the hospital, under sedation. The bags were locked in the trunk of his car. His car keys were in his burned pants, hanging in the tiny closet with what was left of the shirt he'd been wearing. Every few minutes, a nurse came into his room, checked the saline solution laced with morphine being pumped into his body, making sure that he wasn't losing more fluids than were being replaced. For all intents and purposes, Solomon Tutuola was teetering on the verge of death.

ONE

Six weeks later: Dallas, Texas

The faint cry of her neighbor's new baby was barely audible from where bounty hunter Cat Dupree was sitting in her apartment, and yet, for some reason, it was all she could hear. She'd blocked out the thunder of her own heartbeat and was ignoring the sick, helpless feeling that had taken root in the pit of her stomach. Her entire focus was on the wanted posters plastered over the walls of her office — that and the baby's continuous wail.

Her laptop was sitting on top of a file cabinet by the door. The GPS program that was running showed a map of Mexico and a blip that, for the past thirty-six hours, had continued to move steadily westward. It was her worst nightmare come to life, yet she chose to ignore it for the faces on the wanted posters.

After all these years, the faces were as

familiar to her as her own, and yet none of them matched the face of the man who, since childhood, had haunted her dreams. The man who had killed her father and left a six-inch scar along the base of her throat. The same man she'd seen only a few weeks ago and had been certain — so certain — was finally dead. She glanced back at the laptop and winced. Now she wasn't so sure.

Wind rattled the windowpanes behind her, signaling the oncoming storm heading for Dallas. Rain was imminent, but the temperature was in the high thirties, which meant no accompanying ice or snow. After the ice storm they'd endured during Christmas, a simple rainstorm was welcome news. As the wind gusted again, she shivered, then folded her arms across her chest and hunched her shoulders, thankful for the central heating in her apartment. As she did, her focus shifted to the wanted poster tacked above the doorway.

The poster of Justin "Mad Dog" Bailey was the first she'd hung more than fifteen years ago. He'd been singled out as worthy of posting for the simple fact that he had tattoos all over his face and body, one of the identifying features of her father's killer. She'd known immediately that he wasn't the man she was looking for, but she'd had to start somewhere, so she'd tacked him up. She tunneled her fingers through her hair. Her head ached, and the muscles in her neck and back were miserably tight, but that was of no importance to her. It was revenge that had driven her to where she was in life, and it was revenge she needed. Her gaze slid to the next poster.

Edward John Forrest. Edward was too young to have committed the attack on her family, but she'd felt compelled to hang his booking photos anyway, and so it had begun. Over the years, she'd acquired an impressive collection.

As she stood, she realized the neighbor's baby had quit crying. Either someone had poked a bottle in its mouth, or it had finally given up and fallen asleep. The silence was oddly uncomfortable. Now there was nothing to sidetrack her awareness of that damned laptop and the map on its screen.

Frustrated by her lack of willpower, Cat glanced up again, squinting slightly as the light glared on the monitor, blurring the geography through which the blip continued to move. Even though she couldn't see it clearly, she knew it well.

It was Mexico — the place where she'd run her best friend's killer to ground.

She glanced back at the wanted posters all

over her office walls. After Mexico, they were redundant, because there she'd come face-to-face with not only the man who'd killed her friend Marsha, but the tattooed man she'd spent half her life looking for. His name was Solomon Tutuola, and while, for the third time in her life, she had unexpectedly lived to see another day, she had been under the assumption that Tutuola had not. Then this damned blip had resurfaced, taunting her with the possibility that her assumption had been wrong.

Feeling defeated, she moved slowly toward the doorway, then paused under Mad Dog's poster and reached up. The paper crackled as she slipped a fingernail beneath the edge. For some reason she hesitated, discovering it was more difficult to remove than it had been to put up.

Finally she pulled it down and dropped it into the trash, then reached for another one. One by one, she pulled them down, until the walls were completely bare and the trash can was full to overflowing. She emptied it, then began dumping the stacks of posters on the floor into another bag.

Almost an hour passed before the task was finished, and then she finally allowed herself another look at the laptop. The blip was motionless. Whoever was carrying the bugged property that was showing hot on the laptop had stopped for the night.

She grimaced. The bastard was getting more rest than she was. Frustrated, she looked back at the filled trash bags littering the floor and sighed. Those images had been such a part of her life, it seemed strange that she didn't need them anymore.

Last month she'd finally put a name to the face of the man who'd killed her father.

Last month she'd watched the house he'd been in blow up and then burn.

Last month she'd been certain he was dead.

Now she wasn't so sure.

The motionless blip was like a taunt — a "come and find me if you can" dare that she couldn't ignore.

Cat sighed. It was time to see if the devil was dead, or if — as she feared — he'd resurrected himself. But before she absented herself from Dallas again, she had to tell her boss, Art Ball. Just because she had an agenda, that didn't mean he could put his bail-bond business on hold for her. There would always be bail jumpers to find. She just wasn't going to be the one doing it for him — at least not for a while.

And then there was Wilson McKay. She wasn't sure what she was going to do about him. She refused to admit that he deserved any kind of explanation of what she was up to. Just because they'd had sex — unbelievable sex — didn't mean she owed him anything. And just because he'd helped her bring in Mark Presley, the man who'd killed Marsha Benton, that didn't mean she had to keep him updated on the rest of her life.

Part of her wanted to blame Wilson for this uncertainty. When the house where Presley and Tutuola had been hiding out down in Mexico caught on fire, she'd captured Presley, then wanted to go back to make sure Tutuola was dead.

But Wilson had stopped her.

The fact that she would most likely have died if she'd gone back into the burning house was beside the point. When she was being honest with herself, she knew there was no one to blame. But she couldn't live with herself until she knew for sure if her father's killer had survived.

Tomorrow she would call Art and then head south to the border. She had to know who was behind that blip. If it was some Mexican local who'd come across some of Mark Presley's bugged property, then so be it. But if it was Tutuola, then her job still wasn't done. As much as she dreaded another long road trip, she was satisfied with her decision. Within moments, Cat walked out of her office and headed for her bedroom to pack.

It had been almost a week since Wilson McKay had seen Cat. When he was rational, he told himself to just let her go. It was obvious she didn't want anything from him except the occasional round of sex. He should have been happy to just take what she gave out with a thank you and a pat on her butt. Any other woman and he would have. But not her. She'd gotten under his skin in a way no other woman had done and, despite everything he believed in and every instinct he had that told him to let her go, he just couldn't — which explained why he was on his way to her apartment unannounced, with a pizza and a six-pack of beer.

Traffic was heavy on the bypass, but nothing out of the ordinary for Dallas on a rainy Saturday night. The smell of pepperoni wafted under Wilson's nose as he took the exit leading to Cat's apartment building, while the constant sweep of windshield wipers kept the view clear. His radio was tuned to a country station — its style matched his mood and the dark and stormy weather. He needed a Cat fix — at the least, a long session of kissing and cuddling, at the most, a long night with the wildcat in his arms. Just the thought of how it felt to bury himself deep inside her made him ache with want. She was a handful between the sheets, always giving back as good as she got. He had yet to understand how a woman with that much passion in bed managed to stay so cold and distant from everyone she knew. He suspected it had to do with all she'd endured at such a young age, and because of that, he just wasn't willing to give up on her — yet.

The glow of headlights from the heavy flow of traffic was refracted by the rain, while the constant swish of wipers gave the night streets a garish appearance. Wilson thought of the comfort waiting for him inside Cat's cozy apartment and refused to consider the fact that her welcome might not be as warm.

When he pulled into the parking lot and circled her building in search of a space, he couldn't help but notice that the lights were on in her apartment. Now it came down to the crunch. She was home, but would she welcome him in or send him packing with a sharp word and a glare from her cold, blue eyes?

He parked, grabbed the pizza and beer,

and headed for the door. He would know soon enough how warm his welcome would be.

Cat was on her hands and knees in the back of her closet, searching for the matching boot to the one already sitting next to her suitcase, when she thought she heard the doorbell ring. Frowning, she rocked back on her heels and listened again.

There!

This time she heard the chimes clearly and frowned.

"Who in the —"

Wilson.

She knew without a doubt that it was Wilson McKay. He was the only person who visited her and the only one she knew who would come without calling. Probably because he figured she wouldn't answer the door if she knew he was coming, and she almost didn't answer it now. Despite her instincts telling her to leave him standing there, she headed for the living room, hating herself for the spurt of excitement she was feeling. She didn't really have time for this, but ignoring him might raise more suspicion than if she just let him in and got it over with. At least, that was what she was telling herself as she reached the front door.

A quick peek through the peephole was all she needed to see that her guess had been right. It was Wilson — and to her disgust, the sight of him made her pulse skip.

"Hey," she said, as she opened the door.

Wilson breathed a sigh of relief. She was in a good mood.

"Hey, yourself," he said, and before she could dodge him, he leaned in and kissed her square on the mouth.

Her eyes were flashing as he pulled back. He couldn't tell if she was pissed or enjoying the passion he'd put in the kiss.

"Have you eaten?" he asked, offering the pizza.

Cat inhaled deeply, surprised by the hunger pangs she was feeling.

"No, and for that reason *only,* you can come in," she said, then lifted the pizza box from his hands and headed to the kitchen, knowing he would follow.

"I should have called," Wilson said, as he set the six-pack of beer on the kitchen counter.

Cat set the pizza box down and turned to face him.

"Why didn't you?"

He shrugged. Truth had served him well thus far in life. He figured he might as well continue the process.

"I figured you would tell me no."

Cat frowned. She hadn't expected his honesty. Now she had no choice but to respond in kind.

"You would have been right," she said.

Despite a stab of regret, he grinned and shrugged.

"So I saved us both some guilt and anxiety. Do you want your beer in a glass or straight from the can?"

Cat thought of the trip she was about to make and decided against anything alcoholic. Without answering, she handed him a glass, then filled one for herself with ice and Pepsi and laid out two plates.

Wilson reached for the roll of paper towels. He tore off a couple of sheets to use as napkins and then got a shaker of red-pepper flakes from the cabinet where she kept her spices.

Cat was torn between admiring his good looks and being a bit intrigued with the tiny gold hoop earring he wore in his left ear. As usual, his hair was a style in progress. He wore it in a buzz cut that always seemed to be a week past needing a trim. There was a small scar beneath his right eye and enough of a bump on his nose to know it had been broken more than once. His shoulders were broad, his legs long and muscular, his belly hard and flat.

Cat was well aware of how fit he was beneath the denim and leather, and was thinking of what would come later — after pizza and beer. She wouldn't lie to herself and pretend she didn't want him, because she did. They would have sex. Wilson McKay was damn good at it, and she wasn't a fool. No sane, single, red-blooded woman would turn down a roll in the hay with someone who exuded sex appeal like Wilson McKay. But the moment she thought of having sex with him, she remembered the half-filled suitcase and the chaos in her bedroom.

Shit.

"Uh . . . Wilson . . . go ahead and sit down. I'll be right back."

She flew out of the kitchen and down the hall without looking back. When she got to her bedroom, she stuffed things back in drawers, tossed others in the bottom of her closet and shoved the half-filled suitcase under her bed. She gave the bedspread a couple of brief yanks to smooth out the wrinkles and then went back to the kitchen.

Wilson was standing right where she'd left him with a curious expression on his face.

"Are you all right?" he asked.

"Who? Me? Yes . . . I'm fine," she muttered, and then pasted a big smile on her face, grabbed a piece of pizza from the box and took a big bite. "Yum."

Wilson arched an eyebrow.

"Yum?"

"Have some," she said, and pointed to the box.

Wilson knew something was going on, but it was obvious she wasn't going to talk about it. Finally he stifled his curiosity and sat down, picked up a piece of pizza and took a bite. He chewed, then swallowed.

"Yeah, you're right," he said, and toasted her with the slice. "Yum back at'cha," he said as he took another bite.

Cat grinned inspite of herself. When Wilson McKay wanted to, he could be intriguing — even endearing. Still, there were rules in her world he kept trying to break.

They finished the pizza without serious conversation, but when they began cleaning up, Wilson excused himself briefly to go to the bathroom. It wasn't until he was coming back down the hallway that he happened to glance into her office and saw the bare walls.

Shocked, he stopped, then stepped inside.

He'd seen the office as it had been before, the walls papered with wanted posters. Now there was nothing left but nude walls peppered with pinholes, and he knew what that meant. Through an odd stroke of fate, in running down her best friend's killer, she'd found another, as well. He thought of the walls Cat Dupree kept up between her and the world, and wondered how much thinner they were tonight with the absence of those posters.

The banging of a cabinet door reminded him where he was, and he knew that Cat would view his curiosity as meddling. He slipped out of her office as quickly as he'd entered.

"Did I stay gone long enough to avoid doing dishes?" he asked, as he sauntered back into the kitchen.

Cat arched an eyebrow. "Yes."

"Good," he said, and slipped a hand around her waist and pulled her close.

As their bodies connected, Cat sighed.

Now it began.

She turned until they were facing each other. "I suppose you think we're going to have sex."

Wilson's eyebrow arched as a muscle suddenly jerked near the right corner of his mouth.

"I don't have sex with you."

Cat's eyes narrowed sharply. "Damn it, Wilson, don't play word games about —"

He put a finger on her lips. "I make love to you, Catherine."

She slapped his hand away. "While I, on the other hand, have sex."

"Semantics," he muttered, then fisted his hand in her hair and pulled gently, tilting her lips to his mouth.

She felt his anger as she slid her arms around his neck; then the kiss deepened, and his anger morphed into lust. That, she could follow.

A low moan slipped up her throat, but when it emerged, it sounded more like a growl.

"Damn you," Wilson whispered, and cupped her backside. "Grab hold, or I swear to God that the sex you have with me is going to happen right where we're standing, with your pants down around your ankles."

Cat jumped, wrapped her legs around his waist and slammed her mouth against his. She moaned again, but this time because she tasted blood — her own.

Wilson pivoted with her held tight in his arms and strode down the hallway to her bedroom.

"You make me crazy," he muttered, as he dropped her flat on her bed.

"Shut up and take off your clothes," Cat said, as she sat up and began undressing.

Wilson's eyes narrowed angrily. First she didn't want him here, and now he wasn't getting to her fast enough? If he had a functioning brain, he would turn around and leave her naked and wanting. But the thought left his mind as she sat up, pulled her sweater up over her head and tossed it on the floor.

He grunted. *To hell with pride and dignity.*

Within seconds, his clothes were in a pile on the floor and he was standing at the side of the bed.

Cat rolled over onto her hands and knees and crawled over to him, then rose up and wrapped her arms around his neck.

Wilson tunneled his fingers through her hair, then put his arms around her.

"Witch," he said roughly.

Cat sighed. She loved the feel of him — the hard muscles beneath smooth, warm skin — and she loved the way he made *her* feel. But she wasn't going to admit — ever — that she loved the man himself. She locked her fingers around the back of his neck and pulled until she fell backward, pinned to the mattress beneath the weight of his body. At that point she wrapped her legs around his waist again, and this time, she held on.

"So I'm a witch now?"

"Hell, yes," Wilson said, as he stared down at her, ever conscious of what awaited him in her bed.

"Then . . . hocus-pocus, Wilson. Time to disappear."

He grabbed both her wrists, pinned her arms above her head, then thrust into her without warning, taking satisfaction in the shock, then desire, he saw on her face.

"No more you. No more me. Just us. How's that for a little magic?"

"Doesn't feel so little to me," Cat murmured, and rocked upward.

Wilson gritted his teeth and stifled a groan, then gave back as good as he got. He drove into her without tact or finesse, and took her to a climax so hard and fast that she choked on a scream.

Cat felt as if every bone in her body had just crumbled to dust. She had never — never in her life — been satisfied so completely in such a hit-and-run fashion.

"Oh, man . . . oh, Wilson . . . that was . . . that was . . ."

"That was for you," Wilson said. "That was sex."

He cupped her face with both hands, lowered his head and brushed his lips across her mouth.

Cat inhaled softly.

He swept his lips down the side of her neck, then kissed the valley between her breasts before circling her nipple with the tip of his tongue.

Still reeling from the aftershocks of her climax, Cat was shaken by the sudden urgency she felt to have more.

"Wilson . . . I —"

"Shh," he said, and then lifted his head and stared down into her eyes. "You wanted sex. I gave it to you. Now this time is for me. This is what it means to make love."

Before she could answer, he covered her mouth again, stealing the breath from her body and the good sense from her soul. She would have panicked over what he'd just told her, but he left her no time to think — only feel.

He didn't leave an inch of her skin untouched as he moved across her body with his hands and his lips. Twice Cat tried to take control of the situation by urging him to take her, and twice he refused with a soft whisper, then a sigh.

"Uh-uh," he said, and slid his hands beneath her hips and lowered his head.

When he began circling her navel with his tongue, her heart rate accelerated. But when she felt the tip of his tongue sliding down her belly to the juncture of her thighs, she moaned. This was an intimacy involving trust — something she had never had with a sexual partner, something she had never allowed.

Even though she refused to admit there was more between them than a mutual appreciation for sex, she did know he wouldn't hurt her.

Her muscles began to quiver as the pressure began to build.

"Oh . . . oh, God, Wilson . . ."

Wilson had intended this as a means of showing Cat the difference between lust and intimacy, but the urgency in her voice and the way her body was trembling was like a drug he couldn't quit.

Suddenly he felt the muscles in her body winding up, tightening and tightening toward the inevitable climax. It was the sign he'd been waiting for. He rose up, then slid over and into her body.

The sensation was shattering, and it was only beginning. He took her slowly, burying himself deep, then pausing to savor the sensation. Then Cat moaned, and the sound pushed him over the edge. He rode the feeling as long as he could, and when the orgasm hit, he went with her, coming undone in her arms. When it was over, he lay spent and shaking, unable to move.

A short while later, he glanced over at the windows. Raindrops glittered on the outside of the glass, but it appeared that the storm was over.

Cat moved.

He thought he heard a soft sigh, but then she rolled off him and got out of bed.

"Do you want some coffee before you go?"

His eyes narrowed. His nostrils flared. He sat up and then swung his legs over the side of the bed, staring at her in disbelief.

"Before I go?"

Cat glanced at him, then looked away, well aware of how this sounded, but it was his own damn fault. He was pushing her into corners where she didn't want to go.

Wilson stood, towering over her as he paused at the foot of the bed. Then he grabbed his clothes and started putting them on as quickly as he'd torn them off.

"Hell no, I don't want any coffee, Catherine. I couldn't possibly want anything more from you other than the fucking we just had."

The word was rude, but no ruder than she'd been with him.

"Okay, then," she said, and turned and walked into the bathroom.

When she came out, she paused in the middle of her bedroom, listening to the silence, and knew he was gone. But when she glanced toward the bed, her heart slammed against her chest with a hard, painful thud. She stared until her vision blurred and her throat was thick with tears. Taking a deep breath, she leaned over and picked up the money he'd thrown on her mattress.

A hundred dollars — in twenties.

She didn't know what the going rate for a whore might be, but he'd made his point.

"Damn you," she muttered, then drew a slow, shuddering breath, refusing to admit that he'd gotten to her.

Angry with herself, she threw the money into a drawer and then dragged her suitcase from under the bed and finished packing. Her steps were slow as she headed for her office to check her laptop. The blip was motionless, which was good, but according to the map on the screen, it was in the middle of nowhere.

Too tired and too hurt to think about it anymore tonight, she shut the laptop and took it back to her room. Within minutes, she was in bed, with the alarm set for six o'clock. She closed her eyes, trying desperately to sleep, but it was useless. She couldn't forget the hurt she'd seen on Wilson's face or the fact that she was the one who'd put it there. Then she rolled over on her side, thumped her pillow angrily and, with a skill she'd honed over years of disappointment and despair, blanked everything from her mind and went to sleep.

Two

Still reeling from Cat's rejection, Wilson went straight from her apartment to the office. By daybreak, he had a good lead on Paulie Beach, one of his bonds who'd failed to appear, and was packing to go get him. As always, he wore a bulletproof vest under his shirt and his badge on a chain around his neck. There was a can of mace in one pocket of his coat, a Taser in the other, a pair of handcuffs clipped onto the back of his belt and his handgun in a shoulder holster.

Beach had been arrested for B & E — breaking and entering — his third strike for the same offense. That should have been a warning to Wilson, when he'd agreed to bond him out, that Paulie wasn't the type of man who learned from his mistakes.

Wilson grabbed the file he had on Beach and was walking out of the office as his secretary, LaQueen Baldwin, was coming in.

LaQueen was six feet and two-hundred pounds of Jamaican beauty, and had an opinion about everything, including Wilson's single state. She had worked for him for four years, was the best secretary he'd ever had and reminded him of that fact on a daily basis.

Even though he never talked about his personal business, she knew all about his fascination with Cat Dupree. She knew when they'd been iced in together during Christmas and when he'd taken off to West Texas in the middle of the night to help Cat after she had discovered her best friend Marsha Benton's body. She knew when Wilson followed Cat Dupree to Mexico to aid her in catching Marsha's killer, and, after one look at his face this morning, she knew Wilson McKay was not in a good mood, and she promptly attributed it to Cat.

"Good morning to you," she said briskly, as he held the door back for her to enter.

"Yeah, it's a doozy," he muttered, as he pointed to her desk. "I left you a note."

LaQueen glanced toward her desk, then back at Wilson.

"Yes. I see that. However . . . since you are still here, and since I have arrived at this marvelous establishment to devote the next eight hours of my life to it and to you, you may tell me in person just where it is you might be going."

Wilson caught the tone of her voice and realized he'd pushed one of LaQueen's buttons, which figured. During the past twenty-four hours, he hadn't gotten much of anything right with women.

"Paulie Beach was a no-show at court a couple of days ago, and the phone numbers I had on him are disconnects. His mother's going to lose her house unless I can find the bastard. She cried for ten minutes before finally admitting she might know where he'd gone. I'm going to go get him."

LaQueen's lips parted into a smile. She nodded approvingly as she patted him on the arm.

"Ummm . . . that is good! You go find that sorry excuse for a son and lock him up. His momma hurt enough when she gave birth to him. She don't deserve to lose her home over the pain he's causing her now."

Wilson grinned in spite of himself. LaQueen did have a way with words.

"I'll do my best," he said. "Sorry if I was abrupt."

LaQueen arched an eyebrow. "So. Is that what they are calling it these days?"

Wilson's smile slipped. "Calling what?"

"You called it abrupt. I call it a bad night with a woman."

Wilson snorted lightly. "Am I that transparent?"

LaQueen frowned. His pride was damaged. She didn't intend to make it worse.

"If you might be going past a deli on your way back to the office, I would appreciate a bite of something sweet."

Wilson grinned in spite of himself. "A sweet for a sweet lady . . . hmm, yes, I think I can do that."

LaQueen nodded, then gave him a royal wave as she sailed past him toward her desk.

"Be off with you then. You're letting in the cold air."

Wilson's grin widened as he pushed the door shut, then headed for his SUV. She was maddening, but she really was the best damned secretary he'd ever had.

Paulie Beach was a user. He used people and drugs and situations to slide through life with as little effort as possible. For the second time in his life of crime, his mother had put her home up as collateral to bond him out of jail. Only this time, he'd skipped out on his court date, knowing full well that he would be on his way to prison again if he showed. It bothered him some that his mother was in a bind, but so was he. He couldn't afford to go back to lockup. He'd left too many enemies behind.

Wilson pulled around behind the Western Trails Motel and parked. According to Paulie's mother, who'd finally decided her son wasn't worth losing her home for, he'd called her from here the night before last. Wilson didn't know if he was still in residence, but he was going to find out soon enough.

He got out and headed for the office. The woman behind the counter glanced up as he walked in, then stood a little straighter when she got a better look.

"Need a room?" she asked, and fingered a loose bleached-yellow curl.

He flashed his badge. "I'm looking for Paulie Beach. Is he still in room 216?"

Her smile turned into a frown. "We're not supposed to give out —"

Wilson leaned across the counter. "Lady, the man I'm after is willing for his mother to lose her home rather than show his ass in court. I'm not in a very good mood, so don't start making excuses for your clientele. You and I both know most of them rent by the hour, so if you want me to notify some friends in vice that you're running a little something on the side, just say the word."

Her expression shifted to one of defiance, but she didn't mince words.

"Yeah, he's still in there, but if you bust somethin' up when you take him down, you're payin' for it."

"And by the same token, if you call and warn Paulie I'm coming up, I'll come after you for aiding and abetting a fugitive."

She blanched, then held up her hands and stepped back as Wilson left the office.

He quickly moved into the shadows of a stairwell, glancing up to the second-level balcony and the long row of motel-room doors. The cold air, mixed with the warmth of his exhaled breath, was marked by small, cloud-like vapors. Despite the chill, he could smell something rotting from a nearby garbage bin and wrinkled his nose in disgust.

As he started up the stairs, he saw the corner of a maid's cart and knew she was already on her rounds, cleaning rooms. He didn't think Paulie was armed, but he couldn't take a chance on getting an innocent person hurt. Once he reached the second level, he hurried down to the open doorway where the maid was cleaning and flashed his badge.

"Stay inside," he said quickly.

The woman's fear was evident as he closed the door between them, then hurried down to 216.

The curtains were pulled, and there was a thin layer of frost on the windows. He stood to the side of the door and listened, but heard nothing, no one moving around. Too cold to linger, Wilson knew there was only one way to rouse Beach and only one way out of the room.

Wilson made a fist and pounded on the door, but got no response. He pounded again, this time louder and longer.

"Get lost!" someone shouted from another room.

"Paulie! It's Wilson McKay. Get your ass out here now."

There was a long moment of silence; then Wilson heard foot steps hit the floor. He put his hands on his hips and stared at the curtains, knowing that Paulie would look out. When he saw the curtains move, he yelled again.

"Open the door, Paulie. You jumped bond on me. I've come to take you in."

Paulie Beach's expression was a mixture of surprise and anger as he stared at Wilson in disbelief.

"Like hell," he yelled, as he let the curtains

fall back in place.

It was all Wilson needed to see. Impatient and cold and ticked at the world in general, he kicked the door with a vicious blow. It flew inward, revealing Paulie in the act of pulling on his pants.

"Son of a bitch!" Paulie yelped, and bolted for the bathroom.

Wilson caught him by the back of the pants. "Shut your mouth," he said, as he grabbed the man by the arm and shoved him facedown on the bed.

He snapped on handcuffs and dragged him back up on his feet while Paulie cursed and argued.

Wilson wasn't in the mood to listen.

"Just shut up, Beach! You're one sorry bastard, you know that? What the hell were you thinking . . . pulling a no-show in court and putting your mother in danger of losing her house?"

"Piss off," Beach muttered.

Wilson grabbed Paulie's shirt, coat and shoes, and dragged him out the door.

"Hey! It's cold out here. Give me my shoes, damn it. You can't take me —"

"Yes, I can," Wilson said.

The little maid was peeking out past the door when Wilson dragged Paulie Beach out of the room and onto the landing.

"He's checking out," he told her, and then pulled Paulie down the metal stairs, taking satisfaction in the fact that the little bastard wasn't wearing any shoes.

He dropped Paulie off at the jail, spent a few minutes listening to the jailer talk about his first Christmas as a father and tried not to hate the man's guts. It wasn't the jailer's fault that Wilson's personal life was one big mess.

Then, as if fate wasn't through messing with him, he met Art Ball coming in as he was on the way out. All it did was remind him of the female bounty hunter who kept tearing a hole in his heart. Still, he managed to be cordial without making an ass of himself and asking about her. It wasn't Art's fault that Cat was a loner.

Once inside his truck, he jacked the heater up to high, taking comfort in the flow of warm air on his feet, and headed out of the parking lot.

Remembering his promise to LaQueen, he picked up a sack of doughnuts from a deli counter as he filled up with gas, then headed back to the office.

While Wilson was plying his secretary with doughnuts and coffee, Cat was pulling out of a drive-through ATM. She had three-hundred dollars cash in her pocket, a suitcase with several changes of clothes and a pair of tennis shoes, besides the boots she was wearing. There was a to-go cup of coffee in the cup holder on her dash and a small sack of fresh hot pretzels on the seat beside her. Every now and then she took a bite, savoring the crunch of salt between her teeth, as well as the warm, chewy bread.

The rain from last night had passed over, leaving gray but clear skies. The grass in the center median of the interstate was brown and soggy, and there were still a few puddles in the road indentations.

Her cell phone was in the seat beside her, but she'd turned it off. She didn't want to talk to anyone. The only person who knew what she was doing was Art, and only because she'd had to come clean with him to keep from getting fired. He hadn't been happy with her news, but he understood how Cat's mind worked. He had the number to her cell phone, and her promise that she would call him at least every other day, so he would know she was all right.

Once again, Cat was the predator, after her prey.

Solomon Tutuola was not the same man who'd driven Mark Presley into Mexico.

The burns on his face and neck had been serious and, though they were finally healing, they would leave scars. Most of the hair on the left side of his head was gone and, from the consensus of the last two doctors he'd seen, it wasn't going to grow back. There was a large portion of flesh underneath his chin and on the right side of his neck that had burned deep enough that the tattoos he'd had since his eighteenth birthday were gone. The healing flesh was red and tender, and the web-work of scarring was visible there, as well. The last two doctors he'd seen had recommended he be sent to Tulsa, Oklahoma, to their burn center. It was one of the finest in the country, and Solomon was in serious need of some rehabilitation. However, Solomon had his own reason for ignoring their advice, and he'd found it in Mark Presley's big duffle bag.

It was money.

One-hundred-dollar bills banded in five-thousand-dollar stacks — hundreds and hundreds of them. More money than he'd ever seen in his life. He'd given the bound bills a quick count, then quit counting after he'd gone past a million dollars.

Originally, when Presley had contacted him for a ride into Mexico, he'd had no idea why Presley was on the run, nor had it mattered. His focus had been on the money he was going to get for the job. But if he'd known Presley had been carrying this, he would have killed him outright, taken the money and saved himself a world of pain. He would also never have met up with that damned long-legged woman who'd been after Presley. She'd been like a bulldog. Every time they thought they'd lost her, she would reappear. He had no idea what her thing was with Presley, or what had happened to any of them after the explosion. For all he knew, the man who'd been shooting at him had burned up in the explosion, along with Presley and the woman. He certainly hoped so. He couldn't remember seeing any other vehicles when he'd come to and taken himself to the doctor, but it didn't mean one hadn't been there. He'd been so far gone that he could have driven past his own mother and not known it.

Then he'd found the money in Presley's luggage, and he'd begun to look at his misery and pain in a different light. There was enough here for him to retire, which was exactly what he intended to do.

For the last couple of days he'd been heading west, with no particular location in mind. It wasn't until yesterday evening that he'd realized he wasn't far from Agua Caliente, a tiny little village in the middle of nowhere. He'd been there before, years earlier, and had hooked up with a woman named Paloma Garcia. He didn't know if she was still there, but he was going to find out. He needed a place to rest up, and her hospitality would be just what the doctor ordered.

Today was Paloma Garcia's birthday. She had been born in her little house thirty-two years ago today. It was no surprise to anyone in Agua Caliente that she was no better off now than her parents had been when they were alive. No one there was.

She had no means of income other than the colorful serapes she wove and sold to her uncle, who periodically took them to Mazatlan during tourist season for resale.

She woke with no sense of anticipation as to what this day would bring other than that she was officially a year older and still unmarried. The man she'd been seeing had left town over a month ago for the border. She had no idea whether he'd made it into the United States or not. All she knew was that he was gone and she was, once again, alone. Her reputation in the little town had been colored by her careless lifestyle with too many men, and while she refused to consider herself a *puta,* most of the residents looked upon her as one.

She wet a cloth to wash the sleep from her face, then gave herself a sponge bath, bathing from the metal washbasin on a small table beneath her bedroom window. She dressed with no special care, choosing an old but comfortable red dress with colorful embroidery around the neck and sleeves. Her long black hair was her best feature. She enjoyed the heavy weight of it between her fingers as she made a braid, then tossed it over her shoulder. Her movements were slow and thoughtful as she walked through the tiny adobe house to the kitchen. With no electricity and no utilities, her cooking was done over a small fire that she built on the floor in the corner of the room. As she put some coffee on to boil, she laid a couple of tortillas she'd made yesterday onto a flat stone by the fire to reheat, then filled them with some leftover beans. She dipped the bean tortilla into a mole sauce between bites, and ate while considering what she would do today.

Her uncle had just picked up a dozen of her serapes last week, so there was no urgent rush to begin another. As she ate, she peered through a crack in the wooden shutters she had yet to open, judging the time by the height of the sun in the sky, and decided it was just after eight in the morning.

Today was not only her birthday but market day. Maybe she would treat herself to something special — maybe a melon — or maybe not. She didn't feel much like celebrating.

As she was finishing her meal, a knock sounded on her door. Frowning, she took a last sip of coffee before getting up to answer it. The second knock hit the door even as she was opening it.

When she saw the man standing on her doorstep, her eyes widened in disbelief.

He smiled.

She gasped, then fainted.

Solomon was pissed. This was not the reception he'd imagined from Paloma. He picked her up, kicked the door shut behind him, then carried her to her bed. As he carried her through the three tiny rooms, he realized nothing had changed.

A small chalk statue of the Virgin Mary still sat in a dirty alcove someone had long ago chipped out of the thick adobe walls. The walls themselves were patched in a dozen places and badly in need of whitewash. There were two chairs and a tiny wooden table in the kitchen, two chairs and a wooden bench in the front room and, in her bedroom, a single bed and some pegs in the walls where her clothes were hanging.

She owned one pair of shoes, which she was wearing. When Solomon laid her down on her bed, both shoes fell off. His nose curled in distaste as he saw how dirty the bottoms of her feet were. It seemed as if the years had not been kind to Paloma. The woman he'd known would never have let herself go in this way.

There was a wet cloth wadded up in the bottom of a metal basin. He picked it up and then laid it across her forehead.

Within moments, she began to rouse.

"What . . . ? Who . . . ?" She sat up, then gasped.

"Don't go all wacky on me again, woman. I've come too far and I'm too hungry to play nursemaid again. Besides . . . I'm the one in need of help here."

Paloma's heart was hammering so hard she could barely hear herself think. She recognized the voice and the face — at least part of it. They belonged to a man she'd hoped never to see again, yet here he was, looking more than ever like the demon he was.

"Solomon . . . is that you?"

"Yes, it's me," he snapped.

"What has happened to you?"

He didn't like being reminded that his face looked like something from a horror movie.

"I had a little accident," he said, then cupped himself suggestively and added, "but it didn't affect what matters most. It's been a long time since I've had me some ass. Do me first, then I want something to eat."

Paloma swallowed nervously. The last thing she wanted was to put her mouth anywhere on this man's body, but denying him wasn't wise. Not if she wanted to keep herself in one piece.

She took the wet cloth from her forehead and laid it aside as she reached for his belt buckle.

"Remember how I like it?" Solomon said, as she unzipped his pants and then reached for him.

"Yes, Solomon, I remember," Paloma said, and then nervously licked her lips before taking him into her mouth.

The faint scent of urine wafted up to her nostrils. She struggled not to vomit as he grabbed her by the back of the head and pushed himself down her throat.

She choked.

He slapped the back of her head to remind her to tend to business, then let go of every thought but how good her wet, warm mouth felt on his hard dick.

It wasn't the way Paloma had planned on spending her birthday, but she made a quick mental adjustment and concentrated on the task at hand. It was decisions like this that had kept her alive this far, and since she planned on having many more birthdays, she saw no reason to fight back.

THREE

Cat spent her first night on the road in what Art would have called a no-tell motel. As she was checking in, she couldn't help but remember the last time she'd been this far south of Dallas. Then it had been an all-out race down highways and interstates, trying to catch Mark Presley before he left the country. Retracing the journey felt surreal. Even though she was once again trailing a blip on a computer screen, this time she was uncertain as to who was behind it. Bottom line, she needed to make sure the devil she'd thought was dead had not resurrected himself.

By the time she parked and got to her room, she was exhausted. The furnishings were about twenty years out of style but clean enough. Once inside, she locked the door behind her and sat down on the side of the bed, wearily taking in her surroundings. There was a black velvet painting of a bullfight on the wall above the headboard of the bed. The bed spread was pink-and-green cabbage roses larger than the size of her head, and upon closer inspection, she could tell that the carpet wasn't actually carpet at all but artificial turf. Cat scooted the soles of her boots against the surface and then grimaced, well aware that walking barefoot wasn't going to be cushy. Her belly grumbled hungrily, but she was too tired to go looking for a place to eat. Instead, she washed her face and hands, lay down on top of the bed spread and rolled over onto her side. Just to rest. Just for a few minutes.

The next thing she knew, it was two in the morning and she was still in her clothes. She rolled out of bed with a groan. After a quick trip to the bathroom, she kicked off her boots and undressed in the dark. Too tired to look through her suitcase for her pajamas, she crawled back into bed naked, this time beneath the covers.

And she dreamed.

He was behind her. She could feel the warmth of his breath against her neck.

"Wilson . . . I —"

When he lifted the hair from the back of her neck, she choked.

"Shh," he whispered, as he cupped her breasts and pulled her close against him, then

rolled her nipples between his fingers.

Heat shot through Cat so fast she gasped, then staggered.

"Is that good, baby? Do you like that?"

All she could manage was a groan.

When his hands went south, Cat shuddered, then closed her eyes and let herself go. Wave upon wave of unbelievable pleasure began to build, adding to the aching, white-hot pressure already deep within her. Cat wasn't accustomed to letting anyone control her body, but she couldn't find the words to make him stop. The feeling was so good it was frightening, and when she heard Wilson groan, she knew she wasn't the only one affected by their lovemaking.

A minute passed, then another and another, while Wilson's hands and mouth marked a trail of heat all over her body, leaving her almost blind with need. Then, between one breath and another, she began to burn and Wilson sensed it. Before she could think, he dropped to the side of the bed, pulling her with him until she was sitting in his lap, riding his erection.

She wanted to turn around — to watch his face while they did it — but she was coming so fast she couldn't breathe. She didn't want it to be over, but she needed it to stop. And then she screamed.

Cat woke up with a jerk just as the orgasm rolled through her. Breath caught in the back of her throat as she grabbed onto the sheets. A moment passed in a wave of confusion as she tried to orient herself within the starkness of an unfamiliar motel room — along with the place she'd just been in her head.

"Damn, damn, damn," she said with a groan, then rolled over and sat up in the bed.

She'd left Wilson McKay behind for a reason, only it seemed he wasn't as easy to ignore as she'd planned. The digital clock on the bedside table clicked over onto six o'clock just as she glanced at it. It was early, but after that dream, there was no way she was going back to sleep.

Still weak and shaky, she pushed herself up and off the mattress and staggered to the bathroom.

It was a plain, inconspicuous room about the size of a small closet. The dripping showerhead had left a rusty streak down the side of the tub, which should have been a warning for what was to come.

Deciding that the wisest thing to do would be not to look into corners too closely, she unwrapped the tiny complimentary bar of soap, then palmed it as she stepped into the shower. She pulled a clean washcloth down from a small shelf, then turned on the water. When she had it adjusted to the warmth she wanted, she pulled up the shower button on the faucet and then gasped when it sputtered rusty water in her face before emitting a somewhat steady stream.

"Fucking perfect," Cat muttered, as she washed the rusty gunk from her face.

A short while later she emerged from the shower and dressed in a warm, comfortable turtleneck sweater and a pair of jeans. She packed, then headed out the door, leaving her room key and a couple of dollars on the bed for the cleaning lady. The air was chilled, the sky gray and overcast. She pulled the collar of her coat up around her neck and hunched her shoulders as she hurried toward her SUV.

Breakfast came from the drive-through of a doughnut shop, along with an extra-large cup of coffee. Cat ate with one hand while driving with the other. By the time she was finished, her dark blue sweater was dotted with bits of sugar glaze. She brushed the sugar from her clothes onto the floorboard, washed down the last bite of doughnut with the last of her coffee, then took out her cell phone. There were two messages, both from

Art, one telling her to call and let him know she was okay, the second complaining that she hadn't returned his first call. She grimaced, then shook her head as she laid the phone back down on the seat. Art was a good friend, as well as her boss, but sometimes he treated her like a helpless girl and not the self-possessed woman she really was. She would call him later when she was further down the road. Right now there was nothing to tell.

The laptop she'd come to rely on was on the passenger seat, powered up and running. Every so often she would glance down at it, just to make sure the blip she was following was still where it had been the night before. It was. It was not lost upon her that this whole trip could turn out to be a bust. The blip could be nothing more than a leftover bug that her friend Pete had placed in a piece of clothing or a pair of shoes belonging to Mark Presley. After she'd taken Presley into custody outside of Nuevo Laredo, Mexico, anyone could have come across his belongings. She had no way of knowing what had burned in the fire and what had survived. Someone could have come along and claimed the discarded clothing, unaware that some of it had been bugged. One way or another, she would soon find out.

About an hour south, she began to be aware that the traffic in front of her was slowing down. When she drove up over a hill and saw that there'd been a wreck, and that for now both lanes of the highway were being shut down, she frowned and pulled off to the shoulder.

One highway patrolman was stopping traffic. Another was down in the ditch with the wrecked cars and a tow truck. She eyed the situation carefully, then put her vehicle back in gear. While the patrolmen were otherwise occupied, she shifted her SUV into four-wheel drive, wheeled around the parked vehicles and drove onto the center median, bypassing the line of cars and the wreckage. When she was clear of the pileup, she drove back onto the highway and continued her trip south.

Wilson had nightmares all night and, in one way or another, every damn one of them related to Cat Dupree. His first phase of sleep revolved around Cat ordering him from her house. That nightmare evolved into a good two hours of being lost in a maze and hearing Cat screaming for help, but being unable to find her.

He got up before daybreak feeling like

he'd been run over. The last time he'd been this bummed about a woman, he'd been all of thirteen and learning to come to terms with the fact that his pretty, eighteen-year-old neighbor was probably never going to return his affections. Back then, a big breakfast of blueberry pancakes had gone along way toward curing the heartache. Unfortunately, it would take more than his mother's cooking to assuage the pain that loving Cat Dupree had left behind.

By the time he got out of the shower, the streets outside his apartment were already beginning to fill with traffic. As he went to the kitchen to start the coffeemaker, he glanced out the living-room windows, judging the weather by the thin wisps of clouds and the gray, overcast sky. Whatever was going to happen today wasn't going to be good. He could feel it.

He poured his first cup of coffee, thinking of how his mornings used to be when he was a kid back home. The kitchen had been warm and full of noise and great smells. His mom would be standing at the stove cooking bacon or pancakes or something equally tasty, while keeping her rowdy, growing family down to a dull roar.

In comparison to that, his place was a mausoleum. He turned on the small TV he kept on the corner of a kitchen counter just so he could add some voices to the silence, even if the news they were broadcasting was less than heartwarming. As usual, in a city the size of Dallas, the night had not been kind. Someone was dying, while others were already dead. He listened just long enough to assure himself that the suspected perps were none of his bonds, then opted for food.

But when he went to the fridge to get some eggs, he saw a half-empty bottle of beer on the lower shelf and, once again, lost focus. His heart kicked painfully against his chest as he stared at it — remembering.

It had been in his fridge for at least two weeks, maybe more, but he knew who it belonged to. It was Cat's. She had been drinking from it to wash down a bean-and-beef burrito when he'd taken it out of her hands, picked her up in his arms, then carried her to his bedroom. The ensuing session of lovemaking had been gut-wrenching — a mixture of passion and lust that he wished to hell he could forget. Frustrated with himself for being such a loser, he emptied the beer into the sink. The desire for food was gone. If only he could rid himself of Cat's memory as quickly as he'd dumped that bottle, he would be a lot better off.

"Christ Almighty," he muttered, then threw the bottle in the trash. "How in hell do I get past this?"

Frustrated with himself for letting a woman get under his skin to this degree, he turned off the coffeepot, ignored the ache in his gut and went back to his bedroom to dress for the day.

Solomon Tutuola sopped up the last of the beans with his last bite of tortilla, then eyed Paloma as he licked his fingers.

"Got any more?"

Paloma frowned as she shook her head. This food had been meant to last her at least through tomorrow. He'd eaten it without thought for her situation.

"No more," she said, frowning as she glanced at his teeth then looked away. It seemed unnatural to file one's teeth like a wild animal, but, as she remembered, Solomon was as close to an animal as any human could be.

Solomon frowned. The pain pills he'd taken earlier were beginning to wear off, and what wasn't hurting was itching. He glanced around the simple dwelling, frowning even more as he looked back at Paloma herself. Years ago, when they'd first met, she'd been a curvaceous woman with dark, flashing eyes and a rowdy laugh. The woman before him had run to fat, and the displeasure she was feeling was reflected on her face. He was tempted to say to hell with her and take his leave. But he still needed to rest, and he needed some help doctoring his healing wounds.

"I'm going to sleep now," he announced, and rose abruptly.

"But the day is just beginning," Paloma said.

Solomon glared at her. "Then maybe I need some entertaining to keep me awake in this no-place of a town."

"No one asked you to come here," Paloma muttered.

Solomon slapped her.

"Don't backtalk me, woman. You're not pretty enough to get away with it anymore."

Paloma's chin lifted. She might not be pretty anymore, but age had given her something else — something she'd been lacking when she'd first known him. Backbone.

"You don't talk about pretty to me, Tutuola. Your face looks like your heart . . . dark and ugly."

Solomon grabbed her by the throat and squeezed.

Paloma glared back at him.

Suddenly he shoved her aside and strode from the room. She watched him go, then turned and left her house as abruptly as he'd left her kitchen.

Solomon heard her leave and thought nothing of it. She was of no consequence to him other than furnishing a free place to rest. He popped some pain pills, downing them without water, and lay down on her cot. Within a few minutes, he'd fallen asleep.

Paloma was not as easily assuaged. Still, the crisp, coolness of the morning air was calming as she stormed from her little house out into the dusty streets. She paused in her front yard, glancing back one last time at her doorway, then doubled her fists and headed south to the casa of Maria Sanchez. Maria was a witch, and Paloma needed a sure cure for the devil who'd darkened her doorstep.

Cat was less than an hour from the border when she glanced up into her rearview mirror and saw a police car bearing down on her with lights flashing.

"Crap," she muttered, and checked her speedometer. She wasn't speeding — much.

Rolling her eyes at yet another delay, she tapped on her brakes and began slowing down to pull off onto the shoulder. As she slowed, the cruiser caught up with her, then passed her at a high rate of speed. Her foot was still on the brakes as she watched the taillights of the patrol car disappearing over a rise.

Breathing a quick sigh of relief, she glanced down at her laptop, then pulled back on to the highway and turned on the radio, tuning it to a satellite station that played oldies from the eighties. The next few miles passed with a song from Boy George, then one from Michael Jackson. But when Mike and the Mechanics came on with an oldie called "All I Need Is A Miracle," she frowned and turned it off. Her hopes of a miracle had died when she'd found Marsha's body. She knew better than to hope for another one. She drove for about a mile without consequence; then everything began to happen at once.

The eighteen-wheeler about a quarter of a mile in front of her was suddenly heading for the ditch. The church van that had passed her a couple of miles back swerved onto the center median, as did a pickup truck and a small compact car. She couldn't see what they were dodging, but something had to be wrong. Either there was a road-block from another wreck or something more — something potentially deadly for the people on the road.

Seconds later, another vehicle ahead of her swerved, and as it did, she finally saw what was causing the panic. There was a northbound car coming fast — but in the southbound lane.

She tapped on the brakes and began slowing down. It wasn't until she realized there was a phalanx of Texas Highway Patrol cars barreling up behind the northbound car that she realized the enormity of the situation. Someone was on the run from the cops with no care for the innocents heading south. When she saw the windshield of a patrol car suddenly shatter, she realized that the occupants of the car were shooting at the cops in pursuit.

Slamming on her brakes, Cat pulled over to the side of the road, killed the engine, then grabbed her handgun from the glove box. She got out of her SUV on the run and took cover on the passenger side.

As the chase came closer, she heard a series of rapid gunshots and winced when the windshield of another patrol car shattered. The patrol car fishtailed, then swerved into the ditch, barely escaping being rear-ended by the cars giving chase behind it.

Bracing herself, she went down on her belly at the rear of her vehicle, using it as cover while waiting for the fleeing vehicle to draw near. Seconds later it was on her, with the police cars only a few yards behind.

Her first shot hit the left front tire, her second, the left rear. There were two loud pops as they blew in quick succession, then a cloud of smoke and the scent of burning rubber as the driver tried to keep the crippled car on the road.

Helpless, without control, the car quickly fishtailed, then slid onto the center median, rolling several times before coming to a stop upside down.

Cat heard tires squealing as the patrol cars began stopping. From where she was lying, she could see the smoking car upside down, with the tires still spinning.

She got up slowly, laying her gun on the bumper of her car and raising her hands as she stood.

"I'm unarmed! I'm unarmed!" she shouted, as two officers came at her with guns drawn, shouting for her to drop her weapon.

The other officers converged on the wrecked car before the passengers had time to crawl out and run.

Cat stepped out from behind her car.

"My weapon is on the bumper," she said, well aware of what was coming next.

"Hands on the back of the vehicle! Legs spread! Do it now!" one of them shouted, while the other began patting her down. When the handcuffs went around her wrists, she winced.

"Some thanks," she said, as the handcuffs clicked.

The patrolman in front of her frowned as she began to speak.

"My name is Cat Dupree, and I have a permit for the gun. It's in the glove box. I thought it was prudent to stop this crazy bastard before someone got killed, but if I messed up your race, boys, I'm real sorry."

The officer who'd patted her down asked her to repeat her name.

"Cat Dupree. I work for Art Ball Bail Bonds, out of Dallas."

The officer's eyebrows arched as he opened the wallet he'd taken out of her pocket.

"You're a bounty hunter?"

She nodded, then tilted her head toward the wrecked car.

"How long have they been on the wrong side of the highway?"

The patrolman sighed wearily.

"Too long."

Cat frowned. "Someone get hurt?"

"Yeah. The guard at the bank they just

robbed and a woman and two kids about six miles back."

Cat stifled a shudder. "Bad?"

"As bad as it gets."

"Lord," Cat said, watching as the cops began pulling two men out from the overturned vehicle.

The patrolman escorted her to his car, put her in the backseat and then went about the business of checking her credentials. A few minutes later he opened the door, helped her out and took off the cuffs.

"Sorry. Procedure," he said, and dropped the gun into her hands.

"No problem," Cat said, absently rubbing at her wrists as she took her pistol, walked back to her SUV and put the gun back in the glove box.

It was at that point that she realized there was more going on than what was happening on the ground.

"Damn news crews," the highway patrolman muttered.

Cat glanced up. A helicopter with a Channel 4 logo on the side was hovering overhead.

"Smile pretty," the cop said. "I can guarantee they got all of this on tape."

Cat frowned, then looked away. "Well, crap," she muttered.

"Exactly," he said, then glanced into her

SUV and saw the laptop and the program running on it. "What's that?" he asked.

"Bounty."

He arched an eyebrow, then looked back at her and grinned.

"Damn, lady . . . you don't even give them a fighting chance, do you?"

"Not if I can help it," she muttered, then put her hands on her hips. "Are we through here?"

"Yeah. We have your info if we need more from you later." Then he smiled. "Watch your back."

"Always," she said.

She was opening her door when the cop added, "Hey . . . by the way . . . thanks."

"No problem," she said, then with one last glance up toward the hovering helicopter, got in and drove away.

Solomon was still sleeping when Paloma returned, carrying the items that Maria Sanchez had given her in a basket, along with a chicken she clutched under her arm. The chicken clucked nervously. Paloma walked into her bedroom, frowning as she saw Solomon stretched out on her little bed. The mattress was sagging almost to the floor, and he'd gone to bed without covers or removing his shoes, leaving a dark, dirty streak on the bedclothes.

"Animal," she muttered, and set the basket down on the floor, then took the chicken out from beneath her arm. Without hesitation, she grabbed it by the neck and twisted violently, quickly separating the chicken from its head. It flopped about on the floor beside the bed, splattering blood and gore in its death throes.

Solomon woke up as Paloma was taking a cross out of the basket.

"What the hell's going on here?" he shouted.

Paloma continued her spell by sprinkling the contents from a tiny bag Maria had given her onto the pooling blood beneath the now-quivering carcass of the chicken.

When she began to chant in a singsong voice, Solomon realized what was happening. He was as cold and vicious as a man could be, yet Paloma had unknowingly hit upon his Achilles' heel. He was superstitious to a fault, and now he went into a panic at what she was doing.

"Stop! Stop!" he begged, and bounded off the bed, only to find himself blocked from the exit by the blood and carcass of the chicken.

Paloma completed her chant, emptied another tiny bag on Solomon's feet and then looked up at him. The challenge was in her eyes. Solomon crumpled beneath her gaze. His heart was hammering so hard he could barely hear his own voice, and his legs were trembling to the point that he had to grab at the wall to stand.

"What have you done? My God, woman . . . what have you done?"

"You came into my home, availed yourself of my body with no thought for my feelings, took my food without invitation and threatened me with harm if I did not do as you wished. You want to know what I've done? I want to know what the hell you were thinking."

Solomon's eyes were wide, his expression one of shock. He kept looking at the floor, then back up at Paloma.

"What did you do to me?" he begged.

She lifted her chin as she met his gaze head-on.

"You will never hurt another woman as you've hurt me, that I promise you. Your manhood will fester, then wither. Running sores will cover your body. Worms will devour you as you lie in your grave."

Solomon dropped to his knees and began to beg.

"Please . . . please, no, no . . . Paloma. I'll leave. I'll leave right now. I didn't mean to

70

offend you. I didn't mean to frighten you. Take away the curse, I beg of you. Take away the curse."

Paloma threw back her shoulders, taking strength from his weakness.

"It's too late. I'm a poor woman, and the damage to my person and my place has been done."

Solomon's eyes suddenly widened. He held up his hands in a beseeching manner as he scrambled to his feet.

"Wait! Wait here! I'll pay for the damage. I'll pay for shaming you."

His pants were blood-soaked, dotted with herbs and feathers, as he pushed past her and ran from her house. Thinking that he was running away, she was surprised when he came hurrying back. He thrust something into her hands and then began backing out of the house, still begging.

"That will take care of the damage I've caused. Take it with my good wishes . . . just take away the curse. I'm begging you, Paloma. Please, take it away."

Paloma forgot her sense of injustice when she realized he'd handed her the money — more money than she'd ever seen at one time in her life.

"Will you?" he begged. "Will you take away the curse?"

Stunned by the amount of money she was holding, she was momentarily silenced.

Reading it as another refusal, Solomon thrust another stack of money on top of the first one.

"Please!" he begged.

Paloma's heart was pounding as she clutched the money to her breasts.

"Get out," she said.

"Yes, yes, I'm going, I'm going." He began backing toward the door, his arms outstretched. "The curse. Please, Paloma . . . the curse."

"I will remove it . . . but only when you're gone."

He tried to draw a deep breath of relief, but it sounded more like a sob.

"God . . . oh, God . . . thank you, Paloma. I'm leaving now, and I wish you a long and happy life."

"Get out," she repeated. "Get out and never come back."

"Yes. Yes, I'm going," he said, and then turned on his heel and made a run for his car.

Before Paloma could move, she heard the sound of his engine starting. By the time she got to the window, all she could see were the taillights of his car.

She looked down at the money, then back

up at the rooster tail of dust he was leaving behind him, and grinned.

"Fool," she muttered.

Then, realizing she was standing in full view of the streets with an armful of money, she suddenly backed up, slammed the shutters shut and ran to the little niche in the wall where her Madonna figurine was placed. She picked up the figurine, then lifted the shelf on which it was sitting, revealing a large opening in the wall beneath. With one quick glance behind her, she stuffed her money into the hole, then replaced the shelf and statue.

The scent of fresh blood was strong in the air, along with the foul smell of chickenshit. Still, she couldn't blame the chicken. If someone had wrung her neck as she had the chicken's, chances were she would have messed herself, too.

She went back into the bedroom, eyed the chicken she'd just killed, then picked it up and carried it out back and buried it near the corner of her house. Then she went back inside, poured some water into a basin and began cleaning up the mess.

She was going to have to wash her sheets along with the walls and floor, but it was worth it to be rid of Tutuola and his evil ways.

FOUR

Three times during the day, Wilson caught himself about to dial Cat's number. The first time he chalked it up to habit. The second time, he decided it was a habit he needed to break. The third time, he actually dialed the number and didn't come to his senses until he heard her voice on the answering machine. He was so startled that he actually stammered what started out to be an apology until he realized he was talking to a recording.

"Damn it to hell," he mumbled, then disconnected and dropped his cell phone back in his pocket. He stomped out of the restaurant where he'd been eating lunch, slammed his butt into the driver's seat of his car and then hammered his fists on the steering wheel in mute frustration.

After a few moments the hopelessness of his situation passed, leaving him with an empty, helpless feeling. He sat within the silence of his vehicle, watching the sun go down on Dallas, and for the first time wished he'd never met Cat Dupree. A dark gray sedan pulled into the parking space beside him, interrupting his thoughts. He took one look as what appeared to be a happy family of five got out and headed toward the restaurant, then he leaned forward, started the engine and drove away.

LaQueen had locked up and was already gone when he stopped by the office, although the lingering scent of her jasmine perfume was a faint reminder of her presence.

He picked up his messages, taking note that, for once, there were no failures to appear to deal with. He sat down at his desk and started returning the calls, leaving some messages of his own, then left some paperwork on LaQueen's desk to be filed in the morning. He was getting ready to go home when his gaze settled on a picture hanging on the wall. He stared at it until the edges blurred and his eyes burned with unshed tears.

Home.

It had been a long time since he'd thought of his childhood home that way. For him, home was his apartment in Dallas and the place in that picture was where he'd grown up. But it was his unreturned feelings for Cat that reminded him of how shallow his life was here. He'd been at this job, in this city, for the better part of his adult life, yet if he left tomorrow, there would be fewer than a handful of people who would even note his absence. For whatever reasons, he'd neglected his personal life, choosing to chase bail jumpers and the almighty dollar. It was more than humiliating to accept that he'd found someone he wanted to spend the rest of his life with who wasn't even willing to spend an entire night with him.

Cat was still on his mind as he reached across the desk, picked up the phone and punched in a series of numbers. When he heard the first ring, he began a mental countdown of the number of steps it would take someone to get to the phone sitting on the old sideboard in the hall. His answer came on the fourth ring, and unconsciously, his tension eased as he heard her voice.

"Hello?"

"Hi, Mom, it's me, Wilson."

The lilt in her voice was proof of Dorothy McKay's delight in hearing from her oldest son.

"Wilson! How good to hear your voice, son. What's up?"

Wilson smiled to himself. It was typical

that she would get straight to the point.

"Not much . . . just the same old thing. How are things there?"

"Oh, you know . . . your dad's arthritis is an ongoing complaint, and your brothers and sisters keep me busy chasing grandbabies."

"Yeah, I can imagine. Did Charlie's boy, Lee, make the basketball team?"

Dorothy laughed. "Oh sure . . . you know Lee. He's more like you than his own father. When he sets his mind to something, he doesn't stop until he's done it."

Wilson sighed, trying not to think of how he'd missed the boat in this thing called life.

Alice heard the sigh and, like the mother she was, knew there was more behind the phone call than just "checking in."

"Wilson."

"Yeah?"

"What's wrong?"

He flinched. As long as he could remember, she'd always known when something was wrong before she ever heard the words.

"Nothing's wrong, Mom. I just called to say hi. Oh . . . heck, I'm still at the office and my other phone is ringing. I'd better go. Tell Dad I called, okay?"

"Yes, I'll tell him," she said, then added, "I love you, darling."

Wilson closed his eyes. "I love you, too, Mom. Take care."

He hung up, ignoring the fact that he'd lied to her about another call, then locked up and headed for home.

It was dark by the time he reached the parking lot of his apartment building. The temperature had dropped to freezing, and the security light where he normally parked was out. He got out, tripped on an empty beer bottle someone had thrown out, then managed to regain his footing. Cursing the lack of light and the person who'd tossed the bottle, he headed for the building.

There was a puddle of something in the corner of the elevator as he got inside, and from the faint scent, it was probably spilled beer, which just added to his mood. Side-stepping the mess, he reached his floor and got off with his head down, heading for the door at the end of the hall. Once inside, he slammed it, automatically locking himself in, bent over to pick up the mail that had been dropped through the slot, then stalked through the rooms, turning up the thermostat as he passed it.

He showered, grabbed an old T-shirt and a soft pair of sweats, and headed for the kitchen, going through his mail as he walked. Nothing but bills, which he laid aside. Maybe something hot for dinner would change his mood. After heating a can of soup and downing a sandwich, he called it quits. Food was in his belly, but he still felt the emptiness.

He put the dirty dishes into the dishwasher, then turned out the light in the kitchen. He moved into the living room without intent, glanced toward the darkened television screen, then instinctively walked to the windows and pushed the curtains aside.

Night in a city was a world of its own. A different set of citizens emerged to walk different streets. Darkness could be a friend, sheltering the weary from a long, endless day, or it could be something to fear, knowing that there were shadows through which the eye couldn't see, leaving a person vulnerable in so many ways. For Wilson, the darkness just intensified the isolation in which he lived.

It was something deeper and older than time that made him look toward the west — toward the part of the city where Cat lived. He stared at the blinking lights and moving traffic until the lights all blurred together, and while his head said no, his heart still said yes.

At that point his phone rang, pulling his

focus from the window. He walked over to the phone and picked up the receiver.

"Hello."

"Wilson, it is me, LaQueen. Are you watching your television?"

Wilson frowned. LaQueen never called him at home, and certainly not to ask what he was watching.

"No. What's wrong?"

"Turn it on to Channel 4 and see for yourself."

She hung up as Wilson was reaching for the remote. He hit the power button and watched as the screen came to life. It took a few moments for him to catch up to what the storyline and film they were showing was about. He was still trying to figure out why LaQueen thought a police chase on I-35 was something that would be of interest to him when suddenly what the journalist was saying sank in.

. . . identified as Cat Dupree, a bounty hunter out of Dallas. It was mere happenstance that she found herself facing the chase coming toward her, but it was guts that made her react as she did. According to Lieutenant Hooper of the Texas Highway Patrol, Ms. Dupree, without thought for her own safety, shot out the tires on the vehicle the thieves were driving, stopping them from causing further harm.

Unfortunately, Ms. Dupree didn't come along in time to save the three occupants of a car the thieves had forced off the road earlier. They had already been pronounced dead at the scene by the time Ms. Dupree stopped the fleeing suspects.

However, the occupants' deaths resulted in the addition of charges of vehicular manslaughter to the federal charges already pending for bank robbery. Still, the Texas authorities, while grateful to Ms. Dupree for her assistance, want to reiterate that in no way do they advocate citizens involving themselves in police situations.

Wilson didn't know he'd been holding his breath until he felt a sudden need to inhale. When he did, a curse came with it.

He knew exactly where that incident had occurred. It was less than thirty miles from the Texas-Mexico border and, while it could be nothing more than a coincidence that she was back on the same trail they'd taken when they'd gone after Mark Presley, his gut told him different.

He hit the mute button, then grabbed the phone book and flipped to the yellow pages, looking for the number to Art Ball Bail Bonds. Whatever Cat was doing, Art would have to know.

By the time he made the call, his thoughts were racing. He was still trying to come up with a way to question Art without making a fool of himself when Art answered the phone.

"Art's Bail Bonds."

"Art, it's Wilson McKay. Where the hell is Cat?"

Taken aback by the intensity in Wilson's voice, Art spoke before he thought.

"Going to see if the man who killed her daddy is dead."

Shocked by the answer, Wilson was momentarily speechless.

"Did you see her on the TV?" Art asked. "Ain't she a pistol? Just like her to be in the middle of something like that."

Wilson shuddered, then swallowed past the knot in his throat. "Why would she want to go back to Mexico?" he asked. "The house he was in exploded. No way did he survive something like that."

"She seemed to think different."

Wilson stood up and walked back to the window. She wasn't even in the city. She was gone, and he hadn't known it. "Did she say why?" he asked.

Art hesitated. The shock of Wilson's call was passing, leaving him concerned that he'd probably given away more than Cat would have liked. Still, she hadn't told him not to tell. Not exactly.

"Well, she didn't go into details or anything, but I got the impression that it had something to do with a computer and a map."

Wilson groaned. That damned program she'd had on her laptop that they'd used to track Presley. If there was movement on it, she would naturally assume that Tutuola wasn't dead. She'd wanted to go back and see, but he had stopped her. Now she was going on her own. It shouldn't matter. He shouldn't give a damn what she was doing. She was never going to think about anyone but herself.

But it did matter.

"I don't suppose you've heard from her?" Wilson asked.

"No, even though I left a couple messages on her cell. She said she'd check in, so when she does, want me to tell her to give you a call?"

"Hell no," Wilson said. "I'll give her that message myself."

"Yeah, well . . ."

"Thanks for the info, Art. Sorry if I

83

seemed a bit abrupt. It was just that it was a shock to —"

"You don't have to apologize to me for caring about her. I do, too, for all the good it does."

"Yeah," Wilson echoed. "For all the good."

Art disconnected.

Wilson did the same, then dropped the phone onto the sofa. For a few moments he couldn't think. He wanted to scream — to rage at the stupidity she'd exhibited by going off on some wild-goose chase like that without telling a soul where she was going. Then he slammed his fist into the wall, oblivious to the pain in his wrist and the dent he'd put in the drywall. It wasn't that she hadn't told anyone where she was going. It was that she hadn't bothered to tell *him.* If he needed any further proof that he'd been living in some fantasy world where she was concerned, this would be it.

He sat down with a thump, then leaned back and covered his face with his hands. The shock and pain of what he'd learned was turning into anger. The longer he sat there, the angrier he got. An ambulance raced past his apartment building with sirens screaming on the way to someone else's disaster, but it felt like the disaster was his.

He kept remembering the first time he'd seen her, coming out of a burning apartment building with a bail jumper over her shoulder. After that, there was the night he'd found her staggering in the police parking lot, sick as a dog from some bug and about to pass out. Then, when Marsha turned up missing, it had been Cat's persistence that had led the police to Marsha's body, as well as to her killer, and Wilson had been with her all the way. He'd seen her stand as strong through that hell as any man — maybe even stronger — and all through it, the passion between them had simmered. When they'd finally made love, it had been more than lust for Wilson. He had known, almost from the start, that she was going to be something special to him. But he and Cat had been on separate pages when it came to their futures. He'd made love to a woman who was stealing his heart. She'd just had sex with a willing participant. When he'd "paid" her for their last session of sex, he'd promised himself it would be their last contact.

Now this.

He couldn't have her in his life and remain sane. He needed his head examined for caring about what she was doing, but what she'd done was dangerous, and, God help him, he couldn't live with himself if she got herself killed and he did nothing about it.

Suddenly his anger peaked. He grabbed the phone. Art had said she wasn't answering her cell, so he was leaving his message on her home phone. When he dialed her number this time, it was no mistake. He listened to the rings, then took a breath when he heard her voice on the answering machine. As soon as the message beeped, he started talking.

"You made the news tonight. I'd congratulate you on your heroism, but at the moment I'm too damned pissed at your stupidity. I talked to Art. I know what you're doing. And, just so you know, I'm not calling to meddle in your damned business. However . . . going off alone like this to chase a fucking ghost isn't just stupid, it's dangerous. You got lucky when you found Marsha's body. It gave you a chance to bring her back and give her a proper burial. So you brought one killer to justice. Good for you, Dupree. However, if this bastard you're chasing happens to still be alive, it might do you well to remember that when he killed your father, he also cut your damned throat. You survived him once. You might not be as lucky another time. I don't know why I care. I wish to hell I didn't. And just for the record, woman, if it hadn't been for that piece of film on tonight's news, I wouldn't have the slightest notion of where in hell to look for *your* bones. It's obvious you don't give a damn about me, yourself or anyone else. I wish to hell I could return the favor."

His hands were shaking when he hung up. He sat there for a moment longer while his vision blurred and his belly burned. Then he pushed himself up from the sofa.

The apartment was in complete darkness, lit only by the nightlight in the hall and the faint glow of a security light outside the kitchen window. He stood within the shadowy silence, barely aware of the night sounds from the city beyond. All he could hear was the steady thump of his own heartbeat echoing in his ears.

Cat had opted to spend one last night in Texas and then cross the border in the morning, but when she'd come back from the gas station where she'd gone to make a pit stop and fuel up, what she'd seen on the laptop had changed her mind.

The blip that had been stationary for so long was, once again, on the move, but it had changed directions. It was no longer headed toward the coast but had begun moving in a northwesterly direction. Nuevo Laredo was just across the border, but after that it was mostly small villages and a lot of sand and cactus and mountains in the direction the blip was now moving.

She didn't think of the dangers she could be putting herself in by driving through the desert at night. The only thing on her mind was catching up with whoever was carrying some of Mark Presley's property. If it turned out that this trip amounted to nothing, well, she was willing to feel like twelve kinds of a fool just to know the truth.

It was still daylight when she crossed the border, and since bounty hunting was illegal in Mexico, she politely lied about her reasons for entering the country, confident that her weapons were well-concealed under the fake bottom of her console. The fact that she was wearing her tightest sweater and her hair was down and windblown had been distraction enough for the border guards. In fact, they'd even had her exit the car while they did a quick search. Cat had occupied herself with some exaggerated stretches, tightening the sweater across her breasts even more. She knew the guards were watching her, so to add to their interest, she did a couple of deep knee bends, which nicely tightened her blue jeans over her backside.

At that point, one of the guards called out to her.

"Señorita!"

She turned, purposefully arching her back as she looked at him over one shoulder.

"Yes?"

He smiled, then held the door open for her.

"You are free to go. Have a safe trip."

She flashed him a quick smile as she slid behind the steering wheel.

"Thanks so much," she said.

"De nada," he replied.

She was still smiling as she drove into Mexico.

The sun had gone down hours ago. More than once, Cat had thought about pulling off to the side of the road, crawling into the back of her SUV and sleeping until daylight, but she hadn't done it yet. Part of her reasoning was that, even if she stopped, she wouldn't be able to sleep. And even though she was driving on a well-defined road, it wasn't well-kept. The potholes were only slightly less startling than the armadillos and coyotes she kept dodging.

It was sometime after midnight when nature finally called loudly enough that she had to pull over. With nothing remotely resembling a gas station or a diner at which to stop, she chose the nearest cactus. After grabbing a flashlight from the glove box, she aimed the beam all around, making sure there were no snakes nearby before undoing her jeans.

A minute later she was zipping up her jeans and about ready to head back to her car when she heard something that didn't fit in with the night sounds of a desert. She held her breath, waiting to see if she could hear it again, and when she did, a chill ran up her spine. Unless she was mistaken, she'd just heard a baby crying, which made no sense. According to her maps, the nearest village was about twenty miles south.

Still, she listened, trying to convince herself that it must have been an animal — one that just sounded human.

Then she heard it again, and this time, the wail was accompanied by another sound — the yipping of a pack of coyotes.

The implications of those two sounds together was frightening. Cat grabbed her flashlight, then ran for her car. She started the engine, then swerved off the road on which she'd been traveling and headed slowly out into the desert in the direction from which she'd heard the sound. Whatever it was, it couldn't be far. She just had to make sure she didn't drive off into some arroyo and get herself stuck.

As she drove, the rougher ground caused the beams from the headlights to bounce up and down, giving her nothing but brief glimpses of the landscape. Once she braked and hung her head out the window to see if she could hear that same haunting cry, but either the engine was too loud or the sound had stopped. One thing was for certain, her presence had scared away the coyotes. She didn't hear them anymore.

Her fingers tightened on the steering wheel as she ducked back into the car and accelerated slowly. Just when she thought she'd imagined the whole thing, a flash of red and yellow caught her eye. As she turned toward the color, she quickly realized it was a blanket — covering a woman.

The woman was lying on her side, facing the headlights of Cat's car.

She wasn't moving, which any normal person would have done if they'd been faced with headlights coming toward them.

Cat's stomach lurched as she hit the brakes and slammed the car into park. She got out on the run, trying not to think of how she'd found Marsha's body by the color of the coat she'd been wearing. Within seconds, she was on her knees beside the woman, feeling for a pulse.

There was none.

She reached for the blanket, her hand shaking, then pulled it back and shined the flashlight — into the face of a baby, who was looking right back at her.

It wasn't until the baby closed its eyes against the glare of the flashlight that she realized it was still alive.

"Oh God . . . baby . . . poor baby. Poor little baby."

But when she tried to pick it up, the mother's grip — even in death — was so fierce that Cat couldn't pull the baby free. By now the baby was wailing again, but the sound was so weak, it was scary. Cat had no way of knowing how long they'd lain like this — or how long it had been since the baby had been fed. Finally she managed to pull the mother's arms away and gather the baby up into her arms.

The scent of urine and feces was strong as she headed for her car. She opened the back hatch of the SUV, using the flat surface as a changing table, and began a quick check of the baby.

It was a girl. Except for almost certain dehydration and an incredibly dirty diaper, she could see no obvious bruises or injuries.

She didn't know much about babies, but this lethargy couldn't be good.

She tossed the filthy diaper out into the darkness, then began cleaning the tiny child with some of the antiseptic hand wipes she kept up front. Within moments, the baby began to shiver. Cat stripped off her own sweater and, using it like a blanket, covered up the child. She knew the little girl was in need of food and clothing, but short of giving up her sweater, she had nothing. Praying that the mother had the foresight to have been carrying supplies, she made a quick run back to the body.

The headlights were still on, keeping the tragedy in the spotlight. Cat wanted to scream, to cry and rage at the injustice of what was before her, but there was no time. The baby's survival might depend on what she could find.

At first she saw nothing, but she wouldn't give up. She couldn't believe that a mother would be out here, this far from anything, without food and water for herself and the baby.

She crouched with her back to the headlights and searched the darkness with her flashlight. The scent of death and the desert were strong in her nose as she swept the small beam out into the night. Within seconds, she saw what appeared to be a large bundle a few feet away. Lunging toward it, she grabbed it, then ran, dashing past the headlights to the back of her car. She laid the bundle inside, near the baby, and opened it up. Within seconds, a scorpion crawled out from the folds, its upturned tail curled threateningly as it moved.

"Son of a bitch!" Cat yelped, and swept the scorpion and the entire bundle out of the car and into the dirt before anything else could crawl out.

The sweater she'd laid on the baby was now down around its feet, and the night air on the little girl's fragile skin was chilling her moment by moment, reminding Cat that she didn't have time to be squeamish.

She stomped the scorpion into the dirt, grinding it beneath the heel of her boot, then went down on her knees, using the flashlight to search for what she needed. To her relief, she found a handful of disposable diapers. It had been years since she'd diapered a baby, but it did not deter her. The chore had been part of her life while living in foster care. After a few missteps, she finally figured out how to make the little tabs stick and the task was done. The diaper sagged sideways, but it stayed put. Her hands were shaking as she went back to the bundle. When she found a handful of baby clothes, she breathed another sigh of relief. After giving the clothing a vigorous shake, she dressed the little girl in a small T-shirt, then wrapped her up in a clean baby blanket.

A brief sob slipped out from between clenched teeth as she put her sweater back on. For a few silent moments, she stared down at the baby, knowing that her efforts could be too little, too late, and tried not to panic.

The baby's eyes were closed, but her little hands were beating the air as she wailed against the hunger and discomfort of her situation.

Cat felt helpless. What now? Oh. Food. That was it. The baby was surely hungry.

She went back to the bundle. When she found some cans of condensed milk and a plastic baby bottle, she silently praised the dead mother's foresight. Cat had no time to wonder where the woman had been going or how she'd died. Her whole focus was on saving the baby from dying, too. She stared at the cans of milk, knowing it was going to save the baby, but how? The little she knew about feeding babies involved diluting the milk, but to what extent?

The baby squeaked again, raising Cat's anxiety.

"Hey, little girl . . . give me a minute. I don't know what to do with this stuff," she muttered, then brushed her finger against the side of the baby's cheek. As she did, the baby moved toward the feeling with her tiny mouth wide open.

"Okay, honey, I get the message," Cat said, and got down to business.

She popped the top on the can and poured until the bottle was about a third full.

"Water, water, I need water."

Unaware that she was talking aloud, she ran around to the front seat and got her water bottle from the floor-board. There was no time to worry about measurements as she filled the bottle the rest of the way full. She gave it a quick shake, then gathered the baby up in her arms, crawled into the back of the car and pulled the door shut.

The engine was still running.

The heater was still on.

The headlights were still burning.

Cat's heart was pounding as she cradled the baby up against her and pushed the nipple against the baby's mouth.

Again the tiny lips parted in that life-affirming motion, urgently seeking the sustenance that meant life.

Cat watched in awe, seeing how the baby's tongue curled around the nipple, watching the tiny nostrils flare in an effort to breathe and drink at the same time.

At first it seemed that the baby was too weak to suck, and Cat didn't know what to do. But the baby persisted and, when the first trickle of milk slid down her throat and she swallowed, Cat shuddered. It wasn't until the baby settled into a steady, sucking motion, that Cat began to relax.

She listened to the lip-smacking, sucking and swallowing sounds of a feeding baby and tried not to think of the dead mother only a few feet away. The weight of the tiny child was next to nothing in her arms, but the weight of responsibility was huge. For the first time in her life, Cat wasn't focused on her own agenda.

Ghost hunting had just taken a huge backseat to a little girl's fate. She hadn't been able to save the mother, but she would save this little girl's life if it was the last damn thing she did.

Cat sat in silent awe as the baby emptied the bottle and didn't even know she was crying until tears dripped off her face down onto her hands.

FIVE

The bottle was empty, and the baby was asleep. Cat had put what was left of the opened can of milk in her small ice chest, along with the empty bottle. Well aware of the urgency of the situation, she knew she had to get help. Just because the baby was momentarily satisfied, that didn't mean it hadn't suffered something that could precipitate a health crisis.

But for the first time in her life, she'd fallen in love, and for Cat, it was a whole new set of distracting emotions. For every breath the baby took, she took one, too, until their respiration was in sync. When a tiny milky bubble formed on the baby's pursed lips, she didn't know that she was pursing her own lips, as well. When the bubble popped, Cat watched, entranced by the perfection of the baby's dark eyebrows knitting above a perfect little nose.

Cat took a deep, shaky breath, knowing

that, once upon a time. her own mother would have sat like this, watching her breathe and looking for herself in a baby's tiny face.

It wasn't until she saw a pair of dark shadows moving past the rear end of the car that she remembered the mother's body — and the coyotes.

Damn scavengers. In a panic now that she'd delayed the inevitability of dealing with the body, she leaned over between the headrests and laid the baby down on the backseat. When she was satisfied that the child was comfortable and safe, she rolled back to her knees, popped the hatch and jumped out with her handgun drawn. She saw the tail of a coyote disappearing into the darkness and started to shoot, then remembered the baby. The sound would surely wake her, then she would cry, and if that happened, Cat would most likely cry with her.

So she pulled the hatch shut, then circled the SUV, frowning as she realized the coyotes had already been at the mother's body. The red and yellow blanket had been pulled off to the side, and there were bite marks on the flesh. However, with the blanket off, Cat was pretty sure she knew how the young mother had died.

Snakebite.

The skin was all red and swollen around a pair of puncture marks about six inches above her ankle.

The sight made Cat a little nervous, and she began to look around more carefully to see where she was walking, not wanting to end up like this poor woman had.

She looked down, trying to figure out what would be the best way to move the body. Ants were crawling in and out of the woman's nose and mouth. She wanted to throw up. Instead, she gritted her teeth and went after the blanket the coyotes had pulled away.

The woman was small, barely five-feet tall, so when Cat spread out the blanket and rolled the woman's body onto it, the only part of her still hanging off the blanket were her feet. Using the blanket as a sled, Cat pulled the body all the way to the back of the SUV, lifted the hatch door, then looked down.

Decomposition wasn't pretty, but it came eventually to every living thing. Cat's jaw jutted angrily as she bent down, brushed away most of the ants, then began rolling the body up in the blanket.

"Sorry, lady. Life sucks. Death isn't any better."

Gathering all her strength, Cat picked up the body and laid it into the back of the SUV. As she brushed sand and ants from the front of her clothes, she glanced out into the darkness. From where she was standing, she could see light reflecting on the eyeballs of the watching coyotes. Their silence was ominous. But for the safety of her vehicle and gun, she would have been at their mercy, just as the mother and baby had been.

Suddenly anxious to be away from the whole ugly scene, she turned her back on the pack, gathered up everything else that had been with the mother and tied it back up in the bundle, then tossed it in beside the body.

She closed the hatch before circling the car to the backseat to check on the baby. A quick glance confirmed that she was still sleeping. The tragedy of the situation was not lost upon Cat as she glanced from the baby to the body in the hatch. It would be the last time mother and child slept together.

But indulging in emotion wasn't something she could afford right now. She picked the baby up in her arms, got into the driver's seat, then shut and locked the doors.

The baby squirmed a bit, then settled

again. Cat knew there were rules about babies and car seats, but in this situation, rules did not apply. She laid the baby in the seat beside her, then reached for her seat belt. As soon as she was buckled in, she reached for the baby again. Once she had her settled safely in the crook of her arm, she put the car into gear and made a big U-turn before heading back to the old road.

When her tires finally rolled up onto the hard surface, she breathed a sigh of relief. Now all she had to do was find the nearest village and the local police. She didn't know what was ahead of her, but she knew what was behind, and certainty was a better bet than a maybe. She would have to go back to the last village she'd driven through, Casa Rojo.

Cat glanced out the windshield toward the east. The darkness of the sky was beginning to thin. Morning was en route. She didn't know what the day would bring, but whatever it was, it couldn't be worse than what she'd just encountered.

She glanced down at the sleeping baby again, and then, without thinking, bent down and brushed her lips against a ripple of dark curls feathering the little girl's forehead.

Baby skin was soft — softer than anything

she'd ever felt. She suspected a change of diaper was needed again, but as long as the baby was sleeping, she wasn't going to mess up a good thing.

She glanced up in the rearview mirror and imagined she felt the spirit of the dead mother rising up from the back to check on her child. She knew the eerie thought was nothing more than a reaction to hauling a dead body, something she had to get over, but it still gave her a chill.

The laptop was on the front floorboard. She couldn't help but notice that the blip on the screen was still moving northwest as she was moving east. But it couldn't matter — not now. Not until she knew she'd done all there was to be done for a little lost girl.

Sunrise had already come and gone by the time Cat drove back into Casa Rojo. Her first trip through it had been in the dark, so she had no idea if the village had a police station and was in serious doubt about a place this small having a doctor. Still, it was somewhere to start.

The baby had been awake and squirming for a good fifteen minutes, definitely in need of a diaper change, but that would have to wait.

A cat strolled out of an alley and into the

street as Cat drove past, making her brake for its passing. As she did, an old man walked out of a doorway, then stopped, looking at her with a mixture of curiosity and surprise.

Her Spanish was pretty close to non-existent. She hoped his English was better as she rolled down her window.

"Buenos días, señor. Habla inglés?"

He nodded.

"Do you have police here? *Policía?"*

"The tin roof," he said, pointing to a building down the street, where the early-morning sun reflected from a shiny new roof.

Cat accelerated slowly. When she got to the end of the street, she pulled up, parked, then killed the engine. The silence was brief. The baby's discomfort was obvious as she began squirming in earnest.

"I know . . . I know, little girl," Cat whispered, then held the baby closer as she unbuckled her seat belt and got out.

The morning sun was bright on her face, although the air was still chilly. She pulled the blanket closer around the baby, then moved toward the building. There were no curbs, because there were no sidewalks — and only one small, dusty window facing the street. She didn't want to think about

104

handing this baby over to strangers, but it was the only thing she could do. Just a few more steps and then her responsibilities to the dead woman and her child would be over.

The hinges on the door squeaked as she entered. The man behind the desk looked up, then stood. His uniform was rumpled, as was the small cot she could see through the open door to the next room. He'd probably slept here last night, which meant there was, most likely, someone in lockup. His gaze moved from Cat's face to the baby in her arms, and he smiled.

"Señora?"

"Habla inglés?"

"Yes . . . I speak English," he said. "My name is Lieutenant Dominguez. How can I help you?"

"My name is Cat Dupree. Last night I stopped on the side of the road to go to the bathroom and heard a baby crying. This baby. Her mother is dead. Her body is in the back of my car."

"Dead?"

"Yes. Snakebite, I think."

Dominguez's smile disappeared. "Do you have a weapon?"

Cat's eyebrows knitted. "In the car. I have a permit."

"Show me the body," he demanded.

Cat looked down at the baby, then back up to Dominguez.

"Is there a doctor here? The baby . . . I'm not sure if she's okay."

"No, no doctor," he muttered, and pointed toward the door.

"You show me the body now."

Cat backed up, then turned around and walked out. Dominguez was right on her heels.

She pointed to the hatch.

"She's back there. She was covered with the blanket when I found her. Coyotes got to her before I got her loaded up."

The policeman's eyes narrowed. He saw the bundle, and pointed.

"This is hers?"

"Yes. Everything's there except one of the cans of milk she was carrying and some diapers. I changed the baby and used some of the milk to feed her after I found them."

The baby started to cry.

"She's wet and probably hungry again," Cat said.

"Tend to the child," the policeman said, and pulled a cell phone out of his pocket.

Cat laid the baby down on the backseat while she refilled the bottle and got a clean diaper, then headed for the office. At least

106

there was something she could still do for the living.

Solomon had pulled over to the side of the road to piss. Even as he was unzipping his pants, he kept remembering Paloma's curse that his man parts would rot and fall off. His hands were shaking as he pulled out his penis. To his relief, it still looked the same. When a stream of urine began splattering on the dusty ground, he breathed a bit easier. It was working the same, too. Maybe after he'd given her the money and left, she'd taken off the curse, like she'd promised.

As he stood there, he happened to glance up. A lone buzzard was circling the skies to the south. He shuddered, then looked away, afraid it might be a bad omen. As soon as he finished pissing, he opened the trunk of his car and unzipped the duffel bag. He liked looking at all that money — his money. Then he zipped it back up, got a small sack from the trunk with his medicine in it and got back in the car.

It was the last of his antibiotics. He washed them down with the last of the water in his bottle, tossed the empty out into the desert, and then got a tube of ointment from the console and began applying it to his burn scars.

The skin was still fragile, and there were a couple of places on his neck that didn't look right. As soon as he got to Chihuahua, he would find himself a doctor. With all the money he had now, he could afford a good one. He glanced into the mirror, frowning as he ran a hand over his head where hair used to be. He didn't even recognize his own face anymore. He shoved the rearview mirror away from his line of vision, got a fresh bottle of water from the cooler in the seat beside him, then started the engine.

He'd been to Chihuahua many times over the last ten years. It was one of his favorite places to take a little R & R. Now, with his newfound wealth, it would be the perfect place to retire. With one last glance up at the circling buzzard, he put the car in gear and drove away.

Wilson woke up with a knot in his belly the size of his fist. The last time he'd felt like this, his grandfather had died, so apparently accepting that Cat was as good as dead to him wasn't going to be a walk in the park after all. Leaving that angry message on her answering machine had been a sign of weakness, but there wasn't any way to take it back. So what? She knew he'd fallen for her. That was nothing new. So now she'd know he wasn't over her yet. It couldn't hurt any more than it already did.

It took everything he had to get out of bed and go to work, but if he didn't show, LaQueen would be calling, and then he would have a whole new kind of woman trouble.

He turned on the television as he was making coffee, listening absently to the weather forecast, as well as the local news. Ironically, there was an update on Mark Presley, the man Cat had brought to justice for murdering her friend. He upped the volume, catching the last part of the broadcast.

Mark Presley, who was found guilty of murdering his pregnant mistress just before Christmas of last year, was sentenced to death yesterday. Still, with the appeals process, it will most likely be years before the sentence is carried out, if ever. Presley's wife was suspiciously absent from the proceedings, and it's rumored that she's already filed for divorce.

"Sorry bastard," Wilson muttered, then

finished his breakfast and headed for the office.

According to the weatherman, the day would be clear but cold. He couldn't help but wonder if it was cold where Cat was. She had a tendency to go off half-cocked, and he hoped she'd taken the right kind of clothes. Then, the minute he thought it, he cursed himself. What the hell was he doing, wasting time worrying about her?

God. Would he ever learn?

And so his day began.

The baby was crying. Cat had fed her and diapered her and didn't know what the hell was wrong. She was walking in circles inside the police station with the baby on her shoulder.

"I'm sorry, little girl . . . if only you could talk," Cat said, as she cradled the baby against her shoulder.

Suddenly it was quiet. Cat had started to relax, but she'd jumped the gun. Apparently the baby had stopped only long enough to take a big breath. Another wail sounded, coupled with something that could only be called a shriek.

Cat was panicked. This was horrible. Who knew that anything so little could be so loud?

The baby kicked against Cat's hands. Uncertain what to do next, Cat shifted the baby from her right shoulder to her left, and as she did, a sound came up and out of the baby's mouth — a sound so loud and startling that Cat almost dropped her.

It was a burp of magnificent proportions, and with it came silence. The little girl shifted a bit, fussing and rooting her nose against the curve of Cat's neck, and then she settled. Cat could feel the tension in the baby's body melting like butter on hot bread, and she smiled.

"Was that it? Lord, honey, all you had to do was tell me it was a bellyache."

Then she laughed at herself for even talking out loud to someone who couldn't talk back. Relieved that the mini-crisis had passed, she moved to the doorway and looked out.

There were four men near the rear of her SUV. The body had been moved to the back of an old station wagon, and the policeman who'd ordered Cat into his office was inside with it. She could see that they'd unrolled the body, obviously making sure that the woman had died as Cat assumed, and that she hadn't been murdered.

Being a Good Samaritan was more difficult than one might imagine. It would have been just her luck to bring in a body and be blamed for the demise. Thank God it wasn't the case.

But there was still the baby to consider.

Somewhere, there had to be family. There was no way to know why the mother had been out in the desert so far from anywhere with her baby, but surely to God there were people somewhere who loved her and were worried out of their minds as to where she and the child had gone.

As she stood, Dominguez looked up, saw her in the doorway and motioned her over.

She got the blanket, covered the baby and then headed for the street.

"Yes, *señor?*"

The policeman was crawling out of the old station wagon as she approached.

"It is as you said. The little mother suffered snakebite. The marks on her arms are from animals. It was God's grace that led you to the baby or she would have died so, too."

Unconsciously, Cat's arms tightened around the baby as she listened.

"So what happens now?" Cat said.

"Her name was Pilar Mendoza. She was carrying papers that make me believe she was meeting a coyote."

Cat frowned. "You're talking about a man

112

who smuggles illegals into the States?"

"Yes. This is so. Most likely the coyote either turned her away because she brought a baby with her, or he just stole her money and never planned to take her." He shrugged. "Unfortunately, such things happen."

Cat's stomach rolled.

"You mean someone intentionally left her stranded in the middle of nowhere?"

"It is possible," he said, then pointed to the baby. "Unfortunately, the only witness to this tragedy does not talk."

"God," Cat muttered.

"No. It is not God's work. It is the work of the devil."

Cat felt like a traitor. Her heart was already halfway to gone on this baby she'd known for less than twenty-four hours, and she was already dreading the moment when she would be giving her up.

"So what's going to happen to this baby?"

Dominguez frowned. "According to the papers the woman was carrying, she was from Adobe Blanco. It is a little village about two and a half hours southwest of here. Maybe there is family. Maybe not. Who knows? We will take the child and turn her over to the authorities in Nuevo Laredo. We do not have the resources to deal with such things here."

Cat stared down at the baby, knowing full well the tangled chain of legalities that could permanently separate her from any blood family she had left.

"No," she said.

Dominguez's frown deepened.

"What do you mean, no? You do not have the authority to —"

"Don't do this," Cat said. "She will get lost in the system. I know. I've been there."

Dominguez sighed, sweeping his arms outward.

"Look around. Do you see a hospital? Do you see a place for tending to lost children?"

"I see houses. There have to be people in them," Cat said. "Don't tell me there's not even one woman in Casa Rojo who would be willing to take care of a baby girl for a day."

"Why a day?" he said.

"Because that's about how long it will take me to drive to Adobe Blanco, find out if Pilar Mendoza had any family there and bring them back. Surely you would not refuse to give the baby to Pilar's family?"

"Well, I —"

"I need gas. And some cans of gas to take with me. I'll need some water, too. I don't suppose you have ice?"

He shrugged.

"It doesn't matter," she said. "Will you do it? Will you give me until sundown to try and find Pilar Mendoza's family?"

Dominguez sighed. This American woman was pushy, but he had to admit her heart was in the right place.

"Yes. But know this. If you don't come back . . ."

"Oh, I'll be back," Cat said. "With or without Pilar's family, I will be back." Then she laid her cheek against the baby's dark, curly hair and closed her eyes, imprinting the soft, even sound of baby breaths in her heart. "I promise you that, little girl."

Dominguez looked at the body in the station wagon, then at Cat.

"We have no funeral parlor here in this village."

"Just clean the damned ants off her and put her someplace cool. Her family will reclaim the body when they take the baby."

"So maybe we can —"

Cat gave the baby one last kiss on the forehead, then handed her to Dominguez.

"No maybes. You take good care of this baby until I get back, or I swear to God, I will make your life hell."

Dominguez was startled, then angered, as he took the baby.

"Lady, you do not come into my town and threaten me or tell me what to do. This isn't your country. It is mine."

Cat poked a finger against his chest.

"That wasn't a threat. It was a promise. If I'd been five minutes later, this baby would be in some coyote's belly. *Comprende?*"

Her passion deflated Dominguez's anger. Suddenly he got it. The tough woman wasn't so tough after all. The baby had gotten to her. Then he glanced down. The baby was a beauty. It was a shame about the mother. His shoulders slumped slightly as he looked up at Cat.

"Go with Juan. He will help you get fuel and water. Do you have a map of my country?"

She nodded.

"Juan will show you where Adobe Blanco is located on the map. The baby will be here when you get back."

Cat nodded, then turned to the other men who'd been helping with the body.

"Which one of you is Juan?"

A short, swarthy man with a large mustache stepped forward.

"Follow me, *señorita.*"

116

Six

The sun had been up for hours. Cat had no idea how long she'd been driving on what most might consider a trip to nowhere. Looking for a family that might or might not exist, so they could claim the body of a dead woman and the baby she'd left behind, could easily be a lost cause. Cat knew she was playing against the odds in pulling this off. As for the baby, Cat didn't know her name or how old she was — in fact, six hours ago, she'd been unaware of her existence.

But leaving that baby behind in Casa Rojo had been difficult — more difficult than she would have imagined. From the moment she had lifted the baby out of the mother's lifeless arms and realized she was alive, the child had become the most important thing in Cat's life. Seeing that the infant was reunited with family meant more to her right now than finding out if Tutuola was still alive.

She knew from experience what it was like to be a throwaway child. Witnessing the last of her family being murdered — and nearly dying herself in the process — had been a trauma from which she'd never recovered. Even though she was an adult in every sense of the word, an independent, even aggressive, woman, she was still a product of her past. Every day, when she looked in the mirror and saw the ragged necklace of scar tissue around her throat, she was reminded that she belonged to no one. If a wild ride through the Mexican desert was all it took to find a lost baby's family, then it was the least she could do.

The speedometer was hovering between eighty-five and ninety miles an hour, and the rooster tail of dust Cat was leaving behind her was impressive. Her grip on the steering wheel had turned her knuckles white, matching the bloodless set of her lips.

She wasn't just mad, she was furious. And she was scared. Scared for a baby she didn't know, and furious that the mother's death could have been prevented. Granted, the immediate cause of her death was snakebite. But her presence in the desert, so far from anywhere, was suspicious. If it was true that she'd been abandoned to her fate by a coyote, Cat silently wished that man to hell and back once a day for the rest of his miserable life and then to hell for eternity when he died. But she couldn't let her thoughts stray from the greater purpose, which was to get to Adobe Blanco.

When Dominguez had told Cat that Adobe Blanco was pretty much in the middle of nowhere, he'd been right. The landmarks she'd been given to look for were obscure. Still, how many rusted-out 1955 Chevies with a giant saguaro behind them could there be? Once she found that marker, she was to take a sharp turn south and follow what amounted to a dirt road for thirty miles, at which point she would come to a fork in the road, marked by one ancient gasoline pump, what was left of two walls of a building and the skeleton of a roof. It was all that was left of an old gas station that had been abandoned back in the thirties. From there, she would take the left fork and drive the last fifteen miles to reach Adobe Blanco.

The farther she drove, the more afraid she was that she'd somehow missed her turn. When her cell phone suddenly rang, the sound was so startling that she almost ran off the road. Her hands were shaking and her heart was still pounding erratically by the time she got the SUV under control. By then, whoever was calling had either disconnected or left a message. Cat didn't bother to look. Chances were it was either Art or Wilson and she had nothing to say to either one of them, so she kept on driving.

At the point of fearing she'd somehow missed the landmark, she saw the old car and, directly behind it, the giant saguaro.

"Yes!" she shouted, and tapped the brakes until she slowed enough to take the turn.

Dust boiled upward as the thick, gritty cloud that had been trailing her caught up and engulfed the SUV. Moments later, Cat shot out of the morass on a southward route. The sun was on her left and in her eyes. She grabbed a pair of sunglasses and shoved them up her nose, then stomped the accelerator all the way to the floor.

Art Ball hung up the phone, then looked up at Wilson McKay and shrugged.

"She don't answer."

A muscle jerked at the corner of Wilson's left eye as he pivoted angrily and headed for the door.

"Hey, McKay! If I hear anything, I'll let you know."

"Yeah . . . right," Wilson said.

The door banged shut behind him as he left the bail-bond office. It was hard for him to decide which made him the angriest. The fact that Cat still hadn't checked in, or the fact that he was so damned weak-minded where she was concerned that he'd gone crawling to Art Ball for possible scraps of information.

"Hell," Wilson muttered, as he headed for his vehicle. The day was sunny, but the air was frigid. It matched the hard, cold knot in his gut.

His phone was ringing as he got into his vehicle. A quick glance at the caller ID and he answered.

"It's me. What's up, LaQueen?"

The timbre of his secretary's voice was up at least two notches when she spoke. He could tell that she was ticked about something.

"Can you come to the office?" she asked.

"Yes. What's up?"

"We got a phone call from County Jail. A repeat offender named Houston Franks just called for a bond."

Wilson frowned. He knew Franks by reputation.

"What's his bond?"

"Two-hundred thousand."

"What are the charges?"

"There is a whole list of them, including assault. He beat up his mother when she would not tell him where she had hidden her money."

"That's a no-brainer for me. We don't touch him," Wilson said. "If he bonds out, it will have to be on somebody else's dime."

LaQueen sighed, then lowered her voice.

"That is what I knew you would say, but his brother is in the office and he is not leaving until he talks to you."

"I'm ten minutes away. I'll be right there." Then he added, "Are you okay?"

"Not really."

The hair rose on the back of Wilson's neck. LaQueen was the kind of person who could handle anything and, usually, anyone.

"Has he threatened you?"

"More or less."

Her reluctance to elaborate told Wilson that the man was close by. He cursed beneath his breath. "Hang in there, honey. I'm on my way."

He put his vehicle in gear and stomped the accelerator, shooting out into traffic without caution. Within nine minutes of her call, he was pulling into the back of the building where his office was located. He got out at a run and then used his key to let himself in the alley door. He strode into the office just as a blond-haired man with a pockmarked face grabbed LaQueen's arm and twisted her toward him.

LaQueen pulled away, then slapped the man's face just as Wilson stepped between them.

"Get your goddamned hands off her," Wilson snapped, then grabbed the man by the arm and in two moves slammed him belly-first against the wall and cuffed him.

"Hey! What the hell do you —"

"You assaulted my assistant. You're going to jail."

A dark flush swept up the man's neck all the way to his hairline.

"I didn't hurt her none. Hell . . . I've been sitting here for over an hour and getting the runaround. All I want is a bond for my brother."

"I assume you're talking about Houston Franks?"

"Yeah. I'm his younger brother, Jimmy."

"Well, Jimmy, I don't bond out men who beat up their mothers." He yanked at the handcuffs hard enough to make Jimmy Franks wince. "Or mess with men who try to fuck with me and mine. You shouldn't have touched her."

"Come on, man . . . I need —"

Wilson dragged Jimmy Franks into a

chair, then turned to LaQueen, who, for once, was speechless.

"You all right?" he asked.

She took a deep breath, then nodded.

"Call the police," Wilson said.

Jimmy Franks started cursing as LaQueen picked up the phone.

Wilson turned around and pointed a finger in his face.

"Shut up," he said softly. "Just shut the hell up."

Franks hushed, but the expression on his face held more than anger. There was a "get even" look in his eyes that Wilson had seen before. It wasn't the first time, and it wouldn't be the last, that he and some bad-ass had been unable to come to what might be considered a mutual understanding.

A short while later, the second member of the Franks family was carted off to lockup. LaQueen watched until Jimmy and his police escort were out of sight before she turned to face Wilson.

"I should have handled that better."

He frowned, then put his arms around her.

"No, you should never have been put in that situation to begin with." He gave her a quick hug, then pulled back until they were eye-to-eye. "I promise you, it won't happen again."

"You can't make that kind of promise," she said.

"Well, yes, I can . . . and will. You will not be in this office alone again."

LaQueen frowned. "I do not need a babysitter."

Wilson matched her frown for frown.

"I'm not hiring a babysitter. I'm hiring another bounty hunter. You and I both know I could use the help. And when one of us is out, the other one will be on-site. Then, the next time some bastard like Jimmy Franks comes in, you won't be facing him alone."

LaQueen sighed, then laid a hand along the side of his cheek.

"You are a good man, Wilson McKay."

"Yeah . . . and I suspect you and my mother are the only two females to agree on that."

"That Cat Dupree still giving you fits?"

"She's not giving me anything," he said.

LaQueen smiled.

"And therein lies your trouble . . . huh, boss?"

Wilson shrugged. "Since I've never been able to lie to you and make you buy it, there's no need to start now."

LaQueen shook her head.

"I think you quit too soon."

"You don't know what you're talking

about," he muttered.

"I know what I know," she said. "If she is worth it to you, you do not quit."

"There's a difference between quitting and being fed up," he said. "So, do we have a file with potential employees?"

"No."

"Then we need to make one."

"Are we going to put an ad in the paper?"

"No. I'll make some calls."

"You're the boss," LaQueen said.

The sun was shining, which seemed to be a good sign to Tutuola as he entered the outskirts of Chihuahua. The city was so familiar; he was already anticipating stopping at his favorite restaurant. His belly growled as he stopped at a crossroads to let a man on a bicycle pass.

The man eyed Solomon through the windows, then quickly looked away, as if shocked by what he'd seen.

Solomon saw the man's reaction, then cursed and frowned. He was used to people being shocked by his appearance. The tattoos were fierce. In the past, he'd used them to elevate his badass image. But now, with the burn scars and only half a head of hair, there was an air of pity that came with the shock. That, he didn't like. Along with a new home, he was going to have to think about some kind of makeover.

When the man on the bike was through the intersection, Solomon accelerated past him. The first thing on his agenda was breakfast, then a Realtor. There were always places for sale to anyone holding enough money. And this being the off-season for tourists, he might get himself a deal. It was about time something started working in his favor.

By his watch, it was almost noon, but he hadn't reset it since he'd left Texas, and had no idea what time zone he was in or what time it really was. However, he would deal with that later. Whatever time it was, he was still hungry.

As he headed for Abuela's, he kept checking out places he saw for sale, along with areas that were more remote than others. He had no desire to mix with the population. His requirements were no neighbors, no neighborhood, no lawn to care for. He wanted a place apart, and he had the money to buy it.

American dollars went a long way in Mexico, compared to other countries. The way he figured it, he could live comfortably down here for the rest of his life. Finally he tired of shopping for real estate and began looking for a place that served food. Abuela's was on the other side of the city, and he was too hungry to drive that far. By the time he found a place to eat, he was beginning to hurt. He was going to have to squeeze in a visit to a doctor between food and a Realtor.

He wheeled into a parking area beside a small, single-story building and parked. As he exited the car, the scent of tortillas cooking made his stomach growl. When he entered, he had to duck to miss strings of drying red chili peppers hanging from the rafters. He grunted with satisfaction as he noticed there was also a small bar in the corner of the room. A half-dozen posters advertising different beers had been tacked to the walls, and opposite the bar there was an old woman bent over a small fire, slapping raw, uncooked tortillas from hand to hand until they were the desired size and thickness. At that point she flopped them down on an old griddle, letting them cook briefly on one side, then the other, before adding them to a growing stack of freshly cooked tortillas on a small platter beside her.

"Hola," Solomon said.

The old woman didn't look up. He frowned and, this time, yelled.

"Hey! Old woman!"

"Don't yell at her. She cannot hear you."

Solomon turned around just as a heavyset man came out from a back room.

Solomon frowned, then shrugged. No need to make an enemy in the place he intended to live. At least, not yet.

"No offense meant."

The man stared at Solomon long and hard, making no effort to hide his curiosity at Solomon's appearance. Finally he nodded.

"None taken," he said. "Can I help you?"

"Bring me a plate of tortillas and beans."

"You maybe want some *carne asada,* too?"

"Yeah, whatever," Solomon muttered, and sat down, then pointed toward the bar.

"And a beer."

The heavyset man eyed Solomon again, as if trying to decide if it was wise to turn his back to him, then finally nodded before moving toward the bar.

Solomon stretched wearily, then sighed as he kicked back in the chair. Things were finally looking up.

Cat flew past the skeletal remains of the gas station and took the left fork, confident she was still on the right road. As she passed, a roosting turkey buzzard took flight.

By now the sun was directly overhead. She glanced at the gas gauge, then frowned. She had a five-gallon can of extra fuel in the back. It wouldn't be enough to get her back to Dominguez and the baby. She'd have to find more fuel. As isolated as Adobe Blanco was, they must have a gas station for the locals.

As she took a curve in the road, her cell phone slid over and bumped into the console. Several hours ago it had begun beeping at her, signaling unanswered voice mail, so she'd turned it off. There would be time later to check her messages — after she'd located Pilar's family. She picked up the phone and dropped it into a cup holder. When she looked back up, she saw the rooftops of a small village on the horizon.

"Finally," she muttered and, while she wasn't into depending on anyone else for help, she couldn't help but add, "Please, God, help me find that baby's family."

A few minutes later she pulled into the village. As she did, her hopes dropped. Adobe Blanco consisted of less than two dozen houses, all of which were single-story, flat-roofed adobe. Less than half had ever been whitewashed. An emaciated dog wagged its tail as she passed by the doorstep where it was lying. A pair of scrawny chickens pecked in the dirt, while nearby, a woman walked past, balancing a large basket on her head. Cat couldn't tell what was in it but admired her ability. If she could balance her life as well as that woman balanced her load, things would be a lot simpler.

The little village square consisted of a large communal water well. Without electricity, the water was drawn from its depths the old-fashioned way, with a rope and bucket. Cat's frown deepened as she drove even slower. There were no obvious businesses that would give her a stopping point to begin her search. All she could do was get out and hope to God someone here spoke English.

Two women and a young boy who appeared to be in his early teens emerged from the back of one of the houses as Cat pulled to a stop. By the time she got out of her car, the women had stopped, as well, and were staring, obviously surprised by her unexpected appearance.

Cat could tell they were uneasy, but there was no time for delicacy.

"Habla inglés?"

Both women shook their heads. Cat frowned but wasn't ready to give up. Her gaze slid to the boy.

He shrugged.

"Un poquito," he said, holding his thumb and forefinger together to indicate his meaning.

"Is there anyone else here who speaks English?"

"Padre Francisco."

"Where is he?" Cat asked.

The boy pointed down the road. "The . . . how you say . . . temple."

"You mean . . . church?"

The boy smiled and nodded. *"Sí. Sí.* Church."

"How far?" Cat asked.

"Maybe five minutes if you walk."

Cat nodded. *"Gracias."*

"De nada, señorita," he said.

Cat got back in the car and drove in the direction the boy had indicated. Within a couple of minutes, she saw the church in the distance.

"Okay, God . . . please let this work."

Padre Francisco was sitting on a bench beneath a Joshua tree in back of the church, deep in prayer for a sick child in the village, when he heard the sound of an approaching car. The smooth, high-pitched whine of the engine told him it would be a stranger, because no one in this part of the country owned a car that ran as smoothly. He stood, dusted off his robes, then headed for the front of the church. Although the day was sunny, it was cold. In fact, the older Padre Francisco grew, the colder his winters became. He shivered slightly, then poked his hands inside the sleeves of his robes, curious as to who was coming.

Adobe Blanco had been Padre Francisco's first church. He'd arrived in this dusty little no-place over thirty years ago, confident that, once he'd paid his dues to God and the church, he would be assigned to a place more befitting his goals.

The chances had come, but Padre Francisco hadn't gone. He'd been unable to tear himself away from the combination of people and poverty. In truth, he'd learned true humility here, where the only thing people had of any value were their good names.

And so, when he came around the corner of the building and saw the dark, dusty vehicle pulling up at the church, he knew he'd been right. It was a stranger.

To his surprise, the stranger was a lone woman, and when she got out of the vehicle, his first impression was that her beauty was striking but she was far too thin. No one came to Adobe Blanco on purpose, so most likely she was just lost. But when she got closer, and he saw the set of her jaw and the fiery gleam in her eyes, he reassessed his opinion. She might still be lost, but there was an anger in this woman the likes of which he'd never seen.

Cat was looking toward the front door of the church when she realized the man she'd come looking for was already outside. She paused as the priest came toward her and thought to herself that he was taller than most Latinos she knew. His stride was slow but measured, and his face was lined and leathery from the years and the chill of the season. By the time they were face-to-face, she had to look up to meet his gaze.

"Padre Francisco?"

He only nodded.

"You are American?"

"Yes."

"Are you lost, *señorita?*"

She tried to smile, but it didn't quite make it to her lips.

"I've been lost most of my life," she said. "But that's not why I'm here."

The odd, husky quality of her voice was explained once he saw the ugly scar on her neck. He sighed. Life was hard, no matter who you were or where you came from.

"Then how can I help you?" he asked.

"Do you know a young woman named Pilar Mendoza? She would have a baby girl less than a year old."

Cat was more than slightly surprised by the smile that spread across his face. It drastically changed the somberness of his expression.

"Sí! Sí! The little mother."

Cat flinched. The isolation of her life had not prepared her for being the bearer of bad news to anyone but bail jumpers. Still, it was why she'd come.

"It is cold today," the priest said. "Please . . . we will talk more inside . . . okay?"

The priest's smile, as well as his gentle touch, was almost painful to Cat. Still, she let him lead her inside the small one-room church.

Once inside, it was obvious that the priest's life was no better or worse than the other people of Adobe Blanco. The normal ornamentation one expected to see in Catholic churches was absent here. Behind a pulpit there was a single wooden cross hanging on the wall, bearing the crucified figure of Jesus, and there was a small figurine of the Virgin Mary in a niche by the doorway.

135

The priest dipped his fingers in a small metal bowl of holy water, made the sign of the cross, then genuflected, before leading the way down the center aisle to the pews in the front.

"Please . . . sit," he said.

Cat sat down as the priest moved to a small pot-bellied stove near the wall and stirred the coals before adding a small stick of wood. When he was done, he sat down beside her.

"Now then, you mentioned Pilar. Are you a friend?"

Cat took a deep breath. *God, help me do this right.*

"No, Padre. I never met her. Does she have family here?"

Padre Francisco frowned. It seemed strange that this woman would ask about a woman she didn't know, then inquire about a family.

"I'm sorry," he said softly. "Maybe if you explained your true reason for —"

Cat swallowed nervously. "She's dead."

The priest reeled as if he'd been slapped. Again he made the sign of the cross as he whispered some prayer Cat didn't understand.

"Dear God . . . what happened? How do you know this?"

Unaware that her fingers were curled into fists, Cat started talking, wanting to get it all said without coming undone.

"I found her and the baby in the desert last night."

Tears rolled down the old priest's face as he reached for Cat's hands and held them firmly in his own.

"She left only two days ago to meet a man who would take her to her husband, Jorge, who is working for a vegetable grower in the San Fernando valley in California."

"So Dominguez guessed right," she said.

"I'm sorry?"

Cat looked up, meeting his gaze. "Lieutenant Dominguez . . . the policeman in Casa Rojo, figured she might have been robbed and dumped by a coyote, since she was so far from any towns."

The weight of sorrow was heavy on the priest's face and shoulders.

"I am so sorry . . . so sorry . . . for all of you, but how do you become the bearer of such news . . . and how did you learn her identity if she was already dead?"

Cat shuddered as she looked down at his hands, his fingers curling around hers in a gesture of protection. His sympathy was something she hadn't counted on. She bit her lip and looked away, unwilling to let him see how touched she was by his words.

"When I found them, I took them back to the last town I'd been through, which was Casa Rojo."

"Ah, yes . . . I know it well."

"That's where I met Dominguez, and he went through the papers Pilar was carrying. He identified her from those."

Padre Francisco shook his head in dismay.

"Poor little mama . . . poor little baby . . . I can not imagine how this came to be."

Suddenly Cat realized that the priest thought both of them were dead.

"Oh! No! The baby . . . the little girl . . . she's alive. I found them before the animals did. The mother . . . Pilar . . . had been dead for a while. She died of snakebite. It was actually the baby's cries that I heard and that led me to find them. I changed the baby, then fed her with some milk Pilar had been carrying, before I went for help. The baby is the real reason I came. Dominguez is going to turn her over to the authorities in Nuevo Laredo if I can't find family before tonight."

The priest jumped to his feet, clapping his hands to his face, then to his chest.

"Praise be! It's a miracle." He touched Cat's face, then her hair. "You are an angel."

Cat shuddered, then held up her hands as

she stepped away.

"No. I'm no angel."

The priest smiled gently, allowing Cat's denial, and for the first time, allowed himself to stare at the scar on her neck. He frowned, then quickly looked away, fixing his gaze on her face instead.

"What is your name, my child?"

"Cat . . . Catherine . . . Dupree."

"So, Cat Dupree . . . to the Mendoza family . . . you are an angel."

Cat started shaking. Maybe this trip was going to be worthwhile after all.

"You mean there is other family?"

He nodded. "Yes . . . Pilar's parents, as well as her father-in-law, still live in Adobe Blanco."

"Will you go with me to tell them? They need to get to Casa Rojo before the day is over or Dominguez is going to turn the baby over to the welfare department in your country."

"Yes, yes, of course I will go with you. We can't lose little Maria Elena, too."

So now she knew the name of the baby who'd stolen her heart, Cat thought. "That's the baby's name?"

"Yes. She was christened in this very church."

Cat looked around, imagining a much

happier occasion than her visit here today.

"Is there anyone in the village who has a vehicle? You will need to bring back Pilar's body, as well as the baby."

"Yes, yes . . . I . . . the church . . . has an old station wagon. It won't be the first time it is used for a hearse."

Cat glanced at her watch.

"Can we go now? There's not a lot of time."

"Just let me get the keys. You can follow me back into the village to the family home."

"I don't know what to say to them," Cat said.

He nodded, then put a hand on her shoulder.

"Do not worry. I will tell them for you, because they do not speak English. However, it would be good if you were there, should they have a question they want to ask."

"Oh. Sure."

It was the last thing Cat wanted to do, but she could no more have refused the priest's request than she could have driven away and left the baby — *Maria Elena* — without a chance of returning her to her family.

The priest grabbed a coat and some keys.

"The car is behind the church. You go to

your vehicle and wait for me. I'll be right there."

"Yes, okay . . . and, Father . . . ?"

He stopped, then turned to her, a questioning expression on his face.

"Once we start back to Casa Rojo, I will follow you."

He shrugged. "The station wagon is old. It does not always cooperate with our needs. Maybe it would be best if you drove ahead and made sure that the *policía* do not give up the baby before we can arrive."

"Oh. Yes. All right. Don't worry. I'll make sure the baby is still there — whenever you arrive."

SEVEN

Cat glanced in the rearview mirror as she drove out of Adobe Blanco. She could still see the priest with Pilar's family in the old church station wagon behind her, but not for long. Padre Francisco's top speed wasn't going to be more than forty-five miles per hour. All gassed up and good to go, she was shooting for eighty. After a quick look at her wristwatch, she stomped the accelerator. She had the satellite radio in her SUV jacked up on high, hoping that music would drown out the memory of the wails of Pilar Mendoza's grief-stricken parents.

Their faces had been wreathed in smiles when she and the priest had gotten out of their cars. She'd watched their pleasure at seeing the priest at their door turn to disbelief and then horror. Even though she hadn't understood the language, she'd known when Padre Francisco had explained her presence. They'd looked at her, then through her, as if by refusing to acknowledge her presence, the truth of what had happened to their daughter could be ignored.

She'd known, too, when they'd asked about the baby — Maria Elena. She'd seen a break in their grief when they'd been told the baby still lived. When the mother suddenly threw her arms around Cat and hugged her, she supposed the priest had told them about her part in saving the baby's life. She wanted to tell them that she knew how they felt, but she couldn't — not even if she spoke the language. Marsha had been her best friend, not her daughter. And even though she was grieving on her own level for the loss, she had a suspicion that it was nothing to the loss of a child, no matter how old that child might be.

After a few brief moments of having her condolences translated by Padre Francisco to Pilar's family, she'd told the priest she was heading back to Casa Rojo. She wanted to make sure she got back in time to keep Dominguez from turning that baby — her baby — over to the Mexican welfare system. She wouldn't let herself rationalize the absurdity of feeling so protective toward someone else's child. Her emotions had already been ripped to shreds from the brutality of Marsha's death. Maybe she'd subconsciously connected Pilar with Marsha, and Maria Elena with Marsha's unborn baby. If she had, then she'd been no more good to Pilar than she'd been to Marsha. She'd been too late to save either mother, but this time there had been a survivor — a baby only minutes away from becoming food for the animals. It wasn't exactly a fair shake for Marsha and her baby, but like life, it was what it was.

By the time Cat got to the old gas station to make her first turn on the road back to Casa Rojo, she was already shifting her mental focus to the moment when she would see Pilar's baby in her grandparents' arms. Later, she would grieve again for the death of her best friend, but today she was going to see a positive end to a sad beginning. All she had to do to make it happen was get to Casa Rojo before sundown.

The baby kept crying. Dominguez had called in his wife right after the American woman left town, fully convinced that he would never see her again once she got a look at the road to Adobe Blanco. He'd already made a call to Nuevo Laredo informing the authorities there of the woman's death and the baby's presence. They were sending someone to pick up the child but couldn't get there before morning. His wife had gone all soft when she'd seen the baby, but the bloom had soon fallen from the rose. Despite her best efforts, the baby had continued to fuss and cry. Dominguez had said a quick prayer to the Virgin Mary to keep the child well. He didn't want to have to explain to the Nuevo Laredo authorities why a seemingly healthy baby had died on his watch.

He still didn't understand what was wrong with her. She had no obvious wounds and no bruising, so there was no reason to assume she might have internal injuries. Her diaper was dry, and except for the possibility of something effectively invisible, such as insignificant as an earache or the onset of teething, neither he nor his wife could understand why she kept crying.

They'd tried feeding her with the same milk that had been in the dead mother's possessions, and even though she'd downed it, she had soon spat it back up again. She'd been bathed, fed, held and diapered numerous times, yet she remained inconsolable. It was almost as if she knew her mother was dead, even though Dominguez knew that was impossible. The child was too young to understand what had happened, surely. And yet . . .

He glanced out the window, noting the swiftly setting sun, then back at his wife, who was sitting on a cot in an empty cell, rocking the fussy baby in her arms. His expression softened. His wife was a good woman. It was unfortunate that they'd never been blessed with children.

The baby, who seemed to be on the verge of falling asleep, suddenly jerked in her arms, then began to scream all over again. He cursed beneath his breath, and when his wife looked up at him with concern, he shrugged.

At that moment the hinges on the front door squeaked. He turned to see who was coming in, then stared in disbelief.

The American woman — Cat Dupree — was back, and with an angry look on her face.

"What's wrong with her?" Cat asked, as she pushed past Dominguez and headed for the open cell. Without waiting for permission, she lifted the baby out of his wife's arms and clasped her to her breast.

"Hey, hey, no tears, no tears. I found your family, baby girl. I found them for you."

Cat's husky voice softened as she crooned to the little girl, rubbing her hand gently up and down the baby's back as she rocked her in her arms. The baby's hair was soft against the underside of her chin. The sweet, clean smell of her, along with the dampness of baby tears on Cat's neck, washed through her senses, triggering instincts she'd never known she had. Just for a moment, she let herself imagine what it would be like to have a child of her own. Then she shuddered. Those thoughts were for people who had futures. Cat had a job ahead of her that could very easily eliminate any sort of future.

She turned to face Dominguez, only to find him staring at her.

"What?" she said.

"The baby . . . she's stopped crying," he said.

Cat arched an eyebrow, then glared. "Don't tell me she's been crying ever since I left."

"As you wish," Dominguez said.

"Are you serious? The baby has been crying all this time?"

"Maybe she's getting sick," Dominguez said.

Cat laid a hand on the baby's forehead.

"She doesn't have a fever and she's not crying now."

"Yes, I see that," he said, and then pointed at her. "You came back."

She frowned. "I said I would."

He shrugged. "I didn't think you meant it."

"I always mean what I say," Cat said. "Oh . . . by the way. A priest, Padre Francisco, from Adobe Blanco is on his way with Pilar's family to claim the body and the baby, who happens to be their granddaughter."

Dominguez stiffened. "But I've already contacted the authorities to take the —"

Still clutching the baby, Cat took a quick step backward.

"You said you'd wait until sundown."

Dominguez shifted his stance, glancing first at his wife, then back at Cat.

"So . . . I will make another call, okay?"

The glare in Cat's eyes eased but didn't disappear. She was reserving full judgment until she saw, for herself, this baby returned to her family.

"You do that," Cat said, as she continued to pat the baby's back.

As Dominguez went to make the call, his wife moved past Cat, nodding shyly before giving the baby's head a final pat.

"Esta bien," she said.

Cat nodded, then rubbed her cheek against the baby's curly hair. "Yes, it's good. Everything is good."

Cat glanced back at Dominguez. She supposed he was calling off the people who were coming after the baby. It would be at least an hour, maybe more, before Padre Francisco arrived, and she was tired — so tired. The baby had fallen asleep in her arms, clutching a fistful of Cat's hair. She couldn't lay the baby down without pulling the hair out of her hand and feared that would wake her back up again. The cot inside the empty cell looked inviting, and Cat really was so tired.

She moved inside, then eased down on the cot. The baby squirmed but didn't wake. Cat leaned back, then slowly stretched out and turned on her side with the baby still held fast against her breasts.

"Maria Elena," Cat whispered, gently kissing the side of the baby's face, then closed her eyes to rest — just for a moment.

By the time Dominguez finished his conversation, Cat and the baby were both asleep. The silence was welcome, and now that he knew the responsibility of the baby would soon be out of his hands, he, too, began to relax. He sat down in his chair, put his feet up on the desk and then kicked back. He hadn't been any help in putting the baby in a good mood, but in this part of the world, nothing happened quickly. Nothing else was going to happen until the family arrived, and Dominguez knew how to wait.

Solomon Tutuola had found the perfect house to buy. It had been standing empty for over eighteen months, and the owners were eager to sell. He'd spent half the day with a Realtor named Chouie Garza, who was getting on his last nerve.

Chouie Garza had never been afraid of a prospective client before, but after meeting Solomon Tutuola, he could no longer state that claim. He'd gone from shock to fear so fast that he'd excused himself within minutes of their meeting and gone to a bathroom to pee before he wet himself.

Even now, after spending a good half day with Tutuola, showing him first one property, then another, Chouie was still unable to look him in the face for very long without shuddering. When Tutuola had finally settled on a place that had been for sale for almost two years, he was elated — both for the fact that their time together was coming to an end and because he was finally going to get rid of a place he'd considered unsalable.

Tutuola was just as happy to be done with Garza. Every time he looked at the man —

with his dark, beady eyes, long, pointed nose and odd, elongated ears that stood out from the sides of his face like small wings — he thought of a rat.

Pissed off by the man's lack of machismo, Tutuola had given him a slow smile, accentuating the perfectly filed points on his teeth. When Chouie Garza saw them, he literally gasped. At that point, Tutuola laughed out loud. Stretching his slowly healing skin was painful, but Rat Man's reaction was too good to ignore.

"I want to take immediate possession," Tutuola said.

Garza shifted nervously. That was an impossible suggestion. Then he glanced up just long enough to gauge Solomon Tutuola's attitude and decided he wasn't man enough to disagree. Between the burns and the tattoos, Tutuola looked like something out of hell.

He danced from one foot to another, then shook his head.

"The owners . . . they have the final say, but it is customary to wait until the final papers have been signed and money has changed hands."

"How long is that going to take?" Tutuola asked.

"Maybe two weeks."

"No. Hell no," Tutuola muttered. "I'll look elsewhere. I'm not going to spend the next two weeks in some motel. I've been injured, damn it. I need rest . . . real rest."

Garza panicked. He could see his commission going down the drain.

"Wait! Wait. Maybe I could give the owners a call . . . see what they say?"

"Then do it," Solomon said.

Garza walked outside with his cell phone to his ear.

Solomon watched Rat Man's face, well aware that he was afraid of losing a big fat commission. When he saw Garza's expression lighten, he smiled to himself. It was going to work out after all.

Garza came back into the house, all but strutting.

"It is all right, Mr. Tutuola. I have fixed the problem for you. The owners will agree you take immediate possession if you are willing to give more earnest money."

"Whatever," Solomon said.

"Five thousand," Chouie added. "It is furnished, you know, and they don't want their —"

Solomon held up his hand, then strode out to his car with Garza right behind him. He popped the trunk, dipped into the bag with Mark Presley's money and counted out five thousand American dollars.

"Here," he said. "Now where are the keys?"

Garza was stunned. The money was in his hands, but he couldn't quit looking at the car, wondering exactly how much more was in that bag in the trunk.

Tutuola picked the man up by his shoulders until his feet were dangling off the ground.

"I cannot breathe so good," Garza said.

Tutuola let him drop.

Garza landed with a thud, then staggered slightly before regaining his balance. His hands were shaking as he handed Tutuola the keys.

"When the final papers are ready, I will be in touch," Garza said, and made a break for his car.

Solomon didn't bother watching him leave. He was already unloading his car.

It was nearly midnight when Wilson walked into his apartment. He closed the front door behind him without turning on the lights and tossed his keys on the hall table before hanging up his coat. Another cold front had come in just before sundown. According to the weatherman, it was just above freezing, but with the windchill, it felt more like twelve degrees.

Wilson stood in the silence of his home, feeling the emptiness. Somewhere down the hall, he heard a faucet dripping, and the antique clock on his mantle had obviously run down. The steady tick he was used to hearing was missing. He strode to the fireplace for a closer look.

The pendulum had stopped when the clock had run down, which, according to the time, was either two minutes after three last night or two minutes after three this afternoon. Either way, it mirrored Wilson's life. He'd lost all sense of time, along with his sense of well-being. Ever since his last night with Cat when they'd parted on such angry terms, he'd just gone through the motions of living.

After resetting the clock and rewinding the movements, he shoved his hands through his hair in mute frustration, then headed for his bedroom. He hadn't eaten since breakfast, but he didn't want food. He didn't want to do anything but crawl into bed and pray for a night without dreams. He needed to sleep without being haunted by memories of a woman who didn't want him.

"Damn woman," he muttered, as he sat down on the side of the bed to pull off his boots. "Damn . . . hardheaded . . . single-minded . . . ball-bustin' . . . female."

He got up from the bed and began taking off his clothes, tossing them one by one onto a nearby chair until he was completely naked. After a quick trip to the bathroom, he pulled the covers back on his bed and crawled in. The familiarity of the mattress's indentations fit his body perfectly as he let himself relax. He could still hear a faucet dripping as he closed his eyes.

It was the last thing he heard.

Cat was shaking. Wilson could feel her muscles trembling as he slid inside her body. The quick intake of her breath against his ear was a trigger point for his own excitement. When she wrapped her legs around his waist and her arms around his neck, he thought he'd died and gone to heaven.

God, but he loved this woman. Loved making love to her. Loved watching the way her left eyebrow arched when she was trying not to laugh. Loved the constant surprise of seeing that pink butterfly tattoo on her backside. Loved the way she smelled. Even loved to watch that muscle tic near her right eye when she was pissed.

Their bodies fit together like dancers in perfect unison as Wilson began to move, stroke after stroke, rocking back and forth, with only the contours of each other's body visible in the dark.

The digital clock on the nightstand clicked over on the hour. It was one o'clock.

The next time Wilson looked, Cat was beginning to moan. He knew what it meant — knew that she was beginning to come undone. He could do no less than go with her. All the way up — right to the peak of —

Then she screamed.

Wilson sat up with a jerk. Despite the chill in his apartment, he was drenched with sweat.

"Jesus," he muttered, and hit the floor with both feet.

The bathroom tiles were cold, as was the water he splashed on his face, but no matter how long he stood there and how much water went down the drain, it wouldn't take away the memory of that scream. He didn't believe in omens and premonitions, but he didn't like the way that dream had ended.

Moments later, he headed for the kitchen, hoping that a cold beer would take away the bad taste of what had started out as a damned good dream and ended up a nightmare.

It was the last cold beer in the refrigerator. He popped the top on the can and took his first sip before moving into the living room. He stood at the windows overlooking the parking lot and the street beyond while his beer went warm and his feet got colder. Cat was out there — somewhere. He just wished to God she would call. All he wanted was to hear her voice. Even if she was telling him to go to hell for butting into her business, it would be enough. At least he would know she was alive.

Finally he took the nearly full can of beer back to the kitchen and poured it down the drain.

As he started back to his bedroom, he heard the old clock that he'd wound earlier beginning to strike the hour. He paused in the hallway, listening as it struck once, then twice, then the third time, before once again silence ruled.

Three o'clock in the morning.

He'd been in bed less than three hours, and as far as he was concerned, his rest was over. It was too damned early to get up, but he wasn't about to take a chance on reliving that dream.

Instead, he crawled into bed, reached for the remote on his TV and aimed it at the screen. A few moments later, John Wayne's face filled the screen. The irony was not lost on Wilson. John Wayne always saved the day.

Tonight he was going to save Wilson's sanity. He leaned back against the headboard and turned up the volume, willing to do whatever it took to get the sound of Cat's scream out of his head.

It was eleven minutes after eight in the evening when Cat woke up. For a few moments she couldn't remember where she was or why she was behind bars. Then the baby she was holding squirmed, and she remembered everything. She groaned beneath her breath as she eased up from the cot, careful not to wake the still sleeping baby.

"*Buenos noches,* Señorita Dupree. I trust your rest was a good one?"

Cat nodded, then glanced back at the baby on the cot, and took off her jacket, rolled it up and tucked it against the baby's back as a buffer to keep her from rolling off, before moving out of the cell.

She glanced at her watch, then frowned before moving to the other side of Dominguez's desk.

"The priest and Pilar's family have not yet arrived?" she asked.

Dominguez shrugged. "No." His eyes narrowed thoughtfully as he eyed her long legs and slim hips. His gaze was slowly moving upward when Cat toed the desk with her boot.

"I'm up here," she said shortly.

Dominguez smiled slyly.

"You are a beautiful woman. It does not hurt to look."

Cat's jaw tensed as she curled her fingers into fists. "It'll hurt more than you think."

Dominguez didn't miss the warning.

"I meant no harm. As for the priest, you weren't telling me he was coming just to keep the baby here, were you?"

Cat flinched, too tired to mince words and too pissed at the challenge to her veracity.

"I don't lie," she said shortly, then strode to the door and yanked it open.

It was dark — so dark — just as it had been last night when she'd found mother and child. Then she sighed. Had it really been less than twenty-four hours since she'd come upon the body? It seemed much longer.

Come on, Padre Francisco . . . where the hell are you?

It did occur to her as the thought came and went that mentioning hell and a Catholic priest in the same sentence wasn't exactly proper. She stepped outside, grateful for the cool air on her face, then she stilled, tilted her head a bit to the left and

159

listened. It didn't take her long to realize she was hearing an engine. She stepped off the stoop and walked a couple of steps away from the building.

"Someone's coming," she called out.

Dominguez got up from his chair and followed her out. No sooner had he stopped beside her than they both saw an appearing headlight.

"It's them," Cat said.

"A headlight is missing," Dominguez muttered.

"Is that against the law here?"

"I just —"

"Don't give them grief over a headlight, okay? Not unless you're going to help them fix it. They've got a whole lot more to deal with than a burned-out light."

Dominguez frowned, but he kept his silence. He didn't much like this American woman, but he supposed she would be the last one to care. Still, she was a good woman to do what she'd done.

Moments later, the silhouette of the car began to take shape. When it pulled to a stop in front of the open doorway where Cat and Dominguez were standing, the car backfired twice as the priest turned off the engine.

Cat moved forward.

Padre Francisco got out, groaning slightly from the stiffness of old joints as he stretched. Pilar's mother and father emerged from the other side of the car.

"I was getting worried," Cat said, as the priest moved toward her.

"We had a bit of car trouble, but the Lord provided . . . and here we are."

"Padre, this is Officer Dominguez. He's been taking care of Maria Elena."

"Is she all right?" the priest asked.

"Yes. Come see."

The priest said something to the older couple, who looked toward the officer.

Cat sighed. This was all so damned sad and awkward. She knew they were going to have to identify Pilar's body, which was in a small back room, but she figured they should see the baby first.

She stepped forward, took the elderly woman by the hand and tugged gently. "Maria Elena," she said.

The little woman's face was crumpled with grief, yet when Cat spoke the baby's name, there was a glint of hope in her eyes.

Cat led her into the building, then to the back cell where the baby lay asleep on the cot. She reached down, moved her jacket, then picked up the baby.

The little girl's mouth pursed, then made

161

slight sucking motions as she slept. Cat stifled a sob, kissed the dark, tangled curls, then turned and handed her to her grandmother.

The old woman took the baby like a starving man reaching for water, then lowered her head and began rocking and crooning to the baby in a soft, gentle tone.

Cat wouldn't let herself think about how empty her arms felt or the sharp pain in her chest. This had nothing to do with her. She'd done a good deed, and it was time to move on.

"Gracias, gracias, muchas gracias, señorita."

Cat's vision blurred. She started to reach out — to touch for one last time those dark, baby curls — then she stopped. No need prolonging the inevitable.

"Take good care of her," Cat said, and strode out of the cell, pausing at the desk where the others had gathered.

"I'll be leaving now," she said.

Padre Francisco laid a hand on her arm.

"I will pray for you," he said.

It was the last thing she'd expected to hear.

"It will be wasted prayer," she said shortly. "God quit on me a long time ago."

The priest sighed. His voice was soft, but he did not mince words.

162

"God doesn't quit on people. People quit on God."

Cat shivered slightly at the portent in the words, then walked out of the little building without looking back. She poured the last of her fuel from the extra cans she carried into the tank, then got in her car. She picked up her laptop and plugged it into the charger, then booted up her program. The blip that she'd been trailing was in Chihuahua, Mexico, and it was motionless.

"I'm coming," she said. "Whoever you are."

EIGHT

Cat drove through the entire night with a lighter heart than when she'd started this trip. It was strange how fate put people together. She'd been alone in the world, and then she'd met Marsha. They'd bonded so fast, it was as if they'd known each other forever. Just having Marsha in her life had made everything bearable. They'd thumbed their noses at people who sat in judgment of them and managed not to fall into the dark side of life on the streets.

Even now, living with the pain of knowing she would never see Marsha again, she'd learned a big lesson. It was better to have special people in your life, if only for a short time, than to never have had them at all.

For Pilar's family, having baby Maria Elena back with them would go a long way toward healing their pain. And if she hadn't been looking for a ghost, she would never have found Pilar and her baby. She didn't want to think that a higher power might have kept Solomon Tutuola alive so that she would have to come back for him again, but she wondered what the odds were of accidentally being in the right place at the right time to find a baby just before the wild animals could get to her?

She didn't know whether to call it fate or the hand of God or just coincidence, but she had to say, she wasn't sorry. Whoever it was with Mark Presley's belongings, they'd done Pilar Mendoza a great big favor.

Sunrise finally came, along with a sign indicating that she was ten kilometers from some place called Agua Caliente. She was already exhausted by this search, but not quite ready to admit her obsessive need to confirm Tutuola's death might be ruining her life. Nobody could say this trip hadn't already been worthwhile, but Cat wasn't the kind of woman to quit on anything, including herself.

However, her boss, Art, had quit. Calling, that was. She didn't know whether he was pissed or just figured she was dead, in which case there was every likelihood that she would go home to no job — if she got home at all. She'd meant to return his calls. She'd promised she would let him know she was okay. But she hadn't counted on getting caught up in a shoot-out on the interstate, or finding a dead body and a lost baby in the Mexican desert.

She reached for her water bottle, downed the last few drops, then tossed it on the back floorboard, along with the rest of her accumulating trash. When she got to this Agua Caliente, she was going to have to find a place to rest — at least for a while.

Even Wonder Woman ate and slept.

A short while later, she drove into the small, dusty town and, as soon as she did, she began revising her earlier plans. Not only were there no obvious public businesses, she was just praying there was someone here who sold gas.

She braked for a little boy and a dog who ran across the street in front of her, then sat for a moment, letting the heat of the morning sun coming through the windshield warm her body. She shuddered, wishing it could also warm away the permanent chill inside her heart. She was sick and tired of being angry, of distrusting the world in general, even though life hadn't given her much incentive to change.

Then she thought of Wilson. He hadn't given her any reason to distrust him. He'd come through for her time and time again, even when she hadn't asked. Yet she kept pushing him away. What the hell was that all about? If Marsha was still alive, she would be all over her for driving away the only good man she'd come across in years.

Suddenly there was a knock on her window. She jerked, then turned to see a man standing by her car, and rolled down the window.

"*Habla inglés?*" she asked.

He shrugged. "*Un poquito, señorita.*"

A little was better than nothing at all. Cat tossed out a question.

"Does anyone here sell gas?"

He frowned. "*Como?*"

Cat pointed to the fuel gauge.

"Gasoline . . . fuel."

He leaned closer to see where she was pointing. "Ah. *Sí! Sí!* You come. I show."

He crossed in front of her, then motioned for her to follow, which she did, driving through one winding narrow alley after another until he finally came to a stop in front of a small adobe house with a wide-roofed overhang that ran the length of the building. A spindly post at each end of the makeshift porch provided the roof's sole support. Cat resisted the urge to give one a shake as she passed and followed her guide inside the open doorway.

She jumped as a cat hissed at her feet,

then darted past her. Once inside, she had to stand for a few moments to let her eyesight adjust to the lack of artificial light. The little man who'd guided her here was watching her.

She reached in her jacket pocket, pulled out a five-dollar bill and handed it to him.

"Gracias," she told her guide.

Beaming with surprise, he stuffed the money in his hat, then put the hat back on his head.

"De nada," he whispered softly, and slipped away.

She stood for a moment, absorbing the odors and ambiance of what was obviously a small store.

Long strands of red chiles hung from the rafters, while a couple of open crates of onions sat on the floor near a counter. The north wall of the building was stacked eye-high with cartons of Mexican beer, while the opposite wall was the brace for several oversized sacks of dry beans. The shelves behind the counter in front of her held a colorful assortment of cans, the contents of which she could only guess from the pictures on the labels, since her grasp of the language was sparse. She did, however, recognize cartons of bottled water and moved toward them.

The man behind the counter was staring at her. She took no offense. It was probably rare that a stranger ever made it this far, especially a lone woman.

"Habla inglés?" she asked.

He shook his head.

She sighed, but before she fell back on makeshift sign language, a small, stocky woman holding a bag of groceries stepped into Cat's line of vision and spoke up.

"I speak the English," she said.

Cat smiled. "Thank you," she said. "Could you please tell the man I need to buy water for me and gas for my car?"

The little woman nodded, then rattled off a quick sentence to the man behind the counter. He waved in understanding and disappeared into a back room, returning quickly carrying a large five-gallon can and a funnel.

Cat pointed outside.

He sped past her, anxious to make the sale.

Cat glanced around the room, looking for something she could buy that she could eat on the road, but the racks of candy bars and chips that were always available in quick stops in the States were visibly absent.

Once again she turned to the little woman.

"Excuse me, miss."

"Paloma. My name is Paloma," the woman said.

Cat nodded. "Pretty name," she said.

"It means 'dove' in your language."

"They call me Cat."

Paloma's eyes narrowed thoughtfully. *"El gato."*

"Yeah, that's me," Cat said. "Look . . . I've got quite a way to go. What can I buy that I can eat without having to cook it first?"

Paloma frowned. There was nothing in this store like that.

"I am sorry, *señorita,* but this is a small place. We do not have the hurry foods of which you speak."

Cat stifled a smile, knowing that Paloma meant to say fast foods. It was a charming mistake.

"So, how far to the next town?" Cat asked.

Paloma frowned. "A long, long way, and nothing as large as Agua Caliente."

Cat gave herself a mental kick in the butt for not preparing herself better. As usual, she'd gone off half-cocked and was paying for it now. At least she was going to have fuel and water. She would have to go hungry for the time being, but it wouldn't be the first time.

"Oh well, I've been hungry before," she

muttered, more to herself than to Paloma.

Paloma eyed her curiously, wondering how this woman came to be traveling so far and alone.

"You come to my *casa*. I have the tortillas and beans."

Cat was surprised by the unexpected courtesy. "That would be great," she said, then added, "I would pay you."

"Yes . . . okay," Paloma said, then pointed to the door. "I wait for you."

Cat nodded.

The owner of the store came hurrying back inside, grabbed another can of gas and headed back out the door.

Cat followed him out, took her extra fuel cans out of the SUV and set them down beside the car to be filled, as well.

The owner just kept grinning at her, obviously mentally counting the American dollars he was about to receive.

A short while later, her fuel situation had been rectified and she was twenty-four bottles of water to the good. Now all she needed was some fuel for her body. She paid, then came outside to find Paloma waiting patiently beside the car.

"Get in," Cat said. "I'll drive you to your house."

Paloma hesitated only briefly, then got in

Cat's SUV, but not without a bit of effort. The SUV was a four-wheel drive, high off the ground and difficult for a short person to get in. Before Paloma managed to get seated, she'd tried pulling herself up, only to slip and grunt, which had turned her face red with embarrassment. Finally, she was forced into taking the offer of a hand up from Cat.

"Gracias," Paloma said, then pointed to Cat's long legs. "I think you do not have this problem."

Cat grinned. "Where to?" she asked.

Paloma pointed. A couple of minutes later, they pulled up in front of a small adobe house. The little woman got out with no apologies for the way she lived and strode confidently inside, obviously expecting Cat to follow, which she did.

Cat watched Paloma set her small bag of purchases down on a table, then turn and motion toward a chair.

"You sit," she said. "I fix your food."

Cat sat, and within minutes found herself relaxing in the quiet of the simple home. The floor was adobe, just like the walls, and there was a window that had no glass, only some kind of plastic fastened over it. You couldn't see out, but it let light in. The other window was over a small dry sink and was nothing but a hole in the wall that was covered by shutters.

She thought of all the foster houses she'd lived in, all the places she'd been, all the times she'd been hungry. None of them could add up to the poverty in which this small woman lived, yet Paloma seemed at peace with herself and her place in the world.

Cat watched Paloma build a small fire in the dirt hearth, then take cold tortillas from a covered bowl and lay them on a large stone beside the fire.

The smell of wood smoke and the quiet inside the small house were as effective as a sleeping pill. After a few minutes, Cat actually nodded off briefly. The third time it happened, she woke up just before she would have fallen out of the chair to find Paloma watching her.

"You need to rest," she told Cat.

"I know. I'll pull off to the side of the road after a while and get a couple hours of sleep."

Paloma stood there for a moment, judging the wisdom of what she was about to suggest. For some reason, she trusted this woman with the husky voice and the long scar on her throat.

"You sleep here . . . if you want," she said.

Cat stilled. The offer, and the woman, were unexpected. She glanced around the house, saw the small, narrow cot against the bedroom wall, and almost said no. She didn't know this woman. Everything within Cat said not to trust her. But there was something so open about her expression — those dark brown eyes . . . so like the little baby she'd left behind her.

"I would pay," Cat said.

Paloma smiled. "Americans . . . always thinking the money buys everything."

Cat grinned back. "You mean it doesn't?"

They laughed together, and then Paloma took two fresh tortillas from the warming stone, filled them with beans, rolled them up and laid them on a small plate.

"You eat. You sleep. After that, you can pay."

Cat took the food, grateful for the hospitality, and ate quickly, washing down the last bites with a mug of coffee so black she was hesitant to taste it. To her surprise, it wasn't bitter at all.

"Good," she said, as she sat down the empty plate and cup.

"You sleep now," Paloma said.

"I am grateful," Cat said, as she began pulling off her jacket. She slipped her handgun out of the shoulder holster and was about to lay it under her pillow, when Paloma pointed to her throat.

"How did this happen?" she asked.

Cat hesitated, then ran her fingertips lightly along the crooked ridge of flesh.

"A devil did it," she finally said.

Paloma frowned. "Truly a devil?"

Cat shrugged. "Not one with a pitchfork and horns, but a devil just the same."

"Did your devil come to justice?" Paloma asked.

Cat hesitated, then asked herself, what did it matter? This woman would never be a part of her world. Whatever Cat told her would go no further than these walls.

"Not yet," Cat said, knowing "maybe" wasn't going to make any sense to Paloma.

Curious about a woman this unusual, Paloma asked, "So . . . he got away?"

"Not for much longer," Cat said.

Paloma's eyes widened. She folded her hands across her belly, accentuating the roundness of the flesh beneath her clothes, and eyed Cat cautiously. She'd already had one dangerous person in her home this month. She didn't want to unwittingly house another.

"You are the law?"

Cat frowned. "Not exactly." Then she turned and met Paloma's gaze head-on.

175

"Look. If I make you nervous, just say the word and I'm gone."

Paloma thought about it for a moment, then shook her head.

"It is maybe okay. I think you are not like Solomon."

Cat froze. She heard the name, and for a moment couldn't find the good sense to speak. When she did, she didn't even recognize the sound of her own voice.

"You said Solomon. Who is Solomon?" she asked.

Paloma shrugged. "A man I know."

Cat heard her, and still told herself it wasn't possible that it would be the same man.

"This Solomon . . . what did he look like?"

Paloma frowned. "Why do you ask?"

"The man . . . the devil who did this to me is named Solomon."

Paloma gasped, then made the sign of the cross before pointing to the scar on Cat's neck.

"He did this to you?"

"Yes."

Paloma's eyes widened in horror. "This man you seek . . . did he have strange markings on his body?"

Cat's legs went weak. She feared she was about to get an answer to a question that had been plaguing her, and it wasn't going to be what she wanted to hear.

"Tattoos . . . yes . . . all over his face and arms."

"His name is Tutuola?"

"Jesus Christ," Cat muttered, and dropped onto the cot, because her legs would no longer hold her. The tortillas and beans she'd just eaten were threatening to come up. She felt hot and cold all at the same time. "You know him?"

"*Sí, Sí.*"

Paloma pointed to the cot Cat was sitting on.

"He slept there."

Cat vaulted to her feet, unconsciously brushing at the seat of her jeans as if she'd sat in something foul.

Cat grabbed Paloma by the shoulders, unaware that her fingers were digging too deeply into her soft flesh.

"When did he sleep here?"

"Many years ago. He said he would take care of me, but he left," Paloma said, and shrugged out of Cat's grasp, then moved out of her reach. "Then he come back a few days ago like nothing ever happened, wanting things from me I no longer choose to give."

Cat shoved a shaky hand through her hair

and began pacing in a small circle, muttering to herself as she moved.

"He's not dead . . . oh, God . . . he's not dead. Why am I so shocked? I should have known . . . you can't kill the devil. No one can kill the devil . . . not even God."

Paloma crossed herself again. This woman was speaking blasphemy. She wanted her gone.

"You should not speak of such things," she said softly.

Cat stopped pacing and stared at Paloma, wondering what miserable sense of humor God had that would put her in the same room with a woman Solomon Tutuola knew personally.

She grabbed her gun and stuck it back in her shoulder holster, then put on her jacket before digging in her pocket. She pulled out a handful of bills and handed them to Paloma.

"I have to . . . I can't stay . . . uh . . . thank you for the food."

She strode toward the doorway, then paused and turned back.

"About Tutuola . . ."

"What about him?" Paloma asked.

"Did he say where he was going?"

"No. I put a curse on him. He was trying to outrun it when he left."

Cat stood in the doorway, staring back at the small woman with the dark brown eyes, realizing that size had nothing to do with guts.

"Good for you," Cat said softly, and then walked out the door, closing it quietly behind her.

Paloma stood in the silence of her tiny home, waiting for the sound of the American woman's vehicle to disappear. Only after she could hear nothing but the squawking of her neighbor's chickens did she begin to relax. However, she'd had her fill of visitors, and for one of the few times in her life, she locked and barred her door, glad to be rid of them all.

Cat was almost a mile away from Agua Caliente when she suddenly jammed her foot on the brake, slammed the car into Park and staggered out just before she threw up. She retched until her belly hurt and there was nothing coming up but bile. Then she moved to the back of her car, got out a bottle of water, and rinsed her mouth over and over before she dared swallow a sip.

Her belly lurched a bit when the water hit bottom, but it stayed down. She poured the rest on her face and hands, and then squatted down beside the door.

Her head was still pounding, as was her heart. Every breath she took was an ache that went all the way to her toes. She couldn't make sense of what was happening. She'd gotten the answer she needed regarding the mystery blip she'd been following, so she had to put a different mindset to what she did next now that she knew what she was facing. The only thing she knew so far was that she wouldn't leave Mexico until she watched that man die, and she felt no guilt for the thought.

He'd stolen her father's life and left her for dead. It was payback time.

It was instinct that made her take her cell phone out of her pocket and turn it on. Almost immediately, it began beeping, signaling messages she had yet to hear. She flipped through the list, recognizing that every one of them was from Art, and realized she felt somewhat disappointed that none of them were from Wilson.

She would call Art, of course. And there was no time like the present. She'd also better check her answering machine at home. She'd left in such a hurry that there was no telling what she'd forgotten to tend to.

She glanced at her watch, trying to figure out what time it would be back in Dallas, then shrugged off the thought. It didn't matter. She still felt the need to check in — to let someone else know that, at least for the time being, she was still alive.

She dialed Art's number, counted the rings and then, to her dismay, got the answering machine. She'd wanted a voice — a connection with someone she knew — to remind her that there was a part of her world that was still there, but it wasn't to be.

When the message ended, she waited for the ding, then began to talk.

"Art, it's me, Cat. Sorry I haven't checked in before now, but you know me . . . always in the middle of something unexpected. I'll have to tell you all about it when I get back. At least, I will if I *get* back. Got a bit of bad news this morning. Solomon Tutuola is still alive after all. I talked to a woman who not only knew him, but had seen him just a few days ago." She laughed, unaware of how bitter she sounded. "Isn't that a pile of crap? The good ones die, and the bad ones just keep on going. Anyway, just wanted you to know I'm okay. I'll see you when I see you."

She disconnected, then grabbed a piece of paper from inside the SUV before dialing her own number. She rolled her head from side to side, wincing when her neck suddenly popped. Then the messages began to play back, and she forgot her exhaustion.

The first one was from her dentist. She'd missed her appointment, and from the sound of Debbie the receptionist's voice, was on the dentist's shit list for not calling in to cancel ahead of time.

"Well, Debbie, you'll just have to get in line," she muttered, and waited for the next message to play.

There were two hang-ups, then a message from her landlord. She rolled her eyes. Damn, she'd missed paying her rent. Well, hell, she'd never been late before, and he knew she was good for it. He would just have to get in line behind Debbie if he wanted a piece of her ass.

Her mind was already wandering when another message began to play. The sound of Wilson McKay's voice in her ear washed over her and aroused an unexpected wave of longing. She closed her eyes and unconsciously pressed her cell phone hard against her ear, as if it would bring him closer. It didn't take long to realize he was pissed.

When he mentioned he'd seen her shoot-out on the interstate on the news, she could tell by the tone of his voice that he was furious. Tears began burning at the back of her throat, but she swallowed harshly. No need to cry. She already knew he was done with her. She couldn't imagine why he'd even bothered to call.

Then she heard him take a deep breath before the tone of his voice got rougher.

". . . don't know why I care. I wish to hell I didn't. And just for the record, woman, if it hadn't been for that piece of film on tonight's news, I wouldn't have the slightest notion of where in hell to look for *your* bones."

She heard him saying something else, but she'd already lost her focus. When the line suddenly went dead, the disconnect was unmistakable.

There were a couple of other messages, but she hardly heard them. She closed her flip phone, then put it back in her jacket as if nothing had happened. She looked up at the sky. It was gray. A sign that the weather might change, which wasn't good. Even though she was a long way south of Dallas, it was still winter.

Her head began to hurt. She took a deep breath. There was grit in her mouth, and grit in her hair. She needed a bath and a change of clothes, and she needed to sleep for a week.

She strode to the back of her car, got a fresh bottle of water, then closed the hatch and slid back behind the wheel. The silence inside the cab was overwhelming. She reached for the key, intending to turn on the engine, just to hear something besides the thud of her own heavy heart. Instead, she laid her head down on the steering wheel and choked on her next breath.

She swallowed a sob that had come out of nowhere, then wrapped her arms around the steering wheel and let go of the pain.

She cried for outliving her mother and father, for Marsha leaving her behind to face life all alone. She cried for all the years she'd given her passion to hate and revenge, and she cried for herself, knowing that she'd killed whatever it was that Wilson had ever felt for her.

She cried until her chest hurt and her eyes were so swollen that her vision was blurred. Her hands were shaking as she wiped them across her face. Then she felt beneath the collar of her turtleneck sweater to the cat charm on the thin silver chain.

Besides her memories, it was all she had left from her life before Solomon Tutuola had entered their house. She fingered it slowly, then let it drop. She felt the warmth of it against her skin as she leaned back and reached for the laptop. A few moments later, it was up and running. She stared at the map for a long, long time.

So now she knew who was behind the blip, and she knew where he was. She'd never been to Chihuahua, Mexico. As the old saying went, there was no time like the present.

She leaned forward, then reached for the key in the ignition.

NINE

Brothers Houston and Jimmy Franks had finally bonded out of jail, no thanks to Wilson McKay, and now Jimmy had transferred all his anger at the system to Wilson, refusing to consider that they'd gotten themselves into their own messes. They'd spent the last four hours staking out Wilson's office, but he'd never showed. It wasn't until Wilson's secretary left the office with an armful of papers that they decided they'd gotten their break.

They followed LaQueen all the way downtown, watched her go in and out of the county courthouse, stop off at the cleaners, then head back uptown, ostensibly to the bond office. It wasn't until they saw her pull over to the curb in front of a café that they realized she was meeting with McKay. They watched as Wilson got out of his car and went to meet her.

"There he is," Houston said, and

hunkered down in the car so McKay wouldn't spot him.

Jimmy was reaching for the coffee cup sitting on the dash when Houston spoke. He looked away just long enough to knock the coffee over, then caught hell from Houston because the liquid rolled into the defroster vents by the window.

"Damn it, Jimmy! Watch what you're doin'," Houston yelled.

Jimmy began mopping at the spill with a T-shirt he grabbed from the floorboard.

"It was an accident," Jimmy snapped. "And if we're supposed to be watchin' McKay unobserved, then you might want to shut the fuck up. They can hear you all the way across the street."

Houston glared, then looked back. McKay was nowhere to be seen.

"Where did he go?" Houston muttered.

Jimmy took a last swipe at the dash, then shrugged, unable to do a thing about the liquid that had dripped into the vents. He tossed the T-shirt in the back, then rubbed his hands on his pant legs as he looked up. He stared around for a few moments, then pointed.

"There he is . . . inside that café. See? Ain't that him there, with his back to the window?"

"Oh. Yeah. I see him. Damn shame I don't have a piece with me. I'd pop a cap in his back, then we'd see who was in charge. Big son of a bitch . . . had you arrested and left me to rot in jail. And after I wasted my phone call on him an' all."

"Yeah. And that big bitch he's got for a secretary. She's got hers comin', too."

"Yeah," Houston muttered.

Jimmy was fidgeting. He needed a drink, and he needed a fix. Spending all that time in jail had set him on a path to withdrawal that he didn't intend to follow.

"Come on, Houston, let's go. I need to score me some meth."

Houston Franks hesitated, then nodded. "Yeah, all right. We know we can find him anytime we want. I'm thinkin' I could do with a beer or two myself."

Houston started the car, and with one last look at the table where Wilson was sitting, they pulled out into traffic and drove away.

Wilson sat impatiently in the café, waiting for a man named John Tiger. They were meeting for lunch to discuss the possibility of John going to work for Wilson. After what had happened to LaQueen, Wilson was anxious to put safeguards into place so it wouldn't happen again.

It was odd how he'd come to consider John Tiger as a possible employee. If he hadn't been talking to his brother Charlie on the phone last night, he wouldn't have known that John, a longtime friend of Charlie's, now lived in Dallas. Wilson knew John slightly from back home, where Charlie said the man had worked as a deputy sheriff. Now he was a bouncer at a local nightclub. John would be perfect for the job, if he were interested. He had law-enforcement training, and he was big and strong, thus the job as a bouncer. Charlie had attested to his single-minded intent and honesty. If John and Wilson hit it off, Wilson was seriously considering offering him the position.

As Wilson sat there, he got his cell phone out and started checking his voice mail. When he saw there was a message from Art Ball, his eyes narrowed sharply. There was only one reason for Art to be calling him. He'd heard from Cat.

He punched the button to return the call without giving himself time to change his mind. He needed to know she was all right, then he could go about the business of hating her again. Right now, though, he was too damned worried for anger.

"Art's Bail Bonds."

"Art, it's me, Wilson. Have you heard from Cat?"

"Yeah, and damn it, I wasn't here. At least she left a message. Said she'd been delayed a bit, but here's the kicker. That man she went looking for — you know, the one you all thought burned up? Well, according to Cat, he isn't dead."

Wilson's stomach lurched.

"Jesus," he muttered, and dropped his head, then closed his eyes. "She's trailing him, I suppose?"

"Best I could tell. Like I said, it was just a message. I tried to call her back, but I think she's too far away or she turned her phone off or something."

"Perfect," Wilson muttered.

"Well . . . look at it this way, Wilson. She's still alive. It's more than we knew yesterday, right?"

"I guess," Wilson said, then added, "thanks for letting me know."

"No problem," Art said. "Someone's gotta look after her, 'cause she damn well don't look after herself. It might as well be us."

"Yeah," Wilson muttered.

They disconnected just as his waitress arrived with the coffee he'd ordered while waiting for John to arrive.

"Here you go, honey," she said, and slid

the cup in front of him. "Cream or sugar?"

"No, thanks," Wilson said, then leaned back in his chair as he watched her walk away.

The aroma of fried meat and deep-fried potatoes from a nearby table filled his senses and promptly turned his stomach. He'd been hungry when he sat down. Now he just felt sick.

Solomon Tutuola was alive. This was a fucking nightmare. He'd spent just enough time trading gun shots with the man when they'd gone after Mark Presley to know he wouldn't willingly want to face him alone and unarmed. The man was a monolith — a tattooed devil of a monolith.

He leaned forward, put his elbows on either side of his coffee cup, and then covered his face with his hands.

God help Catherine — because he couldn't.

Suddenly, there was a tap on his shoulder. He stiffened, then looked up.

"Wilson . . . long time, no see."

Wilson shifted focus quickly. He stood abruptly and found himself eye-to-eye with the dark-haired, brown-eyed man. The last time Wilson had seen John Tiger, he'd been playing tight end for the local high-school football team back home.

John Tiger had definitely grown up.

"John, thanks for coming," Wilson said, and waved toward the other side of the table. "Have a seat and take a quick look at the menu. We'll talk after you order."

John took off his brown leather bomber jacket and tossed it on an extra chair, then sat. In keeping with his Comanche heritage, he wore his hair long and straight, tied at the back of his neck with a thin strip of leather. His shoulders were wide, his legs long and muscular. When he smiled, his almond-shaped eyes almost disappeared.

"What's good here?" John asked.

"Anything fried," Wilson countered.

John chuckled, and when the waitress arrived, they ordered. Once she was gone, Wilson leaned forward. "I suppose you're wondering why I called you," he said.

"You're going to offer me a job," John said.

Wilson blinked. "What? Are you psychic?"

John grinned. "Naw . . . Charlie called."

Wilson stifled a sigh. Leave it to his family to mind his own business for him. He smiled back. "So . . . let's talk," he said.

"I'm listening," John said.

Cat was less than an hour from Chihuahua. She'd stared at the stationary blip on her computer screen off and on for so long that she had the location memorized.

As she drove, she'd run through scenario after scenario as to how their meeting would go down. Unfortunately, no matter how many times and how many ways she played it, the outcome remained the same. If she didn't go in with guns blazing, the one most likely to die would be her.

She knew he was big. She knew he was deadly. He should have died in the fire, but he had not. If she was ever going to have peace in her life, she had to bring him down. She didn't want to die. But God help her, her daddy hadn't wanted to die, either, and Tutuola had killed him and walked out without a backward glance. The way she looked at it, God had let her live for the sole reason of bringing Tutuola to justice. Trouble was, she'd spent her entire adult life looking for this man without putting enough thought into what would happen after she found him. That was her bad.

A semi-trailer topped a small rise in front of Cat and came barreling toward her, taking its half of the road out of the middle of the blacktop.

She swerved over to the shoulder as the truck sped past, and even though her SUV was heavy, the draft from the truck's passing shook her car.

"Where's a good highway patrolman when you need one?" she muttered, then reminded herself that she was in Mexico. Everything worked differently down here.

She tapped her brakes, then pulled back onto the highway. Road-weary and ready for a good night's sleep, she was thankful she didn't have far to go. Tomorrow would be time enough to face the devil. After that, whatever would be, would be.

During the past few hours, she'd come to an understanding with herself, a sort of fatalistic attitude and, one way or another, she was ready for it all to be over with.

After a while she realized the traffic had picked up quite a bit. At that point a spurt of anxiety kicked in, reminding her how close she was getting to Tutuola. But she set her jaw and kept on going. *Coward* wasn't a name she wore.

By the time she finally reached Chihuahua, she was close to tears, which confounded her. She'd spent most of her life waiting for this day, and now she decided to come unglued? What the hell was that all about? She didn't think about how long it had been since she'd had a really good night's sleep, or eaten a decent meal or had a hot, relaxing shower.

Disgusted with herself, she swiped the

tears away and set her jaw. To hell with it all. She had tonight before she faced her nemesis. She would get a room in a good hotel, treat herself to a real meal, soak in a tub until she was a mass of wrinkles and check what was on TV and hope she could find something dubbed in English. She didn't want to think of tonight as a condemned prisoner's last meal, but she wasn't going to leave anything to chance. It would piss her off to have Tutuola kill her tomorrow when she'd opted out of having cheesecake tonight.

Within the hour, she had reached the city. She stopped at a gas station, got directions to some area hotels and then drove away.

It was the off-season for tourists, which meant the price was right for a suite, rather than a single room, at the Hotel Uno. It was clean but inconspicuous, which was what she wanted.

She registered under a fake name, paid in cash and, once inside, dropped her bag on the bed. She sat down long enough to test the mattress for comfort, then visited the mini-bar and mixed a Coke and whiskey — light on the Coke, heavy on the whiskey. After a couple of sips, she began stripping, carrying her drink to the bathroom as she went.

Steam soon coated the mirrors, signaling the desired water temperature. Cat downed the last of her drink, then stepped into the shower. When she turned to pull the shower door shut, her head reeled. She staggered briefly, well aware that she shouldn't have had the drink on an empty stomach, and then reached for the soap and stepped beneath the spray.

Fifteen minutes later she was out, wearing nothing but a heavy bathrobe she'd found hanging on a hook in the bathroom. She thought about fixing another drink, then picked up the menu and scanned the offers. She was too much of a Texan to consider having anything but beef for what might be her last meal, so when she picked up the phone, she ordered a steak, French fries and a piece of cheesecake. If by some miracle she survived tomorrow, she would make a point of choosing something exotic the next time around.

Once she'd ordered her food, she lay down on the bed, turned on the television and then hit Mute. There were times in her life when she knew that, if given a second chance, she would do certain things a different way. This was one of those times. It hurt her heart to think she might never hear Wilson's voice again, let alone accept that he was so mad at her. She thought she'd read somewhere that it wasn't a good thing to die with regrets, although she didn't know as how that mattered when, so often, death was sudden and unexpected. She wondered how many people died with unresolved anger in their lives.

She glanced at the phone, considering the wisdom of calling Wilson. A part of her wanted to hear his voice so badly that she ached. That in itself was a new experience for her — needing to connect with a man for personal happiness. Twice she reached for the phone, only to stop before she touched it. Just as she'd convinced herself there was no shame in simply saying hello, there was a knock on her door.

Her food had arrived.

Momentarily saved from having to grovel, she tipped the waiter generously and dug into her food without a whisper of guilty conscience. When she had finished, she pushed the room service cart back into the hall and locked herself in.

Now what?

She glanced at her laptop, and out of habit, plugged it in and brought up the tracking program. The blip was still motionless. The tiny blinking light on the screen was a deceptively mild indication of the danger she was putting herself in.

Aware that she was psyching herself out by dwelling on what lay ahead, she turned to the sliding glass door that led to her balcony and walked outside. Mexico was warmer than Dallas, but it was still winter and the night air was chilly. Down below, residents of the city moved about, ignorant of the danger her presence represented.

She stared out beyond the rooftops to a main road a couple of blocks away. There couldn't be any harm in taking a walk down to the bar she saw on the corner. She needed to walk off all the food she'd eaten or she would never get a wink of sleep.

With a quick glance toward the sun sinking in the west, she reached for her bag and pulled out a clean change of clothes. She dressed without care for fashion, leaving her still-damp hair loose, and reached for her room key and wallet.

She thought about taking her handgun, then changed her mind. She was only going to a bar. Surely she could get there and back without any trouble.

She left her room and headed for the elevator, already looking forward to the freedom of a simple walk, and wouldn't let herself consider how much better the walk would have been had she not been taking it alone.

Once outside, her stride was long as she aimed for the lights of the bar. A couple of street vendors tried to catch her eye, one selling serapes, another with a booth of handmade jewelry, most of which was fashioned from Mexican silver and fire opals. She started to walk past when a display of earrings caught her eye. She stopped, backtracked, then began examining the merchandise.

The vendor eyed her clothes, her unusual height and the hard set of her jaw, marking her as an American, before speaking.

"You buy?" he asked.

She shrugged without answering, then spotted a display of smaller earrings and turned her attention toward them. She kept thinking of that single gold loop in Wilson McKay's ear and picturing one of these silver ones instead.

Then she remembered the message he'd left on her machine. He didn't want anything more from her, as he'd made painfully clear. She fingered the earrings one last time, giving them a slight push that sent them swinging, then stuffed her hands in her pockets and kept on walking.

Once she got to the bar, the tension she'd

been feeling began to dissipate. There was a stiff breeze, which had finished drying her hair as she walked. As she stood facing the wind, it lifted her hair from the back of her neck, tugging it until it was in tangles, but she didn't care. The feeling of being unburdened was too precious for her to care about how she looked.

She turned and strode into the bar with her chin up and her shoulders back. She ordered a tequila, neat, and downed it in one smooth gulp, drawing an approving look from the bartender who'd served her.

"Another, *señorita?*"

She shook her head, then turned around to watch the people on the crowded dance floor. A man approached her, offering to buy her a drink. She shook her head without even meeting his gaze. Another came up, slipped a hand around her waist, and moments later found himself on his knees with his fingers bent back to his wrist and a pain running up to his armpit that he wouldn't soon forget.

He was begging her pardon as she turned him loose and walked out. She wasn't in the mood to mess with this. It had been a mistake to come here.

She started back toward her hotel, noticing the rusty red color of the Spanish tiles on the rooftops, as well as the scents and sounds coming at her from all directions.

Somewhere behind the walls of one of the buildings she was passing, a small child cried, and she thought of baby Maria Elena. At least *she* was back where she belonged.

She thought of Marsha and *her* baby, dutifully resting in the finest mahogany casket that money could buy and buried beneath six feet of Texas dirt.

She thought of Mark Presley, wishing every day was pure torture for him during his time in prison before the state of Texas, with its penchant for capital punishment, did what it had promised to do and sent his sorry soul to hell.

Then, as if she hadn't punished herself enough, her thoughts swung back to Wilson. Maybe if they'd met earlier, when their entire relationship hadn't been mixed up in her need for revenge . . . Then she sighed. It was too late for what-ifs.

She stood on a street corner until the sun had set before heading back to the hotel. The cantinas she passed were in full swing, with music and singing. As she passed by an open doorway, she saw more couples dancing. The intimacy of their embraces in the shadowy room made her look quickly away, as if she'd inadvertently intruded in a place where she didn't belong.

By the time she got back to her room, she was both mentally and physically exhausted. She shed her clothes and crawled into bed without another thought of calling anyone.

Oddly enough, she slept the night through in blissful peace.

Solomon Tutuola was in the most peaceful place he'd ever been in his life. He'd found a doctor who'd given him an ointment to keep the new skin supple on the places where he'd been burned and a two-month supply of pain pills to keep him going. He'd hired a local couple as cook/housekeeper and gardener/chauffeur. Most of the land-scaping at this place consisted of artfully placed white crushed rock and cactus gardens, although the back patio was com-pletely shaded by multi-colored bougainvil-lea vines. There was a twelve-foot-high rock wall around the back of the property, and he was thinking of adding the same to the front, so that he would be completely enclosed. He wanted only one way in and out, and he would make sure it was acces-sible only via a pair of iron gates controlled by remote.

The pool in the back of the house had

been in disuse long enough that the water had turned green. He intended to have it drained and checked for leaks.

He'd spent two whole days now as a homeowner and, as soon as he'd healed a bit more, he was thinking of finding himself a woman. He didn't want to marry, but it would be handy to have a woman to bed whenever he wanted, without having to deal with chasing down a piece of tail. His looks had always been an issue with women, but wave enough money in their faces and they willingly went blind and gave him what he wanted. The burn scars had turned the Maori tattoos on one side of his face into what looked like a melted maze. When he grinned, the same corner of his face tilted downward instead of up, revealing only half a smile of those hand-filed lion-sharp teeth.

Now he strutted through the rooms, gazing on the opulence with a sense of having earned his way here, never mind that he'd actually gotten here on the backs and the blood of his victims.

Even though he'd been awake less than an hour, he paused at the wet bar and poured himself a bourbon and Coke, added a couple of ice cubes, then headed for the vine-covered patio. Despite Solomon's massive size, he moved with an odd grace. Just as he was about to exit the house, his new housekeeper, Juanita, came down the hallway.

He paused, waiting for that first look of shock to pass so he could find out what she wanted.

"*Señor* . . . the food . . . it is cooked."

He nodded, then pointed toward the table outside.

"I will eat there," he said.

She looked away quickly, nodding her understanding, and went scurrying back the way she'd come.

Within a few minutes he was enjoying a breakfast of scrambled eggs with a large helping of sautéed peppers, tomatoes and chorizo sausage on the side. He had a stack of warm flour tortillas and a pot of thick, black coffee. As far as Solomon was concerned, it was food fit for the gods and he was in his heaven.

He ate with relish, then called for more coffee before he was done.

Juanita, who was hovering nearby, breathed a sign of relief when she realized her very frightening boss was satisfied with her food and, when he demanded more coffee, she ran to do his bidding.

Once Solomon was through eating, he got up and walked away, leaving her to clean up his mess. His property consisted of the house, the immediate grounds and almost two acres of land, most of which ran behind the house. He liked knowing all of that was his, and especially liked the security features the place already offered. He'd made plenty of enemies in his lifetime, and while he wasn't afraid of the devil himself, he did sleep better knowing there was a rock wall around the bulk of the property. As soon as he had it extended around the front, he would be happier.

He stuffed his hands in his pockets as he began to circle the property, walking with his usual long swaggering stride, making mental notes as to what he would change. He wanted the pool, that was for certain, so he needed to look into someone to do the renovation. Tomorrow he would do a little checking and find some reliable craftsmen. When he got to the back of his property, he lifted his head, then turned, eyeing the house and all that was his.

"Who knew?" he muttered, then began to smile. The smile turned into a chuckle, then a full-blown laugh.

Juanita's husband, Pedro, was underneath Solomon's car, changing the oil, when he heard the laughter. He paused, trying to figure out what was happening. When he realized it was his boss, and that he was all the way at the back of the property, laughing like a man gone mad, he crossed himself, then said a quick prayer. Pedro didn't know what he thought about the job he and Juanita had taken, but as long as they got their pay and the crazy man left them alone, he was willing to give him the benefit of the doubt. He picked up a wrench and went back to work on the car.

It had taken Cat less than two hours to find Tutuola's exact location and learn that he'd paid big money for the property and had two employees, neither of whom stayed over at night. To the best of her knowledge, Tutuola spent the nights alone, although she couldn't count on that. However, even knowing someone else might be there wasn't enough to stop her from what she'd come to do.

The layout of the property gave her few options as to how she would get in, but that was minor. She gave the place a last once-over through her binoculars, then drove away. She would get some food, some rest and wait for nightfall. It wasn't much of a plan, but the way Cat looked at it, it wouldn't take all night to put a bullet between his eyes.

It never occurred to her to call the authorities. There was no evidence linking him to the crime that had left her an orphan other than her word. And there were too many lonely years and bad memories to lay at his feet for her to relent. As she paused at a stoplight, she absently ran her finger along the length of her scar, then swallowed past the knot in her throat as she gripped the steering wheel with both hands.

"Soon, Daddy," she said softly. "Soon the devil will pay for what he did to us."

The light changed. She accelerated through the intersection, on her way back to her hotel.

LaQueen was taken with the new employee. She'd given the big Indian the once-over, then produced a new coffee cup and put it on the extra desk Wilson had set up.

"Last one to empty the pot makes a fresh one," she said, and swept off to her desk with a roll to her step.

"Yes, ma'am," John said, then eyed Wilson, waiting for him to set things in motion.

Wilson was a little stunned by LaQueen's instant approval, but it was a good sign. She was, after all, the boss of all she surveyed, despite the fact that Wilson signed her checks.

"Okay, John. We've got a couple of skips to run down today, so you'll be coming with me to get the gist of how this all works. As time goes on, when one of us is out of the office, the other one will stay close here with LaQueen. I don't want her to suffer a repeat of the other day."

John frowned, as he glanced over at the tall, elegant woman.

"What happened?"

"A client got pissed off at me and took it out on her. Had to have the bastard arrested for assault."

John's frowned deepened.

"Is she all right?" he asked.

Wilson looked at her, then grinned. "Does she look like she's not?"

John blinked, then realized Wilson was teasing him.

"She looks fine to me."

"Yeah, I can see that," Wilson said, and picked up a couple of files. "LaQueen, we'll be out for a couple of hours. Call if you need me for anything. As soon as John gets trained, we'll alternate pickups so you won't be alone in here."

LaQueen sat up even straighter than she'd been sitting and glared at Wilson.

"I have been taking care of myself in here for years now, Wilson McKay. I am not needing a babysitter. I did not know you were hiring just because of me. I thought it was because you wanted help!"

"It's not babysitting, honey. It's simply a matter of taking care of business. I won't have you in danger."

John eyed the flash in her eyes and the tilt of her chin, then spoke. His voice was soft, but it carried easily across the room to where LaQueen was sitting.

"Just so you know . . . there's no danger of anyone mistaking you for a baby. You're one fine-looking lady, and it will be my honor to learn the ropes from you."

LaQueen didn't know whether to bristle or beam. Wilson had never seen her so distracted.

"So . . . John . . . put on this bulletproof vest and clip these handcuffs to the back of your jeans. The can of Mace can go in your coat pocket, and then we're good to go. We'll see about getting you certified as a bounty hunter, as well as a license to carry weapons, later. Right now you're an observer, unless I say different."

"Got it," John said.

Within moments, they were gone.

LaQueen sat in the office, staring blankly into space. It wasn't until the phone rang that she pulled herself together and went back to work.

It was thirty minutes after midnight and there was no moon.

Cat took that as a positive sign as she parked at the foot of the hill leading up to Tutuola's property. She sat for a moment, making sure there was no one around to see her, then got out, locking the car behind her. The last thing she needed was to have her only means of escape stolen.

The night was cold, the wind sharp and unusually strong, but the dark clothing she was wearing broke the chill. She pulled on her latex gloves, patted the shoulder holster under her jacket, checked the batteries in her flashlight again, then lifted her head and started walking. There were no trees to hide behind, no shrubbery in which to shelter. She was out in the open, with only the curtain of night to hide her presence. The steepness of the road made her trek somewhat slower than she'd planned, but it didn't really matter. This might be the last appointment she'd ever keep, but she felt a sense of inevitability. This day had been a long time coming. She was ready to get it over with.

By the time she reached the house, she was breathing rapidly and sweating underneath her clothes. She paused near a corner of the house until her breathing had a chance to even out. Once she had settled, she started searching for a way to get in. She had no way of knowing if the place had security, but if she set off an alarm, then so be it. She intended to introduce herself anyway, before she sent him to hell.

TEN

Solomon was flat on his back in a dreamless sleep when he awakened abruptly. He lay for a moment, listening, wondering what it was his subconscious had heard that had set off his inner alarm. Several long silent moments passed. He'd almost convinced himself that he'd imagined it, when he heard what sounded like a squeaky hinge.

He opened the drawer in the night table and pulled out a gun. Naked as the day he was born, he left his bedroom and started down the hallway. He moved slowly, taking care to stay in the shadows, and stilled his breathing to a whisper.

Cat was inside.

Just the knowledge that she was within shouting distance of this man set her teeth on edge. She stood against the wall near the window she'd crawled through, careful not to step on the broken glass. She'd broken the glass on purpose, knowing the sound would wake him, which was what she'd planned. This time, when they met, he would be the one who was being invaded. This time, she would be the stranger waiting in the shadows.

She stood motionless, listening for a sign that he was up and moving. She didn't have long to wait. A slight creak from a floorboard down a darkened hallway to her left set her nerves on edge. She held her breath, tightened her hold on her gun and slipped farther into the shadows.

Within seconds, she saw what looked like a wraith separate itself from the darkness and move into the living room. From the size of it, she sensed, rather than saw, that it was Tutuola. Her fingers tightened around her handgun, waiting.

Someone was here. He could smell them.

"Who's there?" he called out.

Silence.

He moved a few steps further into the living room, then paused, his finger curled around the trigger.

"I know you're here," he said softly, then chuckled. "I can smell you."

"You smell nothing but yourself," Cat whispered, then went down on her hands and knees only seconds before a bullet whizzed past her head.

Solomon had been so rattled by the sound of a woman's voice that he'd fired off the shot before he thought. When he'd heard nothing that indicated his shot had hit a target, he began backing up, wanting to put something besides space between him and the intruder. When he felt the wall at his back, he froze.

"Who are you? What do you want?" he called out, then silently cursed when he heard the uncertainty in his voice. It wasn't like him to be rattled by anything or anyone.

"I came to watch you die," Cat said, and then dropped flat on her belly and crawled six feet back to the right as Solomon fired a second shot at the place where she'd been.

Solomon fired off another shot in the same direction, then grabbed a crystal vase and threw it. The sound of shattering glass was followed by long moments of silence. He started to shoot again, then realized he'd be wasting his bullets. He started to reach for the light switch, and when he did, a gun went off. The bullet hit the wall right beside his hand. He yanked it back in disbelief. This couldn't be happening. No one got the best of him. No one.

"Who are you? Show yourself, you coward

bitch! I will tear you apart with my hands."

Cat rolled over onto her belly, smiling tightly when she realized she could see the entire outline of Tutuola's body against the white stuccoed walls. Without hesitation, she took aim at his shoulder and squeezed off a shot.

He screamed when he was hit, in shock and rage and pain, and started firing in wild abandon. He fired until his gun was empty, then threw it across the room, cursing with every breath.

At that point, Cat stood up and reached for a light switch.

When the room was suddenly flooded with light, the man Cat saw looked like something from hell. Half of his face and head appeared to have been melted. Everything was sagging and scarred. But the expression of his face was the same. Pure evil.

Solomon gasped. For the first time in his life he was truly defenseless — naked, unarmed, covered in blood from the gushing wound in his shoulder and facing an intruder in his own home. It took a few moments for his eyesight to adjust, and when it did, he realized that he knew the woman — or at least, he'd seen her before.

"You!" he roared, and started toward her.

Cat fired again, this time hitting him in the chest.

When the bullet struck, it spun him completely around. He went to his knees. At that point he leaned forward, bracing himself with his hands, then shook his head like a dog shedding water. To Cat's disbelief, he pushed himself up, staggering as he stood to face her.

Cat flinched. What the hell was it going to take to keep him down?

Tutuola's fingers clenched and unclenched into fists as he stared across the room at the tall, dark-haired woman with the husky voice. When she stepped out from behind his sofa, he shuddered. She was holding a gun aimed straight at his face. No one had ever looked at him without flinching. No one.

Until her.

"Who are you?"

"My name is Cat Dupree."

He splayed a hand across the gunshot wound to his chest, trying to stem the flow of blood. Then he shuddered again. Was this how he died? It didn't seem possible that a total stranger — and a woman, at that — would turn out to be the one who took him down.

"I don't know you," he muttered.

"Oh . . . we've met. Twice before. You know what they say, third time's a charm."

"I saw you at the hacienda . . . outside Nuevo Laredo. Did you come for the money?"

"Hell no," she said softly.

The bitterness in her voice was unsettling. He couldn't help but remember the curse that Paloma had put on him. Was this woman part of the witch's curse?

"Then why?"

"Payback," Cat said.

He frowned. "Payback for what? You are nothing to me."

"Do you remember a man named Justin Dupree?"

Solomon frowned. "You've got the wrong man. I never knew anyone by that name."

Cat moved a quick step to the right and took aim at his knee.

"That makes it even worse," she said softly.

"Why? Why are you doing this?"

"He was my father, and you killed him."

Solomon couldn't believe this was happening. For the first time in his life, he had money. He had property. He had everything he'd ever wanted. He couldn't die now.

"No. No. It wasn't me," he said.

"Yes, it was you," Cat said, and raised her

gun. "I saw you do it."

Solomon shook his head. "Now I know you're lying, because I never left a witness to anything I did."

Cat reached up and yanked down the neck of her sweater, revealing the thick pink curl of scar tissue.

"You left one," she said. "Me. You cut my throat, then left me to watch as you stabbed my father to death. You left me to die. Instead, I have come to kill you."

Solomon realized that his only chance of survival hinged on getting that gun out of her hands before she could fire another shot. There was a piece of Mayan pottery sitting on a pedestal just to his right. Ignoring the pain in his body, he grabbed it by the handle and threw it just as she fired off another shot.

The shot went wild as Cat instinctively ducked. By the time she looked up, he was on her. He knocked the gun from her hand, then began punching her in the face. She fought him hard, kicking and scratching and trying to get her fingers in his eyes. He grabbed her by the throat with both hands and began squeezing.

The pain was immediate. The chance that her hyoid bone was about to be crushed was imminent. Figuring she had about two

218

seconds before he killed her, she drew her knee up sharply, jamming it into his testicles as hard as she could. His scream of pain and rage was deafening, but it worked. He turned her loose. She rolled out from under him, and then, before he could react, kicked him square in the jaw as he leaned over her.

Solomon dropped like a felled ox.

Cat scanned the room frantically, looking for her gun. Suddenly her gaze focused on the sofa. The butt of her gun was visible between two of the cushions. She lunged for it just as Solomon came to and made a dive for her. For a few seconds the gun was in her grasp, and then Solomon landed on her with all his weight.

Every ounce of breath was knocked from her body. He turned her over, then rose up just enough to give himself room to swing a fist.

The first blow landed just below her breastbone. She heard ribs snapping. Pain ripped through her body in shockwaves, but she only grunted as he drew back for the next blow.

Cat was fighting for her life. She scratched at his face, digging her fingers into his skin, and then, finally, pushing her thumbs against his eyeballs.

Again the pain was so sharp that Solomon

was forced to turn her loose. He rose up with a roar as she blinded him, then swung wildly, connecting with the side of her jaw. Cat flew backwards, landing flat on her back. Her head bounced against the hard, tiled floor and, for a few seconds, everything went black. It was an inborn sense of self-preservation that made her move even before she was able to breathe.

She shook her head frantically, trying to clear her vision, as she staggered back to the sofa and grabbed her gun. Blood was pouring out of her nose, she couldn't feel her lips, and one eye was swollen shut. But she was still breathing. When she spun, Solomon was within five feet of her.

For a fleeting second everything seemed to move in slow motion. The tattoos that had marked him as her father's killer seemed to come to life, moving on his skin like geometric snakes. She saw the rage in his eyes, the healing burns on his face and neck and the blood flowing from the wounds on his massive body. His hands were doubled into fists, and one was swinging at her. She knew that if he hit her again, she wouldn't be getting up.

So she fired.

Tutuola didn't even flinch as he grabbed her hair with both hands.

Cat shoved the gun against his belly and fired again.

He shuddered. Then his fingers moved from her hair to her throat, cutting off the oxygen to her body and the blood to her brain.

The gun went off again, but Cat didn't know it. She was on the floor, unconscious. She never saw Tutuola fall. She never saw him reach for his chest, as if trying to stop the blood coming out of the bullet holes.

Cat thought it was the sound of water gurgling in a slow-moving fountain that brought her back to consciousness, but when she opened her eyes, she realized the gurgle was coming out of Tutuola's mouth. She rolled over, then propped herself up on one elbow. For a fraction of a second she thought she saw consciousness in Tutuola's eyes.

"Finally . . . you die," she whispered.

He complied.

Cat managed to sit up, but standing seemed impossible. Pain was in every muscle of her body, in every pore of her skin. The room looked like a war zone, and her blood was all over the place, mixed with his. But she wasn't in the system, so with luck they wouldn't be able to ID her through her blood. And the gun she'd used, which she managed to stuff back in her holster, wasn't registered and couldn't be traced back to her, which meant there was no way forensics could examine the rifling on the shells and connect her to what had gone on. Since she was wearing gloves, there was no chance she would be leaving fingerprints behind, either.

She hadn't really expected to live through this, once she'd decided to give him fair warning that she was there, but since she had, there was enough of her brain functioning to realize she needed to get up and get out. She had no intention of spending the rest of her life in a Mexican jail over a piece of shit like Solomon Tutuola. She'd made sure that he'd fired first. In fact, he'd fired at her numerous times before she'd fired back, leaving her conscience clear. There was the fact that she'd broken in to his house, but he'd broken into theirs, so she considered them even on that score. She'd given him more warning and leeway than he'd ever given her and her dad.

She made it onto her hands and knees, but when she tried to take a deep breath before rising, she almost passed out again. There was no way to know how many ribs he'd broken. All she could do was pray that none of them had punctured a lung.

Stifling a scream, she crawled across the floor to the sofa, then used it to pull herself up. She moaned, then swiped the blood out of her good eye and looked around.

A pair of large fat candles sat on either end of the mantle over the fireplace. A box of matches was nearby.

Fire. That was what she needed. A fire. Fire burned. Fire destroyed. Fire cleansed.

But it took everything she had to move, and when she did, every step was like a knife in her gut. By the time she reached the fireplace, she was sobbing.

"God, please help me do this now and judge me later," she mumbled, then spat the blood pooling in her mouth onto the floor as she reached for the candles and matches.

Her hands were trembling so badly she was afraid she would drop the candles and, if they fell, she knew she would never be able to bend over for them and get back up again. So she clutched them to herself as tightly as she could, then made her way back across the room, ignoring the devil she'd dehorned.

There was a wet bar in the corner of the room, and she needed a starter. The alcohol in the whiskey would work just fine. When she felt herself fading, she took a stiff drink from the decanter of bourbon, then poured the rest of it on the sofa, before emptying the other decanters over the rest of the furniture, saving the last for Tutuola himself.

When she stood over his body and poured the last of his own liquor onto him, years of guilt at surviving when her father had not began to lift from her soul.

She took the two candles, lit them, then scooted one beneath a sofa and the other beneath an upholstered chair. The furniture would soon catch fire, and when it did, the liquor would accelerate the fire, but not before she had time to get out.

She paused over Tutuola's body and struck one last match. The tip flared as it caught. She held it for a moment until she began to feel the heat from the tiny flame, then took a couple of steps backward and tossed the match. It landed on Tutuola's back. The fire caught and blazed on the whiskey pooled at the back of his waist. She tossed a couple of throw pillows next to him, then watched until they also caught fire.

Only after his body was immersed in flame did Cat turn away. She stumbled and staggered all the way to the door, paused, then turned out the lights.

The room was instantly aglow, both from the fire blazing on Tutuola and the two candles beneath the furniture. Already the fabric was beginning to smoke.

"Straight to hell," she muttered, then closed the door behind her.

The night air was cold — a slap in the face that she needed. It was a good hundred yards down the hill to her car, and she didn't have time to waste. There was no way to know how long it would be before someone noticed the blaze, but she was betting her life that it would be long enough to destroy whatever DNA she might have left behind.

She felt in her pocket for her flashlight. It was still there. She turned it on and began stumbling down the hill to her car as the house burst into flames behind her. She never knew when she reached her vehicle or how she found her way back to the hotel. It wasn't until she had parked in the back lot and headed for the door that she realized where she was.

Moving on nothing but pure grit and nerves, she made it inside without being seen, then into her room. She stared down at the "Do Not Disturb" on the knob inside the room, then shakily hung it on the outside instead.

The words were printed in three languages. That should be enough to guarantee that she would be left alone.

Only after the door was closed and locked behind her did she begin to shake. She was covered in blood and all but blind from the swelling and bruising. She couldn't breathe without crying, and blood kept filling her mouth.

She was alive, but she didn't know for how long. Fearing that this might be her last night on earth, there was something she needed to do.

She dragged herself across the room to the sofa and then picked up her cell phone, which she'd left on the table. Twice the room went in and out of focus before she could steady herself enough to see the numbers. There was only one person she needed to call. One person whose voice she needed to hear. One person. Just one.

Please, God, let him be there.

She punched in the numbers with trembling fingers. She wasn't sure that she'd hit the right combination until she heard a phone begin to ring. At least she'd called someone. All she could do was pray it was the right someone.

Wilson was sound asleep when the phone

began to ring. At first he thought it was the alarm clock, and he reached over in his sleep and slapped at the snooze button. But when the ringing continued, he quickly realized it was the phone. He grabbed it, accidentally knocking an empty glass off the end table as he did. The glass thumped as it hit the carpet but didn't break. Wilson lifted the phone to his ear.

"Hello?" he mumbled, still half asleep.

It was the silence at the other end of the line that brought him the rest of the way to consciousness. He rolled over onto the side of the bed.

"Who is this? Hello? Hello?"

Someone sobbed. He heard it as clearly as he heard the catch in his own breath.

"Cat? Catherine . . . is this you?"

"Sorry . . . so sorry."

The hair rose on the back of his neck. Something was wrong with her voice. He could barely hear her, let alone understand what she was saying.

"Cat! Is it you?"

He heard a slow intake of breath, followed by a low, agonized moan, then one word.

"Yes."

His belly rolled. *What in God's name was wrong?*

"Catherine, are you —"

"Wilson . . ."

He stopped. "Yes, I'm here."

"Chihuahua . . . Hotel Uno," she mumbled.

"You're in Chihuahua, Mexico?"

She exhaled the answer, making it sound more like a hiss than a word.

"Yesss."

"At a place called the Hotel Uno? Is that where you're staying? Do you need me? Are you all right? Talk to me, damn it."

"Your message . . ."

Wilson heard her cough, heard her labored breathing, and knew she was hurt. He'd never felt so helpless or so scared in his life.

"What about my message, honey? What are you trying to say?"

". . . said you wouldn't know where to find . . . body. At Hotel Uno."

"Tutuola?"

"Dead . . . and so am I."

The phone went dead in his ear.

"Catherine? Cat?"

She was gone.

Wilson remembered the angry message he'd left on her machine, ranting about being kept in the dark about what she was doing and that he wouldn't even know where to find her body. So now he did, and it didn't make him feel a damn bit better.

"Oh hell," he said, and headed toward his office, turning on lights as he ran.

He grabbed the Rolodex from his desk and began shuffling through the cards, looking for one in particular. The moment he found it, he yanked it out of the file, then reached for the phone.

A few seconds later, the number he'd called began to ring. Only then did he glance at the clock. It was twenty minutes to five in the morning.

He could hear the phone ringing at the other end. It rang and rang until the machine kicked on.

"This is Mike Simms' residence. Leave a message after the beep."

"Mike! Mike! It's me, Wilson McKay! Wake up and answer your goddamned phone."

He kept yelling, demanding his call be answered, but still nothing. He was just about to hang up when he heard someone pick up the receiver.

Mike Simms was a professional gambler with a penchant for pretty machines, but it was his skill as a chopper pilot that Wilson needed.

"Fuck, Wilson . . . do you know what time it is?"

"I need your help," Wilson said.

Two years ago, Wilson had helped bring down the man who'd broken into Mike's home and stolen some valuable art. They'd become friends during the process and had kept in touch on a haphazard basis. Still, Mike wasn't the kind of man who forgot the favors he owed.

"What's up?" Mike asked, and Wilson could practically hear him rubbing the sleep from his eyes.

"I need to get to Chihuahua, Mexico, ASAP. I've got a friend in trouble."

"Shit, boy, you don't ask for much."

"I've never asked you for anything," Wilson said. "But I'm asking now."

Mike sighed.

"I keep the chopper out at Martin's Airfield. Know where it is?"

"Yes."

"Meet you there in an hour."

"Forty-five minutes," Wilson said, and hung up.

Wilson was dressed in under five minutes. He stopped at his office on the way to the private airport, left LaQueen a brief message, then took what cash he had on hand from the wall safe.

He was waiting at the airport when Mike drove up. Obviously Mike had been on the phone himself, because his chopper was fueled and ready when he arrived. Within fifteen minutes, they were airborne.

The fire department was at the estate, but there was no city water service at this location. Once the tanker truck had been emptied, there was no more water left with which to fight. The firemen stood helpless, watching as the burning roof collapsed inward, sending a shower of sparks up into the night sky. It was too bad about the house, but it was, after all, empty. It had been for sale for months, and the Realtor's sign was still stuck in the yard.

It wasn't until the Realtor arrived and got out of his car on the run, screaming a name, that they began to realize they had more to worry about than a burning house, but by then, it was far too late.

It was mid-morning the next day before the ruins could be searched. As the Realtor had claimed, they found a badly burned body in what had been the living room, buried beneath charred rafters and rubble. Their initial search located empty liquor bottles scattered all over the floor near the body. The arson investigator was sick with an intestinal flu and had to keep running outside to throw up. He gave the place a quick once-over, saw the bottles and the candle holders lying near what was left of the furniture and deemed it an accident related to drinking. It was a fireman who found an empty gun. A few minutes later, they found a handful of empty shells that had clearly come from two different weapons. At that point, the fire scene became a crime scene.

Meanwhile, the Realtor had furnished a name for the victim.

Solomon Tutuola was still going to spend his retirement in Chihuahua but with a slight change of address and six feet under.

ELEVEN

The sun came up at their backs, but Wilson was blind to the beauty of the land below them.

Mike had figured out in the first ten minutes that Wilson wasn't about to talk about anything — not the friend who was supposedly in trouble, or the reason he was going after her instead of calling the authorities in Chihuahua to have them look after her themselves. It seemed obvious that this was one of those times when the less he knew, the better off he would be. He'd filed his flight plan and dealt with refueling stops, pretending not to notice that the closer they got to Chihuahua, the tenser Wilson became. Hour after hour, they flew in a southwesterly direction. When they were less than ten minutes out, Wilson suddenly decided to start talking.

"I don't have any right to ask this of you, but I'm not asking for myself."

"Ask away," Mike said.

Wilson nodded. "Okay then, this is it. When we get to Chihuahua, will you hang around until you hear from me? I don't know what shape Cat is going to be in, but from the little I know, I don't think it will be good."

Mike arched an eyebrow. "Cat?"

"As in Catherine, okay?"

"Just asking," Mike said.

"Anyway . . . if you would refuel and file a flight plan . . . you know . . . be ready at a moment's notice . . ."

Mike frowned. "Absolutely. And if you're in trouble, I'm —"

"I'm not the one in trouble . . . yet."

"Come on, Wilson. I'm not afraid of anything. I keep my mouth shut, and you know it."

Wilson's eyes narrowed as he glanced out. He could see the city below them. His gut was in a knot, and his thoughts were racing. Cat was down there — somewhere.

He couldn't get the sound of her voice out of his head, and he didn't want to think about what he might find. An involuntary shudder ripped through him as he took a deep breath, then exhaled slowly.

"Look, Mike . . . it isn't about being afraid. It's about being smart. You just play

234

it by the book, and if anyone asks you what you're doing here, just tell them you're waiting for a fare."

Mike started to argue, then saw the look on Wilson's face.

"So . . . you're just a fare?"

"Right."

He grinned. "Then if you're just a fare and I'm just picking you up, you better know I'm expecting a damned big tip for the ride."

The humor was unexpected. It made Wilson grin; then he gave Mike an easy punch on the arm.

"I owe you a hell of a lot more than a tip for this," he said.

Mike shrugged it off, then pointed. "There it is."

Wilson shifted his gaze. "It" was a small landing strip, obviously not international-level accommodations.

"The airport?"

"One and the same," Mike said, then flipped a switch on his headset to contact the tower for landing instructions.

Within minutes they were down. Mike watched Wilson undo his seat belt, then reach for his jacket.

"You sure you don't need someone at your back?" Mike asked.

Wilson nodded. "I'm sure. Here . . . this is for refueling, and get yourself something to eat. I'll be in touch soon." He tossed a handful of hundred-dollar bills in Mike's lap.

Mike shuffled the bills into a neat stack and then stuck them in his pocket.

"I'll be waiting for your call," he said, watching as Wilson crossed the tarmac and disappeared into the airport.

In a cab on his way to the Hotel Uno, Wilson didn't want to think about how many hours had passed since Cat had called him, or what she'd gone through to be able to tell him that Tutuola was dead.

Along with the ride, the taxi driver seemed bent on giving him a tourist-guide spiel that was nothing short of comic. Still, Wilson couldn't fault him, because the man spoke better English than he did Spanish.

At any other time he would have enjoyed the ride and the scenery — even the odd-ball driver. The day had turned out to be clear and sunny, although the air was cool, but joy was not on his mind. He was scared — damned scared.

He couldn't help but think about how cold it had been back in Dallas when he left, and how far away from home they were. Even after he found Cat — and if she was still alive — it wasn't as if he could take her directly to a hospital and get treatment for her. He knew from the way she'd sounded over the phone that she was in bad shape, which meant wherever he took her, questions would be asked. He needed to get her as far away from here as he could before Tutuola's body was found. Even now, it might be too late — for everything.

The thought hurt his heart in a way he would never have believed possible. Just knowing that Catherine Dupree might have gone off and left him behind in this world made him physically sick. For the first time since he'd known her, he was beginning to understand what had driven her to waste so many years of her life seeking revenge. If he walked into her room at the Hotel Uno and found her dead, he would be deeply inclined to send the person responsible straight to hell — in pieces. However, in this instance, she had already beaten him to it.

He glanced out the window, swallowing past the knot in his throat and willing himself not to panic. After all, she was as unpredictable as the cat for whom she'd been named. If fate stayed true to form, she might only have used up her third life, which meant there should still be six left to go.

Damn the woman. He hadn't meant to fall in love with her. He didn't want to care what she'd done to herself, but it was too late. He cared. God, he cared so much he ached.

He was in such a state of confusion that the taxi driver was pulling into the hotel parking lot before Wilson realized they had arrived. All at once, he panicked. How could he do this? She hadn't told him what room she was in, but he wanted to play this low-key. If she was hurt bad, she wouldn't answer the phone, and they weren't going to tell him her room number outright. He wasn't sure what to do first, and then he saw her car. She might have left a clue in there, he thought.

"Let me out here," he told the cabbie.

The driver hit the brakes and put the car in Park. He was about to get out and open the door for Wilson, but Wilson beat him to it. He handed a pair of twenties to the man, who grinned broadly at the overpayment and quickly drove away before the *Americano loco* could change his mind, leaving Wilson to see if he could spot anything through the windows of Cat's vehicle that might tell him what room she was in. But when he tried the door, to his shock, he found that the car was unlocked.

He opened the door quickly, then froze. Even from where he was standing, the first thing he saw was the dried blood — on everything. On the steering wheel, the floorboards — all over the front seats. He reached toward a dried smear, then stopped and straightened back up, taking long breaths of air, trying desperately to counter the nausea. When he had himself together enough to dare a second look, he found something even more disturbing. The keys were still in the ignition. He couldn't imagine what shape she'd been in to abandon her things like this.

"Oh, God, oh, baby . . . what did he do to you?" he muttered.

In desperation, he began tearing through the papers in the front seat, as well as some that had fallen onto the back floorboard. He spotted a handful of papers on the passenger seat that had the hotel name on them. It didn't take him long to find her room number. Room 204.

Finally . . . the answer he needed.

He took the keys out of the ignition and pocketed them after he shut and locked the car. Within seconds, he was inside the hotel, then running up the stairs. He exited one level up and began moving down the hallway at a fast clip, counting room numbers as he went. It wasn't until he looked down that he realized he was also following a trail of blood drops on the carpet runner. His trek took a turn at the end of a long hallway. His heart was hammering, his gut in knots. He paused for a moment, reading the signs, then took a quick right before he found her room.

The do-not-disturb door-hanger was out. At least she'd been aware enough when she'd gotten to her room to know she had to keep out the maids. But at the same time, he couldn't get in, and picking the lock wasn't possible, not with the computer-generated key cards hotels used these days. That left him with no other option but to knock, then call out.

"Cat! Cat! It's me, Wilson. Let me in!"

He knocked again, then waited. As best he could tell, no one was moving inside. He pounded on the door again, this time louder, this time shouting louder. Again, no one answered.

At that moment a dark-eyed woman in a maid's uniform peeked out of the room across the hall.

Wilson heard the sound and turned abruptly. Thank God. Housekeeping. They had passkeys. He pointed to the door.

"You need to let me in. My friend is hurt."

The little maid shrugged. *"No hablo in-glés."*

Wilson wiped a shaky hand across his face, trying to concentrate on the bits of Spanish he knew. Then he saw the blood spots on the carpet, and grabbed her arm and pointed, showing her that they stopped at the door.

The maid's eyes widened as she recognized the blood.

"Mi amiga . . . muy mal," Wilson said. He couldn't remember the word for hurt or injured, but he'd just told her his friend was bad. Maybe she would put the blood and his broken Spanish together and figure out what he meant. Then he remembered another word that might get him in. *"Muerte . . . muerte."*

She gasped.

He wasn't sure if he'd just told the maid that Cat was dead or murdered, but either way, he saw understanding spreading across her face. He pointed to her passkey, then pointed to the door over and over, until the woman finally relented.

Nervously, she stepped past Wilson, slid the passkey into the slot, then gasped when he jostled past her. Curious, she followed him inside. Both of them saw Cat at the same time. She was lying on her side on the floor, between the sofa and the coffee table. Her clothes were stained with so much dried blood that Wilson couldn't tell what color they'd been originally.

The maid cried out, then covered her face.

Wilson didn't blame her. He wanted to cover *his* face, too. There wasn't a feature on Cat's face that he would have recognized. Everything was swollen, with one eye completely closed. There were deep gashes and cuts on her face that looked as if someone had used brass knuckles on her, but he remembered how big Tutuola had been and knew the man wouldn't have needed brass knuckles to break bones.

Wilson shoved the coffee table aside, then dropped to his knees and put two fingers against her neck. She had a pulse.

"Jesus, honey . . . oh, Jesus," Wilson muttered, as he slid his arms beneath her neck and knees, then stood up and laid her on the sofa.

She was in such bad shape that he was afraid to touch her for fear of doing more harm than good. What he needed was a doctor, but one who would treat her and keep his mouth shut at the same time. The only person who might be able to help him was the maid, and from the look on her face, she was ready to bolt.

He pulled a twenty-dollar bill out of his pocket and handed it to her.

"Doctor? Do you know a doctor who would come here?"

She began to cry, shaking her head to indicate that she didn't understand, and ran toward the door. Wilson was right behind her. The last thing he needed was her spilling the beans and calling attention to the situation.

"Wait! Wait!" he called, and grabbed her by the arm just as she was about to escape.

"Hey, what's going on here?"

The appearance of a redheaded bellman coming down the hall was as surprising to Wilson as the fact that the man had spoken in English.

Everyone stopped in mid-stride. The maid looked relieved, because she obviously knew the bellman. Wilson was just as relieved, because he was going to be understood.

He pointed to the maid. "Tell her I didn't mean to scare her, but I need to get help for my friend."

The bellman glanced past them to the woman lying on the sofa.

"Damn, mister . . . is she still alive?"

"Yes, but she's in bad shape."

"What happened to her?" he asked.

"I don't know," Wilson said. "I just got here."

The redhead frowned, then spoke quickly to the maid, who answered him with quick nods.

"Asuncion says she let you in."

"Yeah, like I said, I just got here. Couldn't rouse anyone and got worried. I don't know what's happened to her, but I would like to keep this quiet. Can we do that?"

Wilson was pulling money out of his pocket while he was talking. He was holding a hundred dollars in twenties when he looked up at the man.

The bellman hesitated, but only briefly. This wasn't the first time he'd been asked to keep his mouth shut and probably wouldn't be the last.

"Name's R.J.," he said, then took the money as he uttered what sounded to Wilson like a brief warning to the maid to keep her mouth shut, too.

She nodded quickly and disappeared without looking back.

Wilson grabbed the bellman by the arm and dragged him into the room, then closed the door.

"Do you know a doctor who would be willing to come here?"

R.J. hesitated. "On the quiet again?"

"Yes."

R.J. glanced at the woman on the sofa, then shrugged. Why the hell not?

"Yeah, I think I do."

Wilson pointed to the phone. "Call him."

The bellman took his own phone out of his pocket.

"I'll use mine," he said, then took the phone book from a nearby table, leafed through the pages and made a quick call.

"Hey, Doc, it's me, R.J. Yeah, I'm all better. Yeah, I took all the pills." He was grinning until he caught the look on Wilson's face and shifted into serious gear. "Say, Doc . . . we got a situation here at the hotel. Got a lady here who needs some serious doctoring, and they want to keep it on the quiet." He paused, looked at Wilson, then asked, "Has she been shot?"

Wilson shook his head. "I don't think so. Just appears as if she's been beaten."

R.J. relayed the information. "Yeah. Now. Okay, I'll tell them. Oh . . . it's room 204 and come in the back way . . . okay? Yeah, you, too, and thanks, Doc."

He hung up, then turned to Wilson.

"Doc's name is Scott . . . Mack Scott. Originally from New Hampshire, I think. He'll be here in about ten minutes."

"Can I trust him?" Wilson asked.

R.J. nodded. "Oh yeah . . . Doc is the kind of man who flies under the radar."

Wilson had a moment's impression of some hack who'd lost his license and had gone across the border where people weren't as apt to check for licenses as they were in the U.S. He grabbed the bellman by the arm and pushed him up against the door.

"Is he some kind of butcher? If he is . . . and he comes in here and does more harm than good, I'll beat the crap out of both of you."

R.J.'s gaze slid past the fire in the man's eyes to the single gold loop in his ear, then shuddered. The man looked like he could make good on the threat. He pulled out of Wilson's grasp as he reached for the doorknob.

"No, he's all legal and everything . . . he just likes to drink a little too much."

"Great," Wilson said, then eyed the bellman. "Sorry. I appreciate your help."

"No problem," R.J. said. "Look, I'd better go or they'll come looking for me pretty soon. I want to make sure Asuncion is keeping *her* mouth shut, too." He pointed toward Cat. "Good luck there, man. I hope she gets okay."

"So do I," Wilson said, and turned back to Cat as soon as the bellman was gone.

246

"Come here, baby," he said softly, as he picked her up from the sofa and carried her into the adjoining bedroom.

He needed to remove her clothes to see the extent of her injuries, but even as he was laying her down, he was starting to dread the answers. She'd groaned out loud with every step that he'd taken, and now, flat on her back and still unconscious, she was weeping. It was almost more than he could bear. He reached for her jacket, then paused.

"Cat, sweetheart . . . it's Wilson. You're hurt. You're hurt bad, and I need to take off your clothes."

He thought he saw her lips move, then decided he was mistaken. Still, he couldn't put this off any longer. She'd been unattended to too long as it was. He reached for the collar of her jacket with one hand, grabbed the sleeve with another, and began trying to ease it down.

Within seconds, she screamed.

He turned loose of her and the jacket as if it were on fire, his voice shaking as he pulled back.

"Lord have mercy, baby . . . it wasn't enough that you had to break my heart. Now you're bound and determined to stop it."

He took a knife out of his pocket, then pressed on the side of the hasp. The blade sprang out, then locked in place. Without wasting any more time, he slid the blade inside the sleeve at the wrist and began to cut. He cut until the jacket was split from the right sleeve all the way to the collar, then began on the left sleeve, repeating the motion. He cut every stitch of her clothing away from her body without moving so much as a hair on her head. The moment her midsection was revealed, he knew she had multiple breaks in her ribs. The swelling and bruising was horrific.

"God in heaven," Wilson mumbled. It was all the prayer he could manage.

He checked her pulse again, making sure that her heart was still beating, and had started to the bathroom to get some wet cloths to clean the blood off her when there was a knock at the door.

"The doctor," he muttered, and took a moment to pull a sheet up over Cat's nude body, then ran out of the room.

Mack Scott had been in Chihuahua for almost fifteen years. He liked to think of it as nothing more than an extended vacation, but truth was, he'd gotten siesta fever and hadn't been able to face any more New

Hampshire winters. Also, there was the booze. He liked it a little too much for the ethics committees in the States. However, the Mexican authorities were a little more lax in their requirements. It hadn't taken him long to get accredited to practice medicine here. Once that happened, he'd had no reason to go back.

It wasn't like he did anything illegal. He just made himself available for people who tended toward keeping their business a bit closer to the chest than the normal. Every so often, R.J. the bellman funneled a little business his way. It didn't hurt anybody and kept him in tequila.

He'd been setting a broken bone on a little boy who'd fallen off his bike when R.J. called. He'd finished up the cast, prescribed some pain pills and sent the family on their way, then packed up his bag for the house call.

Once inside the hotel, the blood trail down the hallway had not escaped his notice. He was already anticipating problems when he knocked on the door. The man who answered looked like someone who'd just stepped out of a pirate movie, right down to the fierce glare and the gold hoop in his ear. Mack took a deep breath and then offered his hand.

"I'm Doctor Scott."

Wilson ignored the hand. "Follow me," he said, and turned away.

Mack walked inside, then shut the door behind him. He paused for a moment to survey the area, noting the smears of dried blood on the furniture and the floor, then kept on going.

"In here," Wilson said.

Mack stepped into the room, then stifled a gasp. The woman on the bed wasn't moving, and her face was a mess.

"Is she dead?" he asked.

Wilson grabbed him by the arm.

"If she was dead, I wouldn't have needed a doctor, now would I?"

"Oh. Yes, right," Mack stuttered, and then hurried toward the bed. "Do you know what happened to her?" he asked, as he pulled back the sheet.

"Best I can tell, she's been beaten within an inch of her life."

"Why not take her to a hospital?" Mack asked, as he got out his stethoscope and began his examination.

"We're not locals, okay? I just need to get her in traveling condition and get her home."

Mack glanced up. "You two on the run?"

Wilson might have laughed, but he was

250

afraid he would start crying and never stop.

"No. We're bounty hunters . . . the ones who usually do the chasing."

Mack frowned, then got down to business.

"She needs X-rays, you know. Her ribs are broken."

"I know they're broken. Can you tape her up enough that she can travel?"

Mack frowned. "Damn, man, moving her when she's like this could finish her off."

Wilson leaned down until he was only inches away from the doctor's face.

"Then make sure you fix her so it doesn't. We need to leave . . . understand?"

The threat was only implied, but Mack didn't feel like pushing his luck.

"Get me a basin and some washcloths. We need to clean her up first so I can see exactly what we're dealing with."

Wilson turned quickly and headed for the bathroom. He filled the ice bucket with water, grabbed two washcloths, then headed back to the bed. Together, they managed to remove the dried blood, revealing even more cuts and gashes than before.

And if that wasn't enough to deal with, sometime during the impromptu bath, Cat Dupree came to.

TWELVE

Cat had shut down hours ago, unable to take the pain. Now something was pulling her back. Once she'd thought she heard Wilson's voice, but then she'd convinced herself it was part of the nightmare she'd created for herself. When she felt hands on her body, her mind went straight to Tutuola. Her first instinct was to fight, but when she moved, pain spilled into every muscle.

She gasped, then groaned.

The doctor was still examining her for injuries, and Wilson was washing blood off her face and neck when he realized she was coming to.

"Thank God," he muttered, then leaned close to her ear. "You're gonna be okay, baby. Lie still and let Dr. Scott help you."

She pushed weakly at their hands.

Wilson was afraid to hold her too tight for fear that he would further injure her already broken bones, but he kept saying her name, talking reassuringly to her.

"Cat . . . baby . . . it's me, Wilson. It's me, honey. Don't fight us. We're just trying to help."

He wasn't sure, but he thought she understood. At least she quit fighting him. Moments later, he watched as she reached toward her mouth, running fingers across the cuts and swellings, then tried to lick her lips.

He grabbed a clean washcloth and dampened it, then held it close to her lips, squeezing lightly and letting droplets of water fall onto her mouth.

When Cat felt the moisture, she turned toward the source like a baby turning to its mother's breast. The droplets on her face and mouth were enough to wake her. Despite the fact that she couldn't see much more than light and shadows from one eye and nothing out of the other, she now knew enough not to try moving again. She also knew she was no longer alone. She reached out, her fingers touching, then curling around, someone's wrist.

"There's a doctor here, honey. He's going to fix you up."

She clutched at him, feeling the thump of his pulse beneath her fingertips. Wilson? Here?

She lifted her arm, her fingers splayed out in the air, searching for confirmation.

He caught her hand and lifted it to his lips, then held it against his face, unable to say what he felt.

It was the tears on his face she felt first, and knowing that he cried for her was humbling. She rubbed her thumb along the curve of his lips, then lightly felt the shape of his eyebrows, remembering the way they arched. From there, it was a straight shot down the length of his nose to that perfect indentation in his upper lip. The sensuality of his mouth was familiar, but it was when she felt that single gold hoop in his ear that she knew for certain he was there.

It was unbelievable to her that, no matter how many times she had hurt him — even shunned him — he had yet to turn his back on her. She was seriously going to have to rethink her life choices.

"Miss . . . I'm going to try and set your ribs now," someone she thought must be Dr. Scott said.

Cat's hands moved to her midsection, remembering the crushing kicks and blows from Tutuola's hands and fists, and she discovered she was naked.

"Clothes?"

Wilson patted her arm. "I started to

undress you, but you couldn't stand the pain. I had to cut them off."

Dr. Scott pulled a syringe from his bag, then paused. "Miss . . . are you allergic to anything?"

Cat could barely form the word. "No."

He filled the syringe, then swabbed an area on her arm with alcohol. "You're going to feel a slight sting."

A sting? Every pore in her body was aching. A sting would just get lost in the crowd. She would have laughed, but she hurt too much to waste the sarcasm.

Wilson pulled a strand of hair away from her swollen eyes, then ran a finger gently across her forehead.

"Can't see," she mumbled.

"I know, baby . . . I'm sorry, but the swelling will go down."

He watched her lick her lips again. When he dampened them once more, her nostrils flared.

"You came," she whispered.

He laid a hand against the side of her face, then leaned close to her ear.

"You had to know I would."

"The pain meds should kick in any time now," Doctor Scott said. "I need to stitch up your cuts, so I'll be numbing those areas after we bind your ribs."

Cat mentally braced herself for what was to come.

She felt hands tracking the lines of bones beneath her skin, then fingers testing — pushing — testing — pushing.

The pain that shot through her went all the way to her back teeth. In spite of her intent to bear it, she screamed, then moaned. The sound cut through Wilson like a knife.

"I'm sorry, miss . . . I'm sorry," the doctor was saying, but he didn't stop working and Cat couldn't stop screaming. She begged him to stop, and she begged Wilson to make him.

Wilson gritted his teeth, wishing to God he could take the pain for her, then, finally, mercifully, she passed out.

Thankful that she was momentarily oblivious, the doctor worked quickly, maneuvering the ribs back in place by touch. When he was done, he bound Cat's midriff as tightly as he dared.

"This isn't a good idea," Dr. Scott kept saying. "I'd feel a whole lot better if we'd gotten X-rays."

Wilson knew there was a body somewhere in Chihuahua that would eventually be found, if it hadn't already. He wanted Cat as far away from the city as he could get her before someone realized the dead man had had help on his way to hell.

"I'll take her to a dozen doctors later, but not here. I need to get her back to the States."

Mack Scott narrowed his gaze as he looked from one to the other.

"I don't want to know what's going on. I'm just giving you my best advice."

"I don't want advice. I want results."

The man's attitude was unwavering. Scott shrugged. It was their funeral. He began numbing the areas around which he would stitch, his entire focus on doing as little damage as possible.

Wilson watched until he was satisfied by what the doctor was doing, then gave the rest of his attention to Cat.

The doctor paused a moment, eyeing his handiwork and trying to decide where to start stitching. Inevitably, his gaze slid to the scar on her neck. Between old wounds and new, he was amazed at the punishment this woman had taken and still lived.

"Look's like she's a survivor," he said.

Wilson sighed, then smoothed a tiny strand of hair away from her neck as the doctor began to stitch up her cuts.

"You have no idea," he said. "You have no idea."

Thirty minutes later, Mack Scott rocked back on his heels and straightened up.

"Okay. That's all I can do for her here."

He began gathering up his things. He dug a handful of samples from his bag, then handed them to Wilson.

"Pain pills. If you're bound and determined to move her, she's going to need them. I've already given her a stiff shot of codeine, so don't give her anything else for at least four hours. After that, she can have two of those pills every three hours until you get her back to the States. Then get her to a hospital ASAP. I'm still uncomfortable about possible internal injuries."

"Yeah. I get it," Wilson said. "What do I owe you?"

"A hundred bucks should cover it."

Wilson dug into his pocket again and pulled out a single bill.

"Well worth it, and then some," he said softly, then shook the man's hand.

"Safe journey," Scott said, then added, "If you two *are* in trouble, don't linger. Mexican jails are not pleasant."

Wilson nodded. "Thanks."

As soon as the doctor was gone, Wilson grabbed his cell phone and made a call.

Mike Simms answered on the first ring.

"What?"

Wilson shifted the phone to his other ear as he moved to the window, eyeing the parking lot below.

"We're coming in. Should be there within thirty minutes, maybe sooner."

"Is she okay?"

"No, but she's alive."

"I'll be waiting."

Wilson hung up, then paused a moment to look around the room. He needed to remove every vestige of Cat's presence. He didn't know if she'd registered under her own name, but he wasn't going to leave anything of hers behind, just in case.

He emptied dressers and the closet, took the stuff she'd tossed into the wastebasket and threw it in her bag along with everything else. He took her room key, then eyed the bloody bedclothes and towels.

The maid, Asuncion, had seen Cat. She would understand and hopefully not raise any unwanted alarms. Just to make sure, he tossed a couple more twenty-dollar bills on the bedside table, and then, after a quick check of Cat's condition to make sure she was still out, he stuffed a handful of wet washcloths into a valet-service bag, then took those along with her suitcase and headed down the back way to her car.

He tossed her bag in the back, then took

the wet cloths he'd brought with him and began to clean out the interior of Cat's car. The water reactivated the coppery scent of fresh blood, and by the time he was through, he was almost sick to his stomach. This wasn't just anyone's blood. It was Cat's. As badly as she'd been injured, he didn't know how she'd managed to get herself back into the hotel. As he began, he soon found a gun beneath the seat. Without a second thought, he wiped off the prints and tossed it in a garbage bag.

Not for the first time, he wondered exactly what had happened to Tutuola, but now was not the time to get curious.

As soon as he'd finished cleaning the car, he tossed the washcloths back in the bag with the gun, then threw the bag in the Dumpster on his way back inside. The closer he got to Cat's room, the faster he moved. By the time he reached the second floor and turned down her hallway, he was running. The only plus to this whole night-mare was that this was the off-season for tourists. If the vehicles around the parking lot were any indication, the hotel wasn't even half full.

He opened the door with Cat's key card and slipped inside. As he did, he thought he heard movement and rushed into the bedroom. Cat was awake. So damned much for the pain shot the doctor had given her.

"Cat . . . honey. What in hell are you trying to do?"

Cat turned her head toward the sound of his voice. "Wilson?"

"Yes, it's me."

"I need to pee."

"Lord have mercy, woman. I don't know —"

"Help . . . damn it."

He sighed. "Don't blame me if you pass out before you can do anything."

"I . . . c'n do it," she mumbled.

He touched the side of her poor battered face, while trying to figure out the best way to help her up.

"Okay . . . can you lift your arms?"

She tried to lift them, then gasped when she reached too high with her right arm.

"Can't . . ."

"One's good enough," Wilson said. "I'm gonna put one arm beneath your shoulders and my other under your knees. When I do, slide your good arm around my neck and hold on. Don't fight me. Don't move. I'll do all the moving for you."

" 'm . . . naked."

He stifled a frown. "One thing at a time, lady. One thing at a time."

He bent down, then hesitated. There was no way to do this without hurting her. Just as well get it over with.

"Hang tough, baby . . . here we go."

He slid his arms between her and the mattress, then lifted her to his chest with one smooth motion. As careful as he was trying to be, she moaned, then hiccuped on a sob.

"Jesus . . . Jesus," Cat mumbled, unaware that she'd said the name aloud.

"I'm sorry, I'm so sorry," Wilson said, as he hurried into the bathroom with her, then eased her down onto the commode. "Can you sit upright without me?"

"Yes."

He hated to let go. "You sure?"

He saw her try to make a fist, and knew that she was angry with herself and the situation as much as with his persistence.

"Yes . . . sure. Can't move . . . can't see . . . still know how to pee."

"Okay, then," Wilson said. "I'll be right outside. Yell when you're ready."

He walked out, then closed the door. The longer he was here, the antsier he felt. As he waited, he heard footsteps coming down the hallway, then loud voices. He caught himself holding his breath, waiting for them to pass. When they did, he exhaled slowly.

As he waited, it dawned on him that every

stitch of clothing Cat owned was down in the car. Then he realized he'd never be able to dress her anyway, so the subject was moot. There was a hotel bathrobe draped across a chair. While he wasn't in the habit of stealing from hotels, the situation called for extreme measures. He picked up the robe just as Cat called out.

He opened the door and hurried in, tossing the card key onto the bed as he passed. "I've got a bathrobe here, honey. We need to get it on you so I can get you outside."

Cat froze. "Out?"

"To the airport. I've got a chopper waiting to get you out of the country."

She nodded once, waiting for him to do what had to be done.

By the time he had her wrapped and belted into the robe, she was in tears. Her shoulders shook with silent sobs, and when he picked her up again, she passed out.

It was God's own blessing. Wilson couldn't take her down the elevator, because that led out into the lobby, and she wouldn't have been able to bear the trip down the stairs without screaming in pain. Even then, as he was carrying her down the hall to the stairwell, he met a guest coming off the elevator who took one look at Cat and gasped.

"Mugged. Watch your back," Wilson muttered, and kept on going.

He got to the parking lot and then opened the passenger's door. He'd scooted the seat back earlier and left it in a reclining position. He laid Cat down without trying to fasten a seat belt around her. By the time he got behind the steering wheel, he was shaking. He glanced at Cat. Thankful that she was still out, he started the car and quickly drove away.

It took fifteen minutes to get to the airport, and it was the longest fifteen minutes he'd ever spent in his life. Every siren he heard made him certain the Mexican police were in pursuit. Every police car he saw, he feared it would make a quick turn in the road and give chase. In spite of every preconceived worry he'd had, none of them came true. Only after he had turned off the main road and taken the smaller road to the airport did he begin to relax. Then he saw Mike standing by his chopper and pulled up beside it.

Mike was smiling, but when he saw the passenger in the car, his expression stilled. He got all the luggage out of the car and tossed it into the chopper, then stood aside, holding the door open as Wilson carried Cat toward him.

When Wilson saw the blow-up mattress on the floor behind the seats, as well as the small pillow and blanket his friend had scrounged, he nodded approvingly as he glanced at Mike.

"Good thinking," he said.

Mike eyed Cat again and then quickly looked away, as if he'd done something wrong. His face was flushed, and his voice was shaking. "Goddamn, Wilson. Goddamn."

Wilson eased Cat down onto the mattress, then pulled the blanket up over her legs.

"I've got to move her car," he said. "Be right back."

"I'll start up the engine," Mike said.

Wilson jumped in Cat's car and drove toward the small building that served the airport. He parked and went inside, heading for the young woman who was standing behind a counter.

She was a curvaceous Latino in her late twenties who was obviously proud of her big boobs and laser-whitened teeth, because she kept smoothing down the front of her blouse and smiling.

"Miss . . . I need to park a vehicle here for a while. Is that a problem?"

She glanced out at the SUV, then shrugged. "No problem."

He took a pen and paper from his pocket. "What's the phone number to this airport?"

She wrote it down for him, then flashed him another toothy smile.

Wilson pocketed the paper and laid a twenty on the counter.

"Thank you for your help," he said. "I'll be in touch about the car."

She palmed the money as she nodded importantly. "It will be safe here, *señor.* We have the twenty-four-hour security here, you know."

"Okay, thanks again," he said, and headed for the door. Once outside, he ran to the waiting chopper. Not until he was buckled in and they were lifting off the tarmac into the air did Wilson finally begin to breathe easy.

He glanced back at Cat a couple of times, reassuring himself that she was still okay, and then thumped Mike lightly on the shoulder.

"I cannot thank you enough for this," he said.

Mike just shook his head and started explaining that he'd filed a flight plan that covered the shortest distance to the border.

"We'll worry about the fastest way to get her home later. Right now, I just want to get back into the States."

Wilson glanced at Mike, eyeing the set to his jaw and the glitter in his eyes.

"Thank you," he said again, softly, then glanced back at Cat. Thankfully she was, for the moment, beyond pain.

They hadn't flown more than a couple of minutes from the airport when Wilson realized they were flying low over some pretty exclusive property. Below, he could see opulent houses with well-cared-for grounds all around.

"Hey . . . look at that," Mike said, pointing down to his left. "That must have been one damned big fire."

Wilson leaned over and glanced at the huge, burned-out shell of a mansion, along with some nearby out-buildings that had suffered roof damage. He didn't think much of it until he happened to notice the long, older model car parked in front of what must have been a garage.

Suddenly his flesh began to crawl.

He knew that car. They'd tracked it into Laredo, then across the border through Nuevo Laredo to that empty hacienda on the outside of town. The last time he'd seen it, Cat had been running past it as she'd apprehended Mark Presley.

Tutuola. That was Tutuola's car.

Dear God, what had gone on down there?

267

He stared at the place until they had passed it by, then looked at Cat once again. There would be time for questions later.

Houston and Jimmy Franks had staked out Wilson McKay's bail-bond business for two days now, and still no sign of McKay. They'd seen his secretary coming and going, and while they intended to show her how to respect real men, they didn't want to tip their hand too soon by messing her up just yet.

Houston was getting bored with their original idea of payback and wanted to leave town. It was Jimmy who wouldn't budge. He'd faced both Wilson and the secretary and come out on the downside. It wasn't in him to forgive and forget, even if he had been responsible for the outcome himself, and with the meth he kept putting in his system, his sense of invincibility was over the top.

The brothers were living out of their car, and it was beginning to smell like Sunday morning in a Saturday night bar. The trash they'd been throwing onto the back floorboard was now piling up and spilling over onto the seats. Houston was reaching for the last beer in the six-pack ring when Jimmy snatched it up, popped the top and downed a good third of it before he came up for air.

"Damn it, Jimmy. You saw me reachin' for that beer."

"Yeah, and you saw me get to it first," Jimmy said, and took another long swig just to prove his point.

Houston snapped.

He slapped the back of his brother's head just as Jimmy was about to take another swig. The last of the beer sloshed up his nose and down the front of his shirt to drip on his pants.

Jimmy cursed, flung the empty can at Houston's head and then doubled up his fists.

"Get out!" he yelled. "Get the hell out of the car now. I'm gonna whip your ass."

Houston slapped the can away and reached in his pocket for a cigarette.

"You've been layin' that claim your whole life, and you ain't done it yet, so 'scuse me if I don't get all panicked over the threat."

Jimmy wanted to fire off a sharp comeback, but he never could out-talk Houston, and that was a fact.

"You still didn't have no claim to do what you did," Jimmy muttered, and then brushed at the wet spots on the front of his jeans.

Houston took a long draw on his smoke, then narrowed his eyes as he blew three perfect smoke rings into the interior of the car.

Jimmy cursed again, but quieter, and rolled the window down enough so that the smoke could escape, but not enough to freeze his butt any more than it already was. He glared at Houston, then channeled his anger to the man they were waiting for.

"I don't know where that damned McKay got off to, but when he comes back, he's mine first."

Houston shrugged. "Fine with me. I just want to get this over with and get out of town."

Jimmy bent over and picked up the paper sack from the floor between his feet.

"Hey! What happened to them last two Ding Dongs?"

"I ate 'em," Houston said.

"Well, damn it all to hell, Houston. I'm hungry."

Houston reached down and started the engine.

"What are you doin'?" Jimmy asked.

"I'm takin' you to get somethin' to eat," Houston said.

"What if we leave and miss McKay comin' back?"

Houston sighed. "Do you want to eat, or do you want to whine?"

Jimmy glared. "Well, hell, I suppose I wanna eat."

"Then shut up and ride."

THIRTEEN

It was the vibration of the helicopter and the whine of the engine that dragged Cat from her drug-induced sleep. Other than the pain, which had become her anchor to knowing she was still alive, she had no idea where she was. The scent of fuel and stale coffee further confused her.

She thought about trying to sit up but soon learned that moving was impossible. When she first looked up, she couldn't figure out why her vision was so blurred. A quick check of her face gave her the answer. Her eyes were swollen, one of them completely shut. Still, she could see what appeared to be the backs of two seats and the silhouettes of two men sitting in them. Then she heard Wilson's voice, and she remembered.

He'd come.

After she'd made that call to him, she hadn't expected to be alive and, even though she was still breathing, she wasn't sure she would ever be the same.

She had a feeling that if she saw herself in the mirror right now, she wouldn't recognize her own face. She had vague memories of hearing someone talking about stitching her back up. Were those just hallucinations, or had it really happened? If it did, was she going to be some replica of Frankenstein's monster?

She'd spent most of her life looking for Solomon Tutuola just so she could watch him die. Now, having accomplished that feat, she wasn't sure but what a piece of her had died with him. She'd lived with hate in her heart and revenge on her mind for so long that, now that they were gone, she didn't know how to fill up that space. She no longer had a purpose. There was nothing left in her life that mattered. Except maybe . . .

Before she could get past the thought, the chopper hit an air pocket and the mattress on which she was lying gave a slight bounce. She groaned aloud, and Wilson immediately turned around. She didn't know how he'd heard her over the roar of the rotors, but he had. Her view of his face was blurred, but she saw enough of his expression to know he was aching for her.

"Sorry about that, baby," he said softly.

Her nostrils flared. It was the only sign she gave that she understood.

Wilson glanced at his watch, matching it against how long it had been since that doctor had given her the pain shot.

"Honey . . . are you hurting? Do you need something for the pain?"

She nodded, then lifted a hand and touched the swell of her lower lip.

"Thirsty, too?"

He took one of the packets of pain pills, popped two pills from the blister pack and then reached for the bottle of water. There wasn't much room to maneuver, but he managed to lean over between the seats enough to help her.

"Open," he said, as he lifted her head to keep her from choking and then popped the two pills between her slightly parted lips. "You need a straw, honey, but I don't have one, so if I pour some of this in your ear, you can bust my chops later."

He tilted the water bottle to her lips just enough to let a small stream flow through, then pulled back and waited for her to swallow.

She tried to get the pills down, but choked.

He lifted her head a little higher, then gave her another sip.

That time the medicine went down.

By the time he eased her back to the pillow, she'd broken out into a cold sweat. To make matters worse, the chopper bucked again.

"Oh, God," Cat mumbled, and started to cry.

The tears were bitter and silent, seeping out from between her swollen eyelids. She didn't know if she was crying for the pain or for what her life had become.

Wilson cursed, then unbuckled himself, climbed over the seat and crawled down next to her. He stretched out on the floor beside the little air mattress, slid his arm beneath her neck and laid his other arm across her hips, careful not to touch the binding around her ribs, then held her. And the next time the chopper hit rough air, he was there, steadying the ride and reminding her that she was no longer alone.

Mike didn't look back, not even when Wilson abandoned him for the woman. He'd been flying for more years than he could count, but he'd never been as antsy as he was today. The woman they'd gone after was so hurt, and Wilson was unusually nervous. Maybe the nervousness was catching.

He knew Wilson's reputation as a bounty hunter. He knew that sometimes bounty hunters put themselves in dangerous situations to bring in bail jumpers. He also knew that bounty hunters were illegal in Mexico, so whatever had gone down with Wilson's lady friend most likely went beyond getting beat all to hell. No wonder Wilson wanted her out of there.

He glanced down, then checked their heading. Just a few more minutes and they would be in U.S. air space. It would be none too soon for him.

Pedro Andehal was the medical examiner who'd received the body from the murder scene. He was fifty-two years old and bordering on burned out himself. The older he got, the more he wanted to be around the living, not the dead. Maybe it was because he was growing nearer and nearer to the day when it might be his own body lying on an autopsy table and someone else about to slice him from stem to stern.

He paused beside the table, eyeing the body before him. At this point, all he knew for certain was that it was male, and that the man had been large — very large. He also knew this wasn't going to be an easy examination. The flesh was charred all the way to the bone, and there was very little of it left on his face. Samples had already been taken and sent to the lab, but they didn't exactly have state-of-the-art equipment. They managed, but the facility could certainly have benefited from an upgrade.

Pedro turned on the tape recorder so that he could record his findings as he worked, pulled the face mask up over his nose, rolled his head from one side to the other to loosen the muscles, then picked up a scalpel.

Solomon Tutuola might be toast, but the world wasn't done with him yet.

Two hours later, Pedro turned off the tape recorder, pulled a sheet back over the charred carcass, wheeled it over to the wall and slid it into a drawer. He turned off the light over the worktable and nodded to his assistant, who began removing surgical instruments and scrubbing the table down.

Pedro tossed his surgical gloves and the disposable footies he wore over his shoes into a disposal unit and the apron he wore over his scrubs into the laundry bin, washed himself thoroughly, then left. He had a report to finish and a date with his wife, and he didn't want to be late.

As he was walking through the hallway on his way to his office, his cell phone rang. He answered absently, concentrating only after he recognized the police chief's voice. The conversation was brief.

Yes, the autopsy was finished. Due to the quantity of gunshot wounds and the destruction of the lungs when the body had burned, it was hard to say whether Tutuola was still alive when the fire had begun. Most of the internal organs had been charred so thoroughly that it was hard to tell what was pre-fire damage and what was post.

It was Pedro's understanding that the roof had also fallen in on the body, which confused the issue as to what bones, if any, had been broken before the fire, or if all the breaks had come afterward. His official ruling was going to be death by gunshot, but the fire would have done him in if the bullets hadn't. Notifying next of kin — if there were any — fell to the police. Pedro's job was over.

As for the police chief, thanks to the Realtor who'd sold Tutuola the mansion, they at least had a name for the victim. This morning he'd begun getting back info in response to the faxes he'd sent out last night. Once he'd read them, it became apparent why the victim might have met such an end.

His full name was Solomon Ranu Tutuola, and his rap sheet in Mexico was staggering, beginning back in the eighties. After further checking, it turned out that Tutuola had a similar arrest record in the United States, and even a couple of arrests in Central America. Not once was there a next of kin listed, and his place of birth, listed as Brisbane, Australia, turned out to be a lie.

He shoved the paperwork into a file folder and tossed it on the edge of his desk. It appeared that a professional hit man had come to their city and died a violent death in what was, most likely, a case of revenge. He would keep the file open and send a couple of officers to interview people in the surrounding area. The houses, because of their size and the occupants' desire for privacy, were separated by as much as a half mile, sometimes more. It was unlikely that anyone would have heard the gunshots unless they'd been outside after midnight, which was when the fire was first spotted. The truth was, they had no witnesses and too many motives, which meant no starting point for an investigation. It certainly wasn't the first time they'd started a case with nothing to go on, and it wouldn't be the last, but he wasn't inclined to put a rush on it. He would never admit it, but he had an inborn prejudice against career criminals and a personal belief that when they bought it, it was nothing more than fate coming back to give them a much-deserved send-off to hell.

At that point, his telephone rang. He answered, frowning as his focus quickly shifted from the dead man to a child who had gone missing. There was no question of where his priorities would lie.

The flight to Dallas was nothing short of agony for Cat. Wilson did all he could, but other than keeping pain pills in her system and steadying her somewhat from buffeting winds, there was nothing more he could do.

Hours later, they were finally within sight of the city. It wasn't the first time Wilson had flown into Dallas after dark, but they weren't landing back at Martin's Airfield. Mike had already made plans to land at the heliport that served Dallas Memorial Hospital.

Wilson breathed a weary sigh of relief when Mike got on the radio and began their descent to the landing pad. Once they were down, everything began happening quickly. The bay doors were yanked open, instantly filling the chopper with blinding lights and cold winter air. There was an emergency team from the hospital waiting with a gurney to take Cat inside, and Wilson wasn't going to let her go alone. As he got out, he stopped long enough to give Mike the keys to his SUV.

"When you get back to the airport, just put all our stuff in my car and lock it up. I have an extra set of keys at the apartment."

Mike nodded. "Will do, buddy."

"I'll come by tomorrow with a check for the ride," Wilson said.

"Yeah . . . and don't forget my tip," Mike teased.

Wilson smiled, then shook his head. "I will never be able to repay you for what you did."

Mike pointed to the woman who was swiftly being wheeled away.

"I'd like to meet her one day when she's got both eyes open and a smile on her face."

"Count on it," Wilson said, then hurried to catch up.

Cat knew she was no longer in the chopper, because the smell of stale coffee was gone. What she did smell was cold air. She heard strangers talking, then felt the motion of the gurney on the concrete as every joint and muscle in her body screamed for relief. Then the gurney rolled over a crack in the concrete, and she passed out.

The next thing she heard was a man calling her name.

"Miss Dupree . . . can you hear me?"

She inhaled slowly, then exhaled a soft yes.

He laid a hand on her shoulder in a reassuring manner. "You're in the emergency room of Dallas Memorial. We're bringing in a portable X-ray for you. After we're done there, you'll be going down to the lab for an MRI."

Cat managed a nod.

"Do you remember anything about what happened to you?"

Wilson had been standing against the wall out of the way, but when he heard the question, he stiffened. If Cat was too out of her head, she might let something slip that could get her in trouble.

As it happened, Cat took care of the situation.

"Ask Wilson," she mumbled.

The doctor looked up, then around. "Is someone here named Wilson?"

"That would be me," Wilson said, stepping closer to the gurney.

"What can you tell me about Miss Dupree's injuries? She's obviously been treated already."

"Not a lot. I don't know what happened to her. I just responded to a phone call. When I got to her, she was unconscious. It appeared to me that she'd been beaten . . .

maybe she was mugged. I don't know for sure. But she's a bounty hunter. She could have gotten in the way of some bad guy she was after."

"So where did this happen?"

"We were in a rural area. The local doctor who bound her broken ribs and stitched her up said to get her to a hospital for X-rays as soon as possible, which is what we did."

Satisfied with the answer, the doctor dropped the inquisition, which suited Wilson.

"Well, then, let's see what we can see," the doctor said, and waved to the orderlies who were bringing the portable X-ray into the E.R.

"Wilson . . . Wilson . . ." Cat mumbled.

Wilson moved past the doctor and then gently cupped Cat's face.

"I'm here, honey. Just let them do their thing. I won't be far away."

"Don't leave," she begged.

"I'm not going anywhere," Wilson said.

Cat couldn't put into words what it meant to her to be back in Texas. She still didn't know how Wilson had made this happen, but she knew one thing for sure. Wilson McKay had saved her life, and in doing so, pulled off a small miracle.

She owed the man.

She owed him big time.

As soon as the doctors put her back together again, there were going to be changes made. She just hoped it wasn't too late to make amends.

A couple of hours later, the tests had been done and Cat had been admitted to the hospital. For the first time in days, Wilson felt his world returning to an even keel. He watched them taking her toward an elevator while listening to the doctor's decisions.

"I want to keep her in the hospital for a couple of days, just to make sure there aren't any surprises."

Wilson frowned. "Besides the obvious, is something wrong that you're not telling me? Are there internal injuries that —"

"No, no, nothing like that," the doctor said. "At least, nothing showed up that would lead us to believe she's in danger. She has a slight concussion but seems to be on the upswing from that. Whoever set her ribs did a good job. Nothing needed to be redone on that front. She may have some slight scarring from the stitches, but a good plastic surgeon can smooth all that out at a later date. As for the swelling on her face, that, too, will subside. Does she have any next of kin . . . someone we need to notify?"

"Just me," Wilson said. "I'll let her boss know." Then he pointed down the hall. "Where are they taking her?"

"Check with the desk. They'll tell you where her room is going to be."

"Thank you, doctor," Wilson said, and headed for the front desk. A few minutes later he was in an elevator on his way to the third floor.

Tutuola was on top of her, pounding his fist into her belly and ribs over and over until she could no longer breathe. She wanted to scream, but the sound wouldn't come.

The gun. She had to get hold of the gun again.

Wilson woke up only seconds after Cat moaned, then screamed. He was instantly out of the chair and at her side. She was dreaming. He could tell by the way her muscles were jerking. He cupped Cat's face with his hands and spoke softly but urgently.

"Cat, you're dreaming. Wake up, honey, wake up."

Cat inhaled swiftly, as if surfacing from a drowning pool, and clutched Wilson by the wrist.

"God . . . Wilson . . . oh, God."

"Are you in pain?"

Cat shuddered. Pain? She couldn't remember a time when she hadn't been in pain of one kind or another. Physical pain, emotional pain — to her, they were one and the same.

"Tutuola," she muttered.

"Shh, baby . . . don't say the name. Don't even think it. So far, no one knows anything about the history that was between you. As far as they know, he was just a man Mark Presley hired to get him out of Texas. Last time you saw him, he was inside a burning house outside Nuevo Laredo, and let's keep it that way."

Before she could answer, the nurse came hurrying into the room.

"What's wrong in here?" she snapped.

Wilson looked up. "I think she was dreaming."

The nurse eyed Wilson suspiciously as she moved toward the bed and began checking Cat's IV hookup, as well as her vitals. Only after she realized that all was as it should be did she ease her guard.

"Miss Dupree, is there anything I can do to make you comfortable? Are you warm enough? Are you in pain?"

Cat lifted a hand to her lips. "Yes," she said, then added, "water."

"Yes, of course," the nurse said, and

picked up the little plastic pitcher. "I'll be right back."

As soon as she was gone, Wilson stepped back to the side of Cat's bed. The ice packs that they'd put on her eyes were taking the worst of the swelling down, and the ointments they'd applied to her bruised and swollen lips seemed to give comfort. But the tears running down her cheeks told him that she was still suffering, and in a way he couldn't make go away.

"You're a tough one. Remember that, baby. You faced down the devil and beat him. Don't quit on yourself now."

Cat licked the edge of her lower lip as she reached for Wilson again. This time her fingers not only curled around his wrist but tightened, then dug in.

"Wilson . . ."

He sensed the determination in her — the struggle she was having with her own need to fade back into an unconscious state.

"What, baby?"

"I . . . don't . . . quit."

He sighed. "Right."

She exhaled slowly, turning loose of the breath carefully so as not to aggravate her bound ribs. She felt herself losing her grasp on reality and tried to hold on long enough for one more thought. It didn't happen.

She slipped back into a drug-induced state of peace just as the nurse came back with her pitcher.

"Here you are, dear," she said.

"She's out again," Wilson said.

The nurse set the water pitcher down beside the bed.

"Well, it will be here when she wakes," she said, and with a brief smile in Wilson's direction, left the room.

Wilson watched Cat's face for a few seconds more, then retreated back to his chair and sat down. After a few seconds, he reached for his cell phone. He probably wasn't supposed to use it in here, but he needed to make a couple of calls and he wasn't leaving her alone.

It was ten minutes after six in the morning at the McKay home outside of Austin. The old horse who'd borne the weight of all the McKay children was waiting in the corral for his morning feed. He stood with his gaze toward the back door, nickering impatiently.

Inside the old two-story home, the sound of the shower could be heard. Carter McKay was getting ready for the day, and the scent of freshly brewed coffee was wafting throughout the house.

Dorothy McKay was a lot slower these

days than she'd been when all her children had still been at home, but there was nothing slow about her instincts. When the phone rang and she saw the caller ID, she knew something was wrong. Wilson was her eldest, but also the one she worried about most. Not only was his chosen profession one she considered dangerous, but he was so very alone. She picked up the phone on the second ring.

"Hello, honey. Are you okay?"

Wilson sighed. Just the sound of her voice was settling to the panic with which he'd been living for the past few days.

"Yeah, Mom, I'm fine. Just checking in with you guys before the day gets crazy."

"We missed you at Christmas. Too bad about that ice storm."

"Yeah, I missed being there, too," he said, remembering the odd day he'd spent with Cat, trying to help her figure out what had happened to Marsha. It seemed like a lifetime ago. "How's Dad?"

"He's fine. In the shower right now. He'll want to say hello."

"Sure thing. So . . . is everyone okay?"

"Your father and I are fine. Your brothers are fine. Your sisters are fine. Your nieces and nephews are fine. You, on the other hand, are not. Start talking. What's wrong, and don't tell me nothing, because I know better."

Wilson wanted to laugh, but he was too close to tears to chance it.

"It has nothing to do with me," he said.

"Is it a woman?"

"You could say that."

Dorothy sighed. "You're in love, aren't you, son?"

Wilson was dumbfounded. It was the last thing he'd expected to come out of her mouth, and yet the moment she said it, he knew he wouldn't lie.

"Yeah."

"So?"

"It's complicated, okay?"

Dorothy frowned. "You listen to me, Wilson Lee. If she's worth loving, she's worth fighting for. Doesn't she care for you?"

"I haven't the faintest idea what's in her head, and if you knew her, you'd know what I mean."

"So talk to her."

"Oh . . . we're way past talking. She's made herself clear more than once in the past."

"So what's happened now that's changed all that?"

"How do you know something's changed?"

"Because you're calling me," she said.

"She's been injured. She's going to be okay, but it's going to take time."

"Oh . . . I'm so sorry. What can I do to help? Does she need a place to recuperate? We've got all kinds of empty rooms, you know. I would enjoy a little female company . . . if you need us, that is."

Tears blurred Wilson's vision as he glanced over at the bed where Cat was sleeping.

"Thanks for offering, but I don't think she would go."

"So don't ask her, Wilson. Just get her down here. We'll do the rest."

Wilson thought about it. It would be a perfect place for her to heal physically. Would she heal emotionally, as well, or would his big, boisterous family send her the rest of the way into her shell?

"We'll see, but you're a sweetheart for offering."

"Wilson . . ."

"What?"

"Are you okay?"

He smiled. "I will be."

"Okay then. Oh . . . here comes your father. Honey, it's Wilson. Come say hello."

Wilson heard his mother whisper something before she handed his dad the phone. Probably warning his father not to pry and promising that she would fill him in later. Their bond was something he'd taken for granted his whole life. But not anymore. What they had was beyond special. He wanted that same relationship, too, and he wanted it with Cat.

Whether it happened or not had yet to be seen.

FOURTEEN

Wilson had sent John Tiger to Martin's Airfield to pick up his vehicle and then leave it in the hospital parking lot.

John had done so promptly. Then he'd come up to Cat's room with the car keys, knocked quietly on the door and waited for Wilson to answer.

When Wilson came to the door, John told him where he'd parked, handed over the keys and walked away without looking back.

LaQueen had filled him in enough to know that the relationship between Wilson and the female bounty hunter was tenuous at best. He also knew that no one was discussing what had happened to her. It was fine with him. Everyone had secrets.

When John showed no curiosity in trying to see the woman on the bed behind him, Wilson knew then that the man had a strong moral streak that would stand him in good stead. Thinking back, he'd been hesitant to hire extra help until Jimmy Franks' assault on LaQueen had forced him to act. Now he and LaQueen wondered how they'd ever managed without John.

John seemed happy enough. It was for damn certain that LaQueen was happy. She liked him. The unexpected bonus to all of it was that John Tiger liked LaQueen, too. Wilson didn't want to think about why he was the only one who couldn't get the woman he wanted.

Once John was gone, Wilson pocketed the keys and returned to Cat's bedside, where he had been for hours, watching her sleep. The swelling in her eyes was going down. Last time she'd awakened, she had been able to see out of both eyes. The stitches on her face were numerous, but looking at them, he realized the only ones that would be visible were the three on her cheekbone. The others were in her hair line, near her right ear and under her chin. Even then, Wilson suspected Cat wouldn't be bothered by new scars. Like the old puckered one on her neck, they were a kind of proof that she'd survived.

Cat herself was undergoing an inner metamorphosis. Losing Marsha and getting justice for her father's death had put her in a different place. She knew she was floundering. She knew she needed a new anchor in her life. And every time she woke up and saw Wilson McKay, scruffy hair, gold earring and several days in need of a shave, her heart would ache. She didn't know if the pain was from regret or a deeper yearning. God knows he'd given her plenty of openings. She just didn't know where he stood on that anymore. Yes, he'd responded to her call and come after her "bones," as she'd put it, but that didn't change what had gone before. There were still five twenty-dollar bills in the table by her bed that he'd left behind the last time they were together, and she'd gotten the message. She'd treated him like a quick fix for sex. He'd paid her in kind. It was her intent, once she was healed, to see if there was anything left between them to build on.

Wilson was centered on the immediacy of the moment. He needed to go home long enough to shower and change clothes, but he was reluctant to leave. He couldn't bear to think about her waking up alone — disoriented and afraid. As soon as he was satisfied that she was on the upswing, he decided, he would make a quick run home. Red Brickman, the man he'd bought the bail bond business from, was sitting in for Wilson. He still had his accreditation, and was helping John Tiger and LaQueen in Wilson's absence.

From the time Wilson had purchased the business from Red, he'd never missed a day of work. Wilson had always claimed there wasn't a woman for the chasing who would be worth dumping his responsibilities onto someone else. That could no longer be said.

Houston Franks was standing in an alley across from McKay's Bail Bonds waiting on Jimmy to show, but he was late. Houston was past wanting revenge and more intent on getting the hell out of Dallas before his next court date. Jimmy, however, was out of his freakin' mind, intent on payback.

It was Houston's personal opinion that Jimmy was a few biscuits shy of a dozen, and he attributed it to his little brother's meth addiction, which was probably why he was late today. More than likely, Jimmy was out trying to get himself a fix. Houston liked to drink, but he'd never gotten messed up with dope and considered anyone a dope who used it. Still, he didn't have it in him to abandon his brother to his own stupidity. The sooner they tapped McKay and got it over with, the quicker they could be on their way.

Houston had been watching the doorway

to McKay's Bail Bonds for over an hour when a big black pickup pulled up to the curb. He saw the man who got out and frowned. He'd seen him several times before. The man looked to be in his late thirties and was obviously Native American. At first he'd thought the Indian was just a customer, but now he wasn't so sure. Wilson McKay had been suspiciously absent from the office, while this man came and went with regularity. And there was an older, heavyset man who now sat at the desk that Wilson normally occupied. It could be that payback for Wilson McKay might prove more difficult than they'd planned.

It was the muted sound of a nurse's call over the hospital intercom that Cat heard first as she began to wake up, and when she did, she needed no reminders as to why she was there. Her body was a ball of pain, but she'd honored a vow she'd made many years ago and would not have changed a thing. Vigilante though it might have been, justice had been served, and without an iota of regret on her part.

Now it was over. Almost.

When she shifted on the bed, Wilson sat up.

"Hey," he said softly.

297

"Hey yourself," Cat said, then reached for her water cup.

"Here, let me help," he said, and poured her some fresh water, then held the straw to her lips.

She drank thirstily, then nodded when she was done.

Wilson eyed her carefully as he set the cup down. The old independent Cat was slowly emerging. He was glad she was healing, but uncertain as to where that would leave him.

"Is there something I can get for you?" he asked. "Want me to check with the nurse and see if you can have something for pain?"

"I'm okay for now," Cat said, then winced from the binding on her ribs as she tried to pull up the covers.

"Let me," Wilson said, and straightened them for her before tucking her back in.

Cat watched the intentness on his face, but she wondered what was going on behind the mask.

"Wilson?"

"Yeah, honey?"

"What are you thinking?"

He was a bit taken aback by her forthrightness, then realized he shouldn't be. Getting straight to business was Cat at her best. He shifted his weight from one hip to the other, then moved to the foot of her bed, needing to put space between them to answer. His gaze was dark, his face expressionless as he stared. Finally he shook his head.

"Hell, Catherine, I'm not sure how to answer that."

"Just tell me what you're thinking right now."

"I'm thankful you're still in one piece."

"Yeah," she said, and looked away.

Wilson knew she was reliving her encounter with Tutuola. He doubted she would ever volunteer what had gone on between them, and he knew he wasn't going to ask.

"Is it over?" he asked.

She nodded, then looked away. A tear slid out from beneath her eyelid and slipped down her cheek.

"You're one hell of a woman. You know that, don't you?"

Cat blinked, then looked up, a little surprised by the passion in his voice.

"I will never ask you what happened," he said. "I don't need to know, okay?"

She nodded, then frowned slightly as her thoughts moved ahead. "Were we in a chopper?"

"Yes. A friend flew me down to Chihuahua. I won't tell you what hell we went through to get you put back together enough to move you, but it wasn't easy."

"I don't remember much after . . ."

"Did you register at the hotel under your own name?"

"No."

He breathed a quick sigh of relief. That was a loose end that had been bothering him.

"I swept the room when we left. Even took your trash with us. Didn't want to leave anything that could be traced back to you, although the blood trail in the hall of your hotel was still there. The best we can hope for is that they never put two and two together."

Cat hadn't even considered the repercussions of that. She'd been too focused on meting out her own justice. Then she remembered her car.

"My car! I left my car! They'll find it eventually . . . and there's a gun in it. I killed — uh — I need to get it out of the hotel parking lot."

"The gun is gone, and your car's not at the hotel parking lot anymore. It's parked out by a peanut-sized airport. Look . . . here's what I've been thinking. I have someone new working for me. I was going to have him fly down and drive it back."

Cat frowned.

"What if someone saw me? What if the

authorities are looking for the car, waiting for someone to try to cross the border with it?"

Wilson frowned, but before he could answer, Cat had come to her own conclusion.

"I don't want it back," she said.

"You don't want it left there, honey," Wilson said. "Eventually, someone will get curious and trace the owner. Then they'll be wondering why an American woman would go off and leave a good vehicle like that behind. They might even be inclined to see if there was any kind of connection between you and an unsolved murder, and you and I both know there's one hell of a connection. If this had happened in the States, we'd be talking self-defense in the act of arresting a wanted criminal. But what we do is illegal in Mexico. They'd throw your pink-butterfly-tattooed ass in jail for life for playing your bounty-hunting cards in their country."

Cat frowned, unsure as to whether she was irked because he'd mentioned the pink butterfly or because she could wind up in a Mexican jail.

"They won't be able to connect me to anything if the car is gone."

"But how?"

"If you'll go to my apartment and bring me the title and a set of keys, I'll tend to the rest."

"Yeah, sure. Just tell me where the stuff is . . . but what are you going to do?"

Cat closed her eyes for a moment, remembering Padre Francisco's old station wagon and the effort it had taken for them to keep it running long enough to come get Pilar Mendoza's baby.

"Give it to a man I know."

"It's your call," Wilson said.

"I don't have my keys," Cat said.

"But I do," Wilson said.

Cat sighed. "I should have known."

"So tell me where the title is."

She did so quickly, explaining which drawer to look in in her desk, and then which file the title was in.

Wilson moved to the side of the bed and gently cupped the side of her face.

"You gonna be okay while I'm gone?"

"Lord, yes. I can't get into any trouble just lying here."

"Only if you don't have any more nightmares."

Cat looked startled. "What? Did I say something I shouldn't have?"

"No, but I was afraid you would."

She covered her face with her hands.

"God, I have made such a mess of my life."

"No, you haven't," Wilson said softly, as he moved her hands away from her face. "Your life was messed up through no fault of your own. You just had a tough time doing cleanup."

"That's one way to look at it," Cat mumbled.

Wilson leaned down, and before Cat knew what was coming, he kissed her.

"Miss me while I'm gone," he said softly, brushing another kiss across her forehead for good measure.

Cat was too stunned by the kisses to answer. By the time she got herself in gear, he was gone. She watched the door swing shut and then closed her eyes.

Miss him? More than he would know.

The FedEx truck was an unfamiliar sight in Adobe Blanco. People paused in the doorways of their homes, staring with curiosity. When the truck sped on through town, they shrugged philosophically and went on about their business.

It was Padre Francisco who was taken unawares when the driver knocked on the door to the tiny church, then entered.

Padre Francisco had been in his quarters, making himself a cup of instant coffee, when he heard footsteps, then someone calling his name. He hurried out, only to find himself the beneficiary of a packet. He signed for it, then sat down on the front pew as the driver left.

At first he didn't recognize the return address, and even when he did, he was puzzled. It was from the American woman who'd rescued Pilar Mendoza's baby, Maria Elena. He couldn't imagine what she would be sending to him and tore into the packet anxiously.

When a set of keys fell out into his lap, he frowned. Then he opened the letter. A car title fell out from between the folds, as did a couple of one-hundred-dollar bills. He stared, trying to make sense of the objects, then unfolded the letter and began to read.

Father Francisco, although my business in Mexico is now behind me, at the last minute, I had to change my plans. I flew home instead of driving. As I thought about how to get my car, it occurred to me that it would be easier to just buy another one than go to all that trouble, especially since I am still healing from some injuries I incurred.

It occurred to me then that you were the ideal person to make good use of the car.

It's free and clear of debt, and I've signed the title over to you. It's parked at the airstrip outside of Chihuahua. The keys are enclosed. The money is for fuel. It will take quite a bit of fuel to get you to Chihuahua, then even more to drive the car back to Adobe Blanco. I hope this isn't too much trouble for you to go through and that you will be able to put the car to good use. I would suggest that you not delay. It has already been parked there for a couple of days.

One thing . . . I would ask that you don't tell anyone where you got the car — ever. If someone asks, just say it was a gift to the church. However, should you have a free moment now and then, it would not be amiss to mention my name in prayer. God knows I need it.

Bless you, Father. Enjoy the car and give my love to Maria Elena.

Catherine Dupree

Padre Francisco couldn't believe what he'd just read and had to reread the letter twice before he completely understood what she'd done. Then he picked up the keys, the money and the title, and fell to his knees in prayer.

He sensed there was far more to the story

than what she'd told, but whatever had happened to Catherine was between her and God. What she'd done for the church and the little town of Adobe Blanco was priceless, but there was still much to be done.

His prayers were fervent, but brief. Something told him not to delay in going after the car. He suspected it would be prudent to remove all signs of her presence from Chihuahua, and after what she'd done for them, it was the least he could do for her.

The next day, he told no one about the bounty that had come their way or where he was going. He just set off for Chihuahua alone, praying all the way that the old station wagon would make it. Hour after hour, he drove — to his surprise, with no car troubles. It was as if God Himself was keeping the old vehicle moving. But by the time he arrived at the airstrip, steam was coming out from under the hood of the station wagon and a tire was going flat.

Immediately, he spied the car that the American woman had driven to their town — the same one that had carried Pilar's body from the desert. He drove straight toward it.

He'd already cleaned out the old station wagon. It didn't have a license plate and he'd never had a title for it, so whoever came across it next was welcome to it. He got out quickly, leaving the keys in the ignition, and headed for the fine new vehicle. After a quick check of the extra fuel cans in the back of the SUV, he discovered to his delight that two of them were full. It was enough to get him on his way.

Once inside, he allowed himself one small breath of relief, then put the key in the ignition. The engine fired on the first turn. He said a quick prayer of thanks for the much-needed vehicle that had come to the little church. The woman was a true angel on earth. A quick glance at the gas gauge revealed a tank nearly two-thirds full.

God was good.

He put the car in gear and drove off without looking back.

Art Ball had been one of the first people Wilson called after he brought Cat back to Dallas. Art had been to the hospital twice since, each time fussing about the extent of her injuries. And as Cat lay in her bed, she knew he was back again, because she could hear him talking to someone as he came down the hall. It couldn't be Wilson he was talking to, because he'd just left to run some errands, so she guessed it was a nurse. One thing about Art, he'd never met a stranger.

Tomorrow she would be released from the hospital, and she was more than ready to go home, yet she was also well aware that taking care of herself was going to be extremely difficult, at least for a while.

She heard a knock on the door and called, "Come in," knowing it was Art.

Sure enough, Art entered with a box of candy and a big smile.

"Hey, Missy . . . you're looking real good today. How you feeling?"

Cat shook her head. "I look like shit, and we both know it. As for how I'm feeling, I guess just glad to be alive."

Art frowned. "Now don't go saying all those bad things about yourself, honey. Lookie here . . . I brought your favorite candy . . . chocolate."

"Is there any other kind?" she asked, as he laid the box in her lap. "As for looking good, what I look like is a fat-faced raccoon."

Art chuckled in spite of himself. "Well, honey . . . except for your two black eyes and fat lip, the swelling is going down real good."

Cat smiled. "Always the optimist."

Art shoved his hands in his pockets and frowned. "When you gonna get out of here?"

"Tomorrow."

"If you need, I got an extra bedroom until

you think you can stay by yourself again."

Cat was surprised and touched. He blushed as she took his hand in gratitude.

"I appreciate the offer, but I'll manage."

Art looked at her, then down at the floor. "What about Wilson?"

Cat tensed. "What about him?"

"He was real worried about you."

Cat sighed. "I know."

Art glanced up at her. "I reckon he cares for you a good deal."

"He did," Cat muttered.

"I don't know what's gone on between you two, and I don't want to. But I can tell you for sure that no one does what he did for you without still having some feelings."

"I hurt him . . . more than once."

Art frowned. "Well, hell, honey . . . he's a big boy. And I reckon if he thinks you're worth it, he can take it."

"Yeah, well, that's the rub, isn't it, Art? He may have decided I'm more trouble than I'm worth."

"That remains to be seen now, don't it? So don't go off half-cocked and make matters worse before they get a chance to get better, you hear?"

Cat sighed, then smiled. "Yes, Art. I hear you."

He scratched his nearly bald head, then

tugged his droopy pants up over his paunch and patted her leg.

"I reckon I'll go on home now. Let you get some rest."

"How's everything going at work? Are you managing okay?"

Art grinned. "Oh, shoot, honey, we're fine, but whenever you're ready to come back to work, just say the word. There will always be a place for you there."

"Thanks, Art. I know I've let you down."

The little man shrugged. "Well, honey, that's just the way life goes. The only way to get past the bad stuff is to get back up and keep going. So . . . rest well and take care."

"I will," Cat said. "And thanks for the candy."

"You're welcome," he said.

A few moments later he was gone, and she was alone with her thoughts again, wondering if it was possible for Wilson to forgive her for all that she'd done to him. Wondering what would happen afterward if he did.

Wilson stood in front of Cat's closet, trying to figure out what to pack. He'd already made all the calls necessary for what he was planning to do, but this was a little beyond his expertise. He knew certain clothes would be more comfortable than others, so he opted for anything loose. He wouldn't let himself think about how pissed Cat was going to be at what he was planning to do. But for the time being, she had called her last shot. Until she was healed enough to take care of herself, he had put himself in charge.

He packed two suitcases, scooped up the makeup and shampoo in the bathroom, tossed her hairbrush in on top of the rest of it and zipped up the last bag. He'd checked the kitchen cabinets, as well as the ones in the bathroom, for any maintenance prescriptions she might be taking. He'd found nothing but a bottle of Tylenol, which he left behind. Where she was going, that would be available, along with anything else she might need.

He glanced around the room again, wanting to make sure that he wasn't leaving something necessary behind. As he looked, he noticed that the drawer on the bedside table was ajar. Maybe there was something in there that she used every night. Maybe that was where she kept her meds. He opened the drawer, then froze.

Five wadded-up twenty-dollar bills lay on top of a phone book, next to a pad of paper and a pen. It was the money he'd tossed on her bed in anger. He knew, because he recognized the happy face someone had drawn on the corner of one bill.

When he'd done it, he hadn't considered how it might have affected her. He'd just been so angry and hurt that he'd acted without thought. He fingered the bills, then dropped them back in the drawer and pushed it shut. He wouldn't think about that now — not when what he was going to do was about to piss her off all over again.

It had taken Cat the better part of a half hour just to put on a pair of sweat pants and an old sweatshirt. She'd asked for them when Wilson had gone to get her some clothes, since she'd come here in a bathrobe filched from the Hotel Uno, which Wilson had promptly taken away and tossed in the garbage because of the hotel monogram, so she'd needed something else to wear home. Her sweats were soft and loose and comfortably familiar. But that was where comfort ended. Her belly and ribs were one solid ache, and the flop sweat on her face was a direct result of trying to get dressed.

She'd managed to crawl back into bed and was now flat on her back, purposefully immobile as she waited for Wilson to come get her. She might not be able, but she was ready — and more than willing — to get out of here.

She dozed as she waited, drifting in and out on the pain pills in her system. Aman's voice down the hall triggered a memory and, before she knew it, she was back in Tutuola's mansion, locked in a death struggle with only one bullet left in her gun and no hope of getting away.

She felt the blackness coming over her, pulling her down, taking her fast. Something bucked against her, then they fell.

She woke up, gasping and swallowing a scream, with Wilson right beside her.

"It's me," he said quickly. "You were dreaming. Take a breath, baby. You're okay."

She was trembling but cognizant as she grabbed for his wrist.

"Crap," she muttered. "I'm okay. It was just a dream." Her chin was trembling, but her voice was clear.

"I'm sorry," Wilson said softly. "I'm so sorry."

"It's my own damn fault," Cat said. "Can we get out of here now?"

He straightened up, then shoved his hands in his pockets. So this was the way she wanted to play it — back to being the tough girl.

"Yeah, sure. Why not?" he said. "They're

getting a wheelchair to bring you down. I'll be waiting in the car."

He turned angrily and started toward the door.

Cat could tell by the set of his shoulders that she'd done it all wrong again.

"Wilson. Wait. Please."

He paused, then turned around. "Yeah?"

"I'm sorry. That was bitchy of me. I hurt. I took it out on you. Forgive me?"

Wilson hoped his jaw hadn't just dropped, because he couldn't believe what he was hearing. She'd apologized, and unless he was mistaken, it was sincere.

He shrugged, then smiled.

"Yeah, sure. No problem. See you downstairs."

The nurse came in with the wheelchair as he was going out. By the time she'd signed all the necessary papers and seated herself in the chair, a good five minutes had passed.

The trip down in the elevator gave her time to pull herself together. She'd made a promise to herself that, if it was possible, she was going to do all she knew how to make it right with Wilson. Unfortunately, this wasn't a very good start.

A few minutes later they were wheeling her out of the hospital. The cold air was a slap in the face and a reminder that winter in Dallas was far from over. By the time they got her seated in Wilson's car, she was shivering, partly from cold and partly from the excruciating pain.

"Sweet Lord," she muttered, and closed her eyes, willing herself to a calmer state of mind.

"Did they give you pain pills, or do we need to get a prescription filled?" Wilson asked.

"I have some samples and a script. The samples are enough to last a couple of days, then I can get the other filled."

"Good enough," Wilson said. "Do you need to take some now?"

"No. I can make it until you get me home."

Wilson set his jaw. "Yeah . . . about that . . ."

Cat's eyes narrowed. "What? You're not taking me home?"

"Oh, I'm taking you home all right, but not yours . . . mine."

She frowned. "I can take care of myself."

"No, you can't, and we both know it."

She sighed. "Damn it, even if you wanted to — which I doubt — you can't take off work to stay home and take care of me."

"That's where you're wrong, Catherine. I'm the boss, so I can do what I want."

He drove away from the hospital and was soon out on the freeway. At first Cat paid little attention to the way they were going. It wasn't until he drove past the last exit that would have taken him home that she spoke up.

"You missed the turn."

"No, I didn't."

"But I thought you said you were taking me home with you."

"I am, Catherine, but not my home here. We're going to my family's home outside of Austin."

Cat panicked. "No, I'm not. You can't make me. I don't know those people. They won't want —"

"Yes, you are. Yes, I can. It doesn't matter, and yes, they do."

Cat's jaw dropped.

Wilson didn't give her time to come back at him again. "Those people are my people," he said. "They want to help you. They want to meet you."

"Looking like this? Lord . . . how perfect," she muttered.

"They know you were hurt. Like me, they're just glad you survived."

"Why would they care?"

Wilson didn't hesitate. He was through playing loose and easy with this woman. He was laying his heart on the line, with no excuses.

"Because I'm in love with you, damn it, and they know it. Through no fault of your own, but it's true, just the same. You've done everything you know to mess it up, but for some reason, it hasn't worked."

Cat was in shock. *Love?* "Are you serious?"

Wilson took his eyes off the road long enough to glance at her expression. She looked scared to death. God. How could the mention of love make someone so brave feel so afraid? He didn't know if this would work, but he was going to give it his all.

"I'm as serious as a heart attack, lady."

FIFTEEN

Cat gave Wilson a mutinous stare. "I don't want to go."

"Duly noted," he said. "The seat reclines. If you want to sleep, feel free. It's a long ride."

Her voice shook. "Why are you doing this to me?"

"Already told you, but you're obviously not listening, so there's no point repeating myself."

Cat's heart rate was off the charts. Panic swept over her, leaving her weak and shaking.

"Wilson . . . please."

"Close your eyes, honey. It will make the trip faster."

"You can't just dump me in a house full of strangers."

"Oh . . . I'm not dumping you. I'm staying, too, at least for a while."

"And that's supposed to make me feel better?" she muttered.

"For God's sake, Catherine, this isn't a punishment. I'm taking you to the one woman I trust to take care of you. Someone I know will feed you and doctor you and baby you mercilessly. My mother is a sweet, gentle woman who offered to help care for you. I didn't ask her. When she found out you'd been injured, she offered." When he braked for a red light, he fixed her with a cool, steady stare. "So while you're there, you will not insult her. You will not be a smart-ass. If you're pissed, remember it's at me and not her. Do we understand each other?"

Cat blinked. She was still considering whether or not to be insulted that he thought she would be rude to his family when she decided to give him a break. It wasn't as if they'd spent all that much time together outside the bedroom, and her track record on attitude was well-known.

"Yes, I understand."

"Good."

She turned her head to stare out the window, unwilling to let him see the tears in her eyes, and thought to herself that she would be heartily glad when she got her act back together. She never used to cry, especially over little things like this.

Wilson suspected that he'd hurt her feelings, but he wouldn't relent. He wanted Catherine to love his family as much as he did, but he wouldn't tolerate her being rude to them, especially when they were only trying to help.

So they drove in silence. After a while Cat reclined her seat and slept, and he drove on through the morning.

It was a few minutes past one when he turned off the highway onto a blacktop road.

It was the change of sound and speed that woke Cat. She roused, looked out through the windshield, then struggled to sit up. Finally she remembered the lever beside the seat and shifted from reclining to upright, wincing as her injured muscles objected.

She glanced at Wilson. He was looking straight ahead.

"Are we there yet?"

It was the universal question that all traveling children asked that caught him by surprise. He looked at her, then smiled.

"Almost."

She nodded, then began smoothing at her hair. Her stomach was a jumble of nerves, and her hands were shaking as she reached for the visor. She pulled it down so she could use the mirror on the back.

"I look like shit."

Wilson figured that after everything else he'd gotten away with today, a lie would be asking too much.

"Yeah, you pretty much do," he said.

She bit the side of her lip, then grinned reluctantly. "Well. Thank you. I feel so much better now."

Wilson chuckled. "Honey . . . they all know you've been hurt."

She eyed the bruising, then ran her fingers lightly over the healing cuts in her hairline. She turned her face slightly, eyeing the stitches on her cheek, then the ones below her ear, then felt the ones beneath her chin.

"What did you tell them about . . . about how I got this way?"

"Mom knows you're a bounty hunter. She just assumed one of the perps you were after did it, which, in a way, is true."

Cat nodded. "Just wanted to make sure we were on the same page."

Wilson pulled her hand away from her face and held it.

"Are you still mad at me?"

Cat sighed. "No."

"It will be okay, I promise."

She shrugged. "It's not like I've never been dumped on strangers before. After Daddy was murdered, that's the way I went through my childhood."

Tears suddenly blurred Wilson's vision. He blinked rapidly to clear it, then pulled her hand to his lips and kissed the bruised and skinned knuckles.

"I am so sorry. I never thought about it that way. I promise my parents will not treat you lightly."

"It's okay," Cat said. "I'm guessing that I'll know all your secrets before I leave."

He frowned. "I don't have any secrets from you."

"Sure you do. Everyone has secrets."

Wilson sighed. There was no use arguing. She was just going to have to live with people who trusted each other for a while before she got it.

A few minutes later they topped a rise. Wilson tapped on the brakes, then stopped. As always, the sight sent a wave of longing through him. This was his favorite place on earth. The roots that had bound him to this land as a child were still deep and thriving.

"There it is," he said, pointing down into the valley below.

A spiral of smoke was trailing from the chimney of a white two-story farmhouse. There was an attached garage on the north side of the house and, of all things, a white picket fence around the yard. Several barns, sheds and corrals dotted the landscape around it, and Cat could see a large herd of cattle in the near pasture, gathered around a half-dozen large round bales of hay. It looked homey and welcoming, and she was surprised at how easily she could picture Wilson growing up in a place like this.

"What do you think?" Wilson asked.

"It looks good." Then her voice wobbled with an emotion she wasn't expecting. "It looks safe."

Shattered by the honesty and innocence in her voice, Wilson had to swallow before he could speak.

"Jesus," he said softly, then turned her hand over and kissed the middle of her palm. "You haven't known safe very many times in your life, have you, baby?"

Cat pulled her hand away, then wadded her fists against her lap, trying to steady her emotions.

"I got by," she said.

"Well, hell, Catherine. Sometimes it isn't enough just to get by."

At first she was puzzled by the anger in his voice, then realized it wasn't aimed at her.

She shrugged. "I managed."

"Well, now it's my time to show you there's a lot more to life than just getting by."

She was struggling with how much to say without making an ass of herself when Wilson leaned over and kissed her on the mouth.

The touch was butterfly brief, but strong enough to go straight to her heart. Wilson loved her, and she was beginning to believe that could be a good thing. She just needed to learn how to trust enough to love him back.

He took his foot off the brake, and down the hill they went. By the time they drove into the yard, Cat's heart was thumping wildly and her palms were sweating. This was a crossroads in her life like none she'd never come to before. Despite the way it had come about, Wilson McKay had just brought her home to meet his parents. The implications boggled her senses.

She was reaching for the door handle when the front door of the house suddenly swung inward. A woman emerged dressed in jeans and a sweater. Her hair was red with snowy-white streaks, and she was smiling as she hurried off the porch.

For a moment Cat froze, searching for Wilson in the woman's face, but when her gaze finally centered on the woman's mouth and she saw her smile, she shivered. That smile was wide and genuine, and aimed right at her.

"Oh, man," Cat mumbled.

Wilson gave her hand a quick squeeze. "That's Mom. Welcome home, honey."

Then he got out, met the woman at the gate and gave her a big hug before the two of them headed for the truck. Wilson opened the door and reached for Cat's hand.

"Cat, honey . . . this is my mom, Dorothy. Mom . . . this is Catherine."

Cat smiled shakily. "Hello, ma'am. You can call me Cat."

Dorothy McKay slid past Wilson and reached inside the truck. "And you can call me Dorothy. Lord, Lord, darlin', look what they've done to you. Come in, come in. You must be tired and hungry. I've got soup and cornbread, and your room is all made up."

Dorothy looked back at Wilson.

"Wilson Lee . . . don't just stand there, bring her in."

Wilson arched an eyebrow, then grinned. "I was just waiting for you to get out of the way."

Dorothy thumped him on the arm.

"Don't be a smart-ass, mister. Just do as you're told."

"Yes, ma'am," he said, and leaned inside the cab to help Cat get out as his mother ran ahead to hold the gate open.

Cat was smiling. He glared.

"Don't say anything," he muttered. "Just help me out here, before I get in to more trouble than I'm already in."

"She's a superwoman, isn't she?"

"She thinks so," Wilson said. "None of us have ever had the guts to argue with her . . . including Dad. Now come on. Let's get in out of the cold and have some of that soup. What do you say?"

"I say yes," Cat said, and slid her arm around Wilson's neck.

He put one arm around her shoulders and the other under her knees, and helped turn her so she could slide out of the truck. When her feet were firmly on the ground, he let her go.

"Are you steady on your feet? If you're not, I can carry you."

"I can move on my own, but since you're here, I'll just lean on you a little, okay?"

"You can lean on me all you want, Catherine. Never forget it."

Cat took a step, then stifled a groan.

"Honey . . . ?"

"I can do this," Cat said. "It's just going to take me a couple of minutes."

"Take your time," Dorothy called.

So they did. By the time they reached the front steps, Cat was trembling and out of breath, but she'd made it. Still leaning on Wilson's arm, she walked up the steps and into the house. The warmth of the house was second only to the wonderful smells filling it.

"Man, Mom, that soup smells great," Wilson said.

"Vegetable beef, your favorite," she said, and then pointed down the hall. "Wilson, take Cat to the extra downstairs bedroom." Then she smiled at Cat. "There are loads of empty bedrooms upstairs, as well, but I didn't want you to have to negotiate stairs all day." She patted Cat on the arm. "Honey, take your time. You have your own bathroom in there. If you don't feel like sitting at the kitchen table, I can bring a tray of food to your room."

"No, ma'am. I'll eat at the table, thank you. Just give me a couple of minutes to wash up and I'll be right there."

"Call me Dorothy, remember?"

"Yes, and thank you again."

Wilson offered his arm again. She grasped it firmly, leaning on him as they went.

"Come on, honey. Just a few feet more. I'll bring your bags to the room while you're washing up."

She nodded, but her focus was on the hallway and the array of photos lining the walls. Baby pictures, then school pictures, of six children, three boys and three girls. Pictures of them at their proms. Pictures that she guessed were their senior photos taken for the school yearbook. And loads of pictures that had to do with sports and holidays.

She searched for Wilson's face among them and then settled on the tallest one in a family grouping. His hair was short, dark and badly in need of a comb, and he was grinning widely as he held up a trophy while his brothers and sisters looked on.

"That's you, isn't it?" she said, pointing to the boy in the photo.

"Yeah. I had just won a punt, pass and kick contest. I think I was about ten or twelve at the time."

"What's a punt, pass and kick contest?"

Wilson looked at her and tried not to let his surprise show.

"Football, honey."

"Oh. Never did get into it myself," she said.

"You would have made a real pretty cheer-leader," he said.

Cat arched an eyebrow. "How sexist of you, Wilson."

"Thank you. I try."

Cat actually laughed, then winced and

grabbed her ribs. "Oh, crap. It hurts too much to laugh."

"So let's get you to your room," he said. "You can look at all of my great pictures later."

Cat was still smiling when Wilson opened the door, but as soon as she stepped into the room, she froze.

The walls were covered in a wallpaper dotted with tiny bouquets of lilac. The curtains at the windows were creamy sheers that would make it appear sunshine was streaming in even when the day was gloomy. The bedspread fabric was a pale butter-yellow with thin lilac stripes, and there was a crocheted afghan folded across the bottom of the bed in a lilac shade the same color as the walls. The dark hardwood floors gleamed as if they'd just been polished, and the lamp beside her bed had little pompons on the shade that jiggled as she walked across the room.

"Oh, Wilson," Cat said, and then sat down on the side of the bed and closed her eyes.

He sat down beside her, then put his arms around her shoulders.

"What's wrong? Are you ill? I can —"

She clutched at his wrist. "No . . . no . . . it's not that."

She drew a slow, shuddering breath. "It's

just . . . when Daddy was still alive . . . my room was this color. It's the last thing I had that was mine before I was swallowed up by the system."

Wilson laid a hand on the back of her head, then pulled her close against his chest. She was trembling.

"So consider this karma, honey. Call this your full-circle moment for the day."

Cat leaned within the shelter of his arms, letting herself feel his strength, accepting everything he was offering as a blessing and not an attempt at control.

"I guess we better not keep your mother waiting too long," she said, and reluctantly stood.

"I'll go get your bags," Wilson said, and left her to get to the bathroom on her own.

By the time he came back carrying her things, she was sitting on the side of the bed again, this time staring out the windows. She looked up as he came in.

"There's a man coming toward the house. Is that your dad?"

Wilson set down the suitcases and then glanced out.

"Yep, that's him, Carter McKay."

Cat watched the older man for a few moments, then looked up.

"You walk like him," she offered.

"I act like him, too, which is why I'm in Dallas and he's here."

"You two don't get along?"

Wilson smiled. "No, nothing like that. We're just both hardheaded and, as long as Dad can take care of the place on his own, he'll be doing it his way. Someday I'll come back here. I promised him."

Cat's eyes widened. She kept staring at Wilson's face, past the scar on his cheek, the hair always in need of a cut and that tiny gold loop in his ear, and tried to picture him on a ranch.

A pirate cowboy? Stranger things happened. Why not?

"Are you ready to eat a little?" he asked.

"Yes."

He held out his hand. She reached for it. The action had been instinctive on his part, but it was a giant step toward trust for Catherine. Wilson led the way to the kitchen, where his mother had set out steaming bowls of vegetable beef soup and hot squares of yellow cornbread. She was at the counter slicing a fresh-baked pie.

"Umm, it smells good, Mom," Wilson said.

"No, it smells fabulous," Cat said.

Dorothy beamed. "Have a seat and dig in before it all gets cold."

Wilson was helping Cat to her seat when the back door opened. The man who came in was tall and vibrant, bringing in the scent of cold air and alfalfa hay with him.

"Hey, boy! 'Bout time you got yourself down here."

The older man hung his Stetson on a peg by the door, then crossed the floor in two steps and engulfed Wilson in a big hearty hug. Then he looked past Wilson to Cat. His smile stilled as his dark eyes swept her face, then took note of the way she held her body. His eyes narrowed sharply as he fixed Cat with a steely glare.

"I hope the bastard who did this to you didn't get away."

Cat flashed on the fire curling across Solomon Tutuola's body.

"He didn't go far," Cat said, knowing by now he was probably six feet under.

"Good job, missy," Carter said, then eyed Wilson carefully. "Good eyes, son," he said softly, before turning to Cat and holding out his hand.

Cat didn't hesitate as she slid her hand into his.

"Call me Carter. Welcome to our home, Catherine."

Cat heard the truth in his voice, and another layer of nervousness disappeared.

"Don't let me stop you," Carter said. "Dorothy's soup will stick to your ribs and get you fit in no time. Ya'll get after that food while it's good and hot, now."

"Thank you," Cat said.

"Don't say thank you until you've tasted it," Dorothy said, then giggled.

Cat sat quietly after that, eating her soup and listening to the banter between Wilson and his parents. She had vague memories of her parents being like this — before her mother's death. After that, her father had changed. He was more serious, less likely to kid around, although she knew she was loved. But she'd forgotten it. She'd forgotten all of it — until now.

As she took a slow drink of iced tea, Wilson reached across the table, snagged a square of cornbread and buttered it lavishly before laying it on her plate. Then, without a word, he kept on talking to his dad about one neighbor who'd filed for bankruptcy and another who'd been arrested for growing marijuana on his place.

Cat stared at the cornbread, then up at Wilson, trying to remember the last time someone had prepared food for her, doing it for no other reason than to make sure she was comforted and comfortable.

She picked it up and took a bite, savoring

the crunch of warm cornbread and the salty taste of melting butter. As she chewed, her gaze moved to Wilson again — and another piece of the armor around her heart fell away. All the while she was eating and listening, she was wondering if this was what love tasted like — warm, comforting, delicious on the tongue.

Cat was asleep in her bed. Wilson had changed clothes and was in the truck with his dad, checking on the cows.

Carter liked having his first son with him, but it had been a while since they'd been alone. Usually, when his children and grandchildren showed up, it was a riot of noise and food. And while he loved the noise that his big family brought with them, he also liked the one-on-one times he could occasionally catch with his sons.

"The place looks good, Dad," Wilson said.

"Yeah. We're doing all right," Carter said, then turned down a narrow lane that led to the far pasture. "Tell me about your woman," he said.

Wilson hesitated. He wouldn't lie to his father, but at the same time, he didn't intend to give away secrets.

"She's a bounty hunter."

"Hell, boy, I already knew that. Is she

special?"

Wilson sighed. "Yeah."

"Does she love you back?"

"I don't know. . . . Sometimes I think so . . . sometimes I'm not so sure."

"She's been hurt before, hasn't she?" Carter asked. "I saw that scar on her throat. That's older than what she's got now."

"Her mother died in a car accident when she was six. Cat was with her. She survived. Then when she was . . . I think thirteen . . . a man broke into their home, cut her throat and stabbed her father to death in front of her, then left her to die. She spent the rest of her growing-up years in the welfare system."

Carter shook his head. "Damn shame. That explains the shadows I saw in her eyes."

"Yeah, that and then some," Wilson said, and let it slide.

"So what are you going to do about her?" Carter asked.

"Get her well, then marry her."

Carter grinned. "Congratulations, son. I think she's a winner."

"Well, don't go congratulating her just yet, okay? Right now, a marriage proposal isn't something that can come out of my mouth. I've got to get past her distrust of the world first."

"You will."

Wilson grinned. "Thanks for the vote of confidence."

Carter grinned back. "Your mama didn't like *me* right off, either."

"Yeah, I know. I've heard the story at least a hundred times in my life," Wilson said.

Carter shrugged. "Well, hell, it wasn't all my fault that a skunk turned up in the home economics room when we were in high school."

"No, but you're the one who brought it to school, right?"

Carter chuckled. "Now, how was I to know it was still alive? It was laying on the side of the road by Daddy's mailbox when I left for school. I just tossed it in the back of my truck, thinking it would be a good trick to put it under Billy Ray Johnson's fancy Corvette for the day. Temperatures had been in the nineties all week. I figured Billy Ray's car would be nice and ripe by the time school let out. But the damned skunk came to and staggered into the school, and the rest of what happened was the skunk's fault, not mine."

Wilson had heard the story off and on his whole life, and the telling was still funny to him.

"Yeah, and Mama was the first person who got squirted when it got into the home ec room, right?"

Carter grinned. "A case of being in the wrong place at the wrong time. She has since forgiven me." He was silent for a few moments, then added, "That's all life is, a whole set of circumstances — some of them good, some of them bad. You get through the circumstances whether you like it or not, but it's what you take from them that keeps you on an even keel."

"Yeah, I've had a few circumstances of my own during the past few years. I suppose I learned from them, because I haven't repeated any of them . . . except Cat. Every time she bats me down, I tell myself to hell with it and to hell with *her*. Then I find myself worrying about her and wanting to take care of her. If I had one wish for the rest of my life, it would be that Catherine Dupree never had another sad day for as long as she lived."

Carter eyed his son carefully. "Sounds like love to me."

Wilson just shook his head, then pointed out the window.

"Hey, is that Old Gray?"

Carter glanced in the direction Wilson was pointing, then frowned. Their old horse had gotten out of his pen and was in the pasture with the cattle — again.

"Hell, yes. That stubborn cuss hates to be alone. He's always finding a way to get out, and every time he does, he heads straight for the cattle. Horses are herd animals, you know. Looks like I would have learned by now what he's been trying to tell me for years. That he doesn't want to be alone."

"Want me to catch him and ride him back to the barn?"

"Naw . . . leave him be. He looks plenty happy out there, and he's not bothering anything."

Wilson smiled as they drove to the pasture gate, while his Dad kept on talking. He listened absently as his thoughts wandered. Most of them wandered toward Catherine.

Cat woke up, dragged herself to the bathroom, then crawled back into bed. The wind had picked up outside. She could hear it gusting as it swept around the corner of the house, rattling the bare branches of the bushes against the wall.

Her bed was warm and comfortable. The flannel sheets were soft and smelled like sunshine. Probably some deftly scented laundry rinse, but it made her think of summer and fresh air just the same.

She lay on her side and snuggled into the pillow, then pulled the covers up over her ear, leaving only her face exposed, and drifted in and out of consciousness. Every so often an unfamiliar sound would be loud enough to get her attention, but nothing prompted her to get up and explore.

She could hear the muted sound of a television playing somewhere off in another part of the house, and occasionally the hum of the central heating as it came on.

She kept picturing the photos lining the walls in the hallway outside her room, and imagined what this house must have been like when all the children were still young and living at home. It must have been loud and fun and frantic, and it would have been impossible to be lonely.

There would have been birthday parties and holiday dinners and cookouts on the Fourth of July. They would have had fireworks and pets to play with, and they would have gone to bed every night unafraid of what the morning might bring.

She scrunched her eyes a little tighter, wishing she could fall back asleep and not think about what it would be like to belong to a family like this. If only Marsha were still alive. She would have been able to tell Cat what to do. She would have injected a dose of reality into the situation and yanked Cat out of the rut she was always in.

As she thought of Marsha, the ache in her heart tightened. She missed her so much. Then she remembered a little dark-haired baby girl looking up at her in the night, and the ache lessened. She hadn't been able to save Marsha, but she had saved a life. Maria Elena would grow up hearing the story of how an American woman found her wrapped in a blanket in her dead mother's arms, and of how strong she was to have survived. She wouldn't grow up with material things, but she would grow up knowing she was loved. No amount of money could buy that kind of blessing.

Finally Cat slept again, and sometime in the late afternoon, when Wilson came into her room, he found her asleep and, without waking her, stretched out on the big bed beside her and closed his eyes.

When Cat woke up again, she found him there, sound asleep.

Sixteen

Wilson was asleep on his side facing Cat. When she opened her eyes, his face was the first thing she saw. Being this close to him without his vibrant personality in any way posing an emotional threat, she felt comfortable studying the man who claimed he loved her.

The first thing she focused on were his eyebrows. They were dark and almost perfectly formed, which was so unfair to women everywhere. All those beauty shop appointments to be waxed and plucked and he'd been born with the look.

His nose had been broken at least once, and there was that scar on his cheek. She frowned, wondering why, during all the time they'd spent together, she'd never asked him how it came to be there. No wonder he'd become disgusted with her. She'd willingly gone to bed with him numerous times but had rarely bothered to ask him a single thing about his life. It had been all about her. Always her and her problems. Looking back, she was appalled to think how terribly selfish and cold she must have appeared.

Her vision blurred, which aggravated her. Here she was tearing up again when there was no obvious reason. It was amazing how she'd existed all these years without emotional connections. She'd gone through life and work with attitude and diligence, but she'd never let anyone close except Marsha — and now Wilson, and that was entirely due to his persistence.

Her gaze slid to his mouth. God, she loved that mouth — the full, sensual cut to his lips, and that sarcastic tilt at the corner when he grinned.

His nostrils flared slightly as he breathed, and there was a faint stubble of black whiskers that she knew he would shave off the first chance he got. There were worry lines between his eyebrows that she felt responsible for, but she resisted the urge to rub them away.

She watched him until she'd looked her fill. The quiet moments had given her a sort of peace — as if she'd finally given herself permission to follow this man and see where he led. Oddly enough, the lost, unsettled feelings she'd been having seemed less pertinent. She thought about what might happen if she kissed him awake, then changed her mind and began to get out of bed. As she started to roll over, the motion woke him, and he sat up immediately.

"Are you okay?"

"I'm just going to the bathroom."

"Need any help getting up?"

"I can manage."

Wilson rolled out of bed, then glanced at his watch. "Dad will be feeding pretty soon. I'll get my boots on and go help, if you don't need me then."

"I'm good," Cat said, as she stood up. Seconds later, she flattened her hands against her ribs and groaned. "God in heaven . . . I hope I never have to go through anything like this again."

Wilson took her in his arms. "It's not about hoping . . . it's about knowing that it can't, because I can tell you for sure, I would be the one who wouldn't live through it the second time."

Gently he threaded his fingers through her hair, combing the dark tangles away from her face before he kissed her.

Cat heard the soft sound of his indrawn breath just before their lips met, then the faint groan of desire that came with it.

"Catherine," he whispered.

"What?"

He sighed, then leaned his forehead against hers. "I don't know . . . just . . . Catherine."

She sighed. He wanted her. That in itself was a miracle. She laid a hand against his face, then rubbed her thumb lightly against the curve of his lower lip.

"Go help your dad," she said.

He glanced at the stitches on her cheek and frowned at the bruising around both eyes. "Be back soon," he said, and left quickly.

Cat made her way to the bathroom. After giving herself a pep talk, she went in search of Wilson's mother. Since she was here, she wanted it to be on congenial terms. She had a lot of experience being in places where she wasn't wanted, and she didn't want to get off on the wrong foot by being standoffish. The easiest way to find out how sincere Dorothy McKay's welcome had been was to spend time with her when no one else was around. It was the quickest way to discover the truth.

Dorothy felt centered. It was always this way when any of her children were home. Even though they were all grown and long gone from the house in which they'd been raised, it didn't mean she didn't love having them back. It was as if they gave her life purpose.

A big pot roast was in the oven, and a berry cobbler was cooling on the cabinet. She'd gotten out her crocheting and pulled her favorite chair close to the living room window for the light. Working with yarn always calmed her spirit. It was all about creating something, even while sitting still.

Just outside the window, one of the barn cats was stalking a meadowlark that had landed on the front gate. Dorothy paused, letting her hands go idle as she watched the drama play out.

As she was watching, Cat came into the room. Dorothy heard her footsteps and looked up, smiling broadly as she motioned Cat over to the window.

"Oh good . . . you're here! Come see, honey. We've got a ringside seat to the drama."

Cat moved as quickly as she could, then stopped beside Dorothy's chair and looked out. Immediately, she saw the big gray tomcat crouched flat on the ground, with only the tip of his tail twitching, his big yellow eyes fixed on the bird on the gate.

Meanwhile the meadowlark continued to trill and call, as if it didn't have a care in the world.

Catherine caught herself holding her breath, watching intently as the big tomcat began making his move. Slowly, slowly, he began to creep forward, move then pause, move then freeze, move then hunker down.

"Watch . . . here goes," Dorothy said.

"How can you tell?" Cat asked.

"Watch the tail," Dorothy said.

The tip of the cat's tail was twitching frantically now, his ears flattened. Then he leaped — just as the meadowlark took flight.

Dorothy clapped her hands together and laughed aloud.

"Old Fritz has yet to catch one of those birds, but he never quits trying. I guess I'll go out and give him a treat to make up for the miss. Want to come with me?"

Dorothy held out her hand, waiting for Cat to clasp it. To Cat's surprise, she did so without hesitation. Dorothy led the way, talking all the way about the lineage of the old tom Cat was about to meet, and, despite his failure with the bird, what a great mouser he was.

Cat watched Dorothy pour a handful of dry kitty treats into an old cup.

"Okay, that should be enough for Mr. Fritz," Dorothy said. "Out we go."

Cat was all the way out the door before she realized how easy Dorothy had made this. She'd included her in the drama, shared the climax, then invited her along to meet Fritz, who was obviously another member of the family. If Cat hadn't been so sore, she would have been enjoying herself immensely.

Dorothy glanced up at Cat as they paused at the top of the back steps.

"Is this too much for you, honey? If it is, just say so. I tend to overwhelm people without meaning to."

"No, no, I'm fine . . . and you're not overwhelming me."

Dorothy beamed. "Good. So come on. I'll introduce you to the main four-legged male around here." She went down the steps, calling the cat.

"Here, kitty, kitty, kitty. Fritzie . . . treats. Treats."

She rattled the treats in the cup. Seconds later, the old tomcat came bounding around the corner of the house. His tail and ears were on point. Dorothy grinned.

"Look. He doesn't know we saw him fail, so he's full of confidence. We should all pull ourselves together so well when we goof up."

Cat wrapped her arms around herself against the chill as she watched Dorothy kneel down and begin feeding Fritz. She fed him one treat at a time, waiting to give him another one until he would meow a request. That went on until the treats were gone. Then Dorothy stood up, brushing the dirt and dried grass from the knees of her jeans as she pointed to the old cat.

"Watch this," she told Cat. "Now he'll sit down and begin giving himself a bath, as if I no longer exist." She was smiling as she added, "Never make a cat your best friend. They'll let you down every time."

Cat thought of her best friend and smiled despite the lump in her throat.

"I can see that," she said, as the cat turned his back on both of them and began to groom himself.

At that point Dorothy noticed that Cat was shivering. "Lord, what was I thinking? You don't have enough clothes on to be out here like this. Let's get back inside. I'll make us some hot chocolate and warm you right up. How does that sound?"

"Great," Cat said, and was slightly surprised that she meant it.

Back in the kitchen, Dorothy washed her hands, then waved the hand towel at Cat as she began to dry them.

"Go on into the living room, honey. Find yourself a soft seat. I'll bring the hot chocolate in there."

Cat wished she were good at chitchat.

Surely there was something she should be saying that would fill the uncomfortable pauses in their one-sided conversation. Instead, she nodded and limped her way into the living room, where she paused for a moment, eyeing the furniture, then chose a large, overstuffed chair with a high back.

She'd barely seated herself when Dorothy came bustling into the room.

"Oh . . . good choice," she said, and picked up a bright yellow crocheted afghan from the back of the sofa and laid it across Cat's lap.

Cat fingered the afghan, delighted by the color and touched by the care. "I'm not used to all this attention," she said. "You're going to spoil me."

Dorothy cupped Cat's cheek. "I spoil all my kids," she said softly, then added, "This chair is a recliner. Want your feet up?"

Cat was still trying to wrap her mind around being included as one of the family and only managed a nod. Moments later she found herself reclining.

Dorothy patted her on the knee as she straightened the afghan. "The milk should be ready. I'll be right back. Are you a marshmallow girl?"

Cat was still distracted by all of the attention and missed the question. "I'm sorry? What?"

Dorothy grinned. "Marshmallows . . . do you like them in your hot chocolate?"

Cat grinned. Marshmallows? In hot chocolate? This was too unbelievably Brady Bunch. "Oh. Yes. Actually, I do."

"Great. Me, too," Dorothy said, and actually waved at Cat as she left.

Cat was still wrapping her mind around Dorothy's sweet nature, the softness of the afghan and the warmth of its weight, when she heard the back door open and someone come in. She recognized the voice, then had to deal with the jump in her pulse.

Wilson.

Her stomach twisted slightly. Was this what wanting to be with someone felt like? A little nervous, anxious to see his face?

Wilson came striding into the room, bringing the outdoors in. Like his father earlier, he smelled of cold air and the fresh scent of alfalfa hay.

"Hey, honey . . . are you comfortable? It's been quite a while since you had your pain meds."

"I'm okay," she said.

He frowned. "You shouldn't miss a dose, Cat. It will just slow you down in getting relief when you do start hurting again. I'm going to go get them."

Cat watched him stride out of the room in the same manner that his mother had a few minutes before. She was thinking to herself how much alike they were in their need to nurture when Dorothy came back into the room carrying a tray with cups of steaming hot chocolate. At the same time, Wilson came in from the other doorway carrying Cat's pills and a glass of water.

Wilson got to Cat before Dorothy did, and watched until she downed the pills. Then Dorothy slid in between them with a cup of hot chocolate, complete with miniature marshmallows.

"Here's a spoon, honey. I don't know about you, but I always like to stir mine until they melt."

"That looks good," Wilson said.

"There's some for you, too," Dorothy said, pointing to the tray.

"I take mine straight," Wilson said, picking up a cup that was minus marshmallows.

Cat's eyes narrowed as she watched Wilson sink into the sofa, cradling his cup as he sat. It was good, she thought, to be seeing him here in this place. He was somehow softer — more approachable. She took a sip of cocoa, smiling with satisfaction when a marshmallow came with it. She leaned back and closed her eyes, enjoying the sensation as the marshmallow finished melting on her tongue.

Or maybe she herself was changing? Maybe she was the one who was softening? And if she was, what would it cost her? She knew, with every bit of her soul, that she would not survive losing another loved one. She could not withstand that much grief and go on living.

She shuddered slightly, then opened her eyes, studying the hominess of the room and watching Dorothy's fingers flying as she continued working the yarn in her lap.

A few minutes later they heard Carter come in the back door and call out, "Hey . . . where is everybody?"

Cat saw Dorothy's face light up and her features soften as Carter entered the room. He walked over to where his wife was sitting, and leaned down and kissed her cheek before he did or said anything else.

"Is there some of that hot chocolate for me?" he asked.

Dorothy pointed to the tray. "Now, sugar, you know there is."

Carter brushed a finger down the curve of Dorothy's cheek, then picked up his cup. As he did, he turned to Cat and winked.

"You doin' all right, missy?"

"Yes, sir." She hesitated for a moment, then added, "It's remarkably generous of both of you to open your house to a stranger."

Carter glanced at his son, then back at Cat, fixing her with a studied stare.

"Well now . . . here's the deal. Wilson thinks you're something special, so that changes your status from stranger to family."

Cat blushed. She didn't know what to say.

Wilson rolled his eyes. "Oh great, Dad. Here I am trying not to put any pressure on her, and you go and open your mouth and set me back a good month."

Carter looked at her and winked.

Cat grinned. Their banter wasn't at all what she'd expected, and it took the seriousness out of the moment.

Dorothy glared at both of them. "For Pete's sake, you two. Drink your cocoa and leave her alone."

Wilson glanced at Cat, then lifted his cup and silently toasted her. Without thinking, she lifted hers, too. Together, they took a sip, silently sealing something that, as yet, remained unsaid.

That night they all sat at the dinner table, talking about the day and Cat's treatment, when she needed to go back for a checkup and when she would get her stitches out. As they were finishing dessert, Wilson's cell phone rang. He glanced at the caller ID, frowned, then got up.

"Excuse me a minute. I need to take this."

Cat had seen the look on his face and recognized it as one of concern. She tried to listen to what he was saying as he walked out of the room but couldn't hear enough to know who he was talking to.

Then Dorothy began cleaning up the table and shooed Cat to the living room. Carter helped her up, then offered her his arm and escorted her to the chair she'd claimed earlier.

As soon as she was seated, he took the same yellow afghan and covered her legs again.

"I don't quite know how to take all this," she said.

Carter stopped, then turned around and sat down on the arm of the sofa. "How so, honey?"

"I'm used to taking care of myself."

He watched her for a moment, then folded his arms across his chest.

"That's an admirable quality to have, but there comes a time in everyone's life when they need a little help."

Cat was unconsciously picking at the afghan as she answered. "I didn't want to come here," she admitted.

Carter nodded. "I can understand that. Hard enough meeting strangers when you're at your best . . . and I'm going out on a limb here by guessing this isn't your best."

Cat laughed, then grabbed her ribs and groaned.

"Oh . . . crap . . . that hurt. Don't make me laugh," she gasped.

Carter grinned, and that was the way Wilson found them when he walked into the living room.

He'd heard her laugh and had an actual moment of jealousy that it wasn't because of something he'd said. But when he saw the true light in her eyes and the joy on her face, he couldn't begrudge a moment of it. Leave it up to his dad to make everything okay. He wished he could say the same about what was happening back in Dallas.

The phone call had been from John Tiger. Something was going on back at the office that had them concerned. LaQueen was getting hang-up phone calls, the tires on John's truck had been slashed and Red Brickman's car had been keyed while in the back parking lot. Someone was sending a message. Problem was, they only dealt with losers, so without actual contact from someone, it was going to be hard to pinpoint who it was.

Wilson was torn between wanting to get back and tend to business and an unwillingness to abandon Catherine when she was in need. Even though his parents could easily take care of her, it was the emotional abandonment he wanted to avoid. He'd told John to have video surveillance equipment installed all around the perimeter of their building and hope for the best. But if things persisted, he would be forced to return.

Cat saw movement from the corner of her eye and realized Wilson had come into the room.

"Is everything okay?" she asked.

"Not exactly, but we're working on it," he said.

"What's wrong?" Carter asked.

Wilson shrugged. "Just a little harassment at the office. Nothing that hasn't happened before. It will work itself out. Don't worry about it."

Cat didn't say anything more, but she knew better. Harassment at a bail bond office was unusual. Perps didn't want to alienate the very people who were responsible for bailing them out of jail time and time again. The knowledge that someone had a personal interest in causing trouble for Wilson made her nervous.

A short while later Dorothy joined them, dragging over a card table and a deck of cards.

"Who's up for a game of cards?" she asked.

"Hey, great idea, sweetheart," Carter said, and began setting up the card table for her, pushing it right up in front of Cat so that she wouldn't have to move her seat.

"What are we playing?" Wilson asked.

"Poker okay with you guys?" Dorothy asked.

Cat stifled a grin. She beat Art on a regular basis when work was slow at the office. It remained to be seen if her skill carried over to other players, but she wasn't going to give herself away. She allowed Wilson to plump up some pillows behind her, then watched without comment as the cards were shuffled and dealt. Dorothy pulled out a large stack of plastic chips, sorted them and doled them out.

Cat picked up her cards. Her heart skipped a beat as she laid them down on the table in front of her and waited for the others to bet. Carter tossed in a chip, as did Dorothy and Wilson. Cat added her chip to the pot.

Wilson pulled three cards out of his hand and laid them aside.

"I'll take three," he asked. Dorothy gave him three new cards.

She dealt two for herself, and two for Carter, as well.

"Cat? Any for you?"

"I'm good."

The others paused, gave her a calculating look, then eyed each other and grinned.

"Dang, Wilson . . . looks like you brought a ringer to the table," Carter said.

Dorothy looked a little nervous. "Are you sure, dear? Do you know how to play the game?"

"Yes, ma'am, I know the rules."

"It's Dorothy, not ma'am," Dorothy reminded her, then giggled nervously.

Wilson didn't take his eyes off Cat, but he didn't challenge her. Instead, he added another chip to the pot.

Carter laid his cards down on the table. "I'm out," he said.

Dorothy fiddled with her cards and chips, then tossed two chips into the pot.

"Oh . . . I'm in and I'll raise you," she said, then smiled apologetically.

Cat met the ante, then upped it without saying a word.

Wilson's eyes narrowed. He met the ante and upped a chip.

Dorothy fussed and then giggled, and laid

down her cards.

"I'm out, too," she said.

Cat looked up. Wilson was staring at her. She stared back without flinching. He looked down at his cards, then up at her. He couldn't tell if it was the bruising on her face that was rattling him, or if it was because she had yet to blink.

"Call," Wilson said, and laid down his cards. He had a pair of twos.

Cat laid down her cards. She was holding three aces.

"Damn," he muttered, as Cat pulled the pot toward her, then began stacking the chips. He looked at his mother. "Did you shuffle that deck at all?"

"Now, Wilson, don't be a sore loser," Dorothy said. "You saw me. It's just luck of the draw."

"Some luck," Carter said, and winked at Cat.

Cat waited for them to deal the next hand. She folded for two hands in a row, then, on the third hand, anted up once before calling and losing to Carter.

Then they dealt another hand, and just like the first, Cat stayed. No extra cards, no nothing. Just that flat expression on her face.

Wilson grinned. She must have a hell of a hand. Unfortunately, he did not, and quickly folded, as did Dorothy. Carter stayed in for another round, upping the ante by four chips.

"Here's your four and two more," Cat said.

Carter stared at his cards, then shook his head and laid them down. "I'm out," he said.

Cat laid her cards face down on the table and reached for the pot.

"Just out of curiosity," Wilson said, and turned over her cards before she could stop him.

"Hey," Cat said, but it was too late.

Wilson stared at the cards for a few seconds, trying to wrap his head around what he was seeing, and then looked up at her and grinned.

Carter's mouth dropped.

Dorothy stared at the cards, then looked up at Cat and giggled.

"You bluffed," she said.

Carter frowned. "That wasn't a bluff. That was a damn massacre."

"You quit fair and square, Dad," Wilson said.

Cat stacked up her chips, then leaned back, exhaling carefully.

Carter looked at her for a few more moments, then started to grin. "You are something, missy, and that's a fact."

Cat arched an eyebrow, then picked up her five cards, none of which matched, and tossed them toward Dorothy.

"Where did you learn to bluff like that?" Carter asked.

An odd expression came and went on Cat's face. "Life," she said, and then looked to Wilson to be rescued from having to say any more.

Wilson read the plea in her eyes and got up from the table.

"I'm going after a Pepsi. Anyone else want something cold to drink?"

"I would," Cat said, and then smiled at Carter and Dorothy. "Deal me out, okay? I'm going to go get my pain pills."

"I'll get them," Dorothy said, and jumped up.

"They're on the table beside the bed," Cat said, as Dorothy hurried from the room.

Carter picked up the cards and began shuffling them absently, eyeing Cat every now and then as he did.

Cat knew he was thinking about her. She just wasn't sure if it was good or not.

Carter laid the cards down on the table and then leaned forward. "Cat . . . Catherine."

Cat met his gaze. "Yes?"

"You're the first female Wilson ever brought here."

Cat's eyes widened. "Oh."

"I think that life you spoke of a while ago has dealt you some really bad hands, hasn't it?"

Breath caught in the back of Cat's throat as her eyes began to blur. She took a breath, then looked away.

"It's okay, kiddo," Carter said softly, then laid a hand over hers. "If you're looking for a soft place to fall, we've got arms to catch you."

The offer was staggering. The only other people who'd been this kind to her were both dead. Cat closed her eyes, then covered her face with her hands.

Carter scooted his chair back from the card table, then paused beside Cat and patted her head before leaving the room.

By the time everyone came back, Cat had her emotions back under control. She sipped her Pepsi while they played a few more hands of poker, listening to the friendly banter and adding a few comments to the conversation.

When the game finally broke up, Cat was exhausted. Carter and Dorothy left, carrying the card table and cards to be put away, leaving Wilson and Cat alone. When Cat stood, she swayed on her feet.

"You're worn out," Wilson said. "I should have put you to bed hours ago."

"I'm fine. I had that nap, remember?"

"You're not fine," Wilson said, and picked her up and carried her down the hall. He toed the door open and carried her into the bedroom, then set her down beside the bed. "Sit down, baby. I'll pull off your shoes and socks."

Cat was too tired to argue. She sat, then braced herself against the pain as Wilson began pulling off her shoes and socks. The next thing to come off was her sweater. He pulled it over her head, then laid it aside.

"You go to the bathroom. I'll turn back the bed and get your flannel PJs."

Cat didn't even bother to ask how he'd managed to pack what she'd needed as she staggered into the bathroom. She came out a few minutes later with her hair in a ponytail and her jeans undone.

Wilson handed her an old T-shirt. "This will be softer against your skin than the buttons on your pajama top," he said as he helped her put the shirt on.

She nodded gratefully, letting him pull the rest of her clothes off for her, then help her into the pajama bottoms. She crawled in between the covers, groaning with relief as she finally settled.

Wilson watched the changing expressions on her face while thinking how stunningly beautiful she really was.

"Catherine?"

The serious tone of his voice got Cat's attention.

"What?"

"Are you sorry you came?" he asked.

"No."

A small grin tilted one corner of his mouth. "Still mad at me?"

"No."

"What do you think of my parents?"

She thought of what Carter had said to her, and of the love that Wilson professed to have for her. If she had the guts to trust her heart instead of her instincts, she might let herself love them back.

"I think . . . if I let them . . . they would be a soft place to fall."

Wilson's eyes widened as a lump came into his throat. "And if you trusted me . . . ?"

"I can't wrap my head around that kind of joy."

"Because you don't trust me?" he asked.

She reached for his hand. "No, Wilson, you've proven yourself worthy of trust. Far more than I deserved."

"Then what can I do to make this all right

for you?"

"I think . . . maybe . . . I just need some time."

His nostrils flared, but he didn't argue. "I can give you that, too."

"Thank you, Wilson . . . for everything."

"You're welcome. So . . . is there anything I can get for you before I go shower?"

"No. I'm fine."

He bent down and kissed her cheek, then groaned and gently kissed her lips, careful not to hurt the cuts and bruises.

"Sleep well, my love," he said, and then he was gone.

The room was in shadow, with the light in the adjoining bathroom left on so that she would be able to see should she need to get up in the night.

For a while she lay with the echo of Wilson's words ringing in her ears, listening to the sounds of people readying for bed, and then, afterward, the silence as the house settled for the night.

Finally Cat slept.

Less than an hour later, Wilson came into the room, pulled the covers back and slipped into the bed beside her. When the nightmares began, he was there, pulling her back from the darkness. She rolled onto her side with a pillow clutched to her chest, her voice heavy with sleep.

"Wilson . . . ?"

"What, baby?"

She sighed softly. "Nothing . . . just . . . Wilson."

He caressed her face, then smoothed her hair away from her forehead

"Rest now," he said quietly.

So she did.

SEVENTEEN

It was Sunday, and the everyday routine of the McKay family was undergoing a drastic change from what Cat was just getting used to after three days. Sunday, she'd been told, was also family day, which meant that, after church, all the grown children and their families came home for dinner.

She was trying not to be nervous all over again.

She had been at the McKay house long enough that she was actually starting to think there might be life after revenge. Being brought here under duress had seemed like a slap in the face at first, but Wilson had ignored her demands to be taken home, and now she was glad he had.

In just the short time she'd spent with Dorothy, she'd come to understand what she'd lost when her mother had died. So much of a woman's confidence came from the example her mother set, she realized. A woman learned by observation that when a crisis occurred, instead of tearing a family apart, it brought them closer together. Learned that, when the world was falling down around your ears and you were positive you'd made the worst mistake of your life, your mother would still be there — loving you, forgiving you, on your side no matter what.

Cat had missed that part of childhood. She'd grown up fast and hard, and never let anyone see her cry. After a while, she hadn't even bothered to cry for herself. Weeping didn't change a damn thing about the miserable hand she'd been dealt, so why bother?

Then Wilson McKay had come out of nowhere, wanting something from her that she didn't know how to give. It was her good fortune that he'd refused to give up. And it was a blessing that he'd loaded her up and brought her to his childhood home. This was not only a place of unconditional love, but a place where she could feel herself healing in body and soul.

However, in a short while she was about to meet the adult versions of the kids she'd seen in the pictures lining Dorothy's walls. She'd also been told that between them, they had given Dorothy and Carter twelve grandchildren, all under the age of fifteen. She didn't know whether to be worried or just plan on losing herself in the crowd.

Dorothy had opted out of church services and had been cooking since daybreak, yet she had still managed to serve waffles with blueberry sauce for breakfast. Cat was in awe of Dorothy's multitasking abilities. And there was another thing through which they'd connected. Cat had been mesmerized by Dorothy's skill at crocheting, and Dorothy had seen it. Two days ago, Dorothy had produced another crochet hook and a fresh skein of pink yarn, and begun teaching Cat how.

At first Cat had rejected the notion, saying she couldn't possibly learn. She'd felt awkward and silly, and couldn't seem to balance the yarn between her fingers while pulling loops through with the hook. But Dorothy didn't know the meaning of the word quit. Finally Cat had given up and given in, and found out that she loved it. So far she had learned how to make a chain and a simple crochet stitch, and she was as proud of the beginnings of her own afghan as she'd been when she'd become certified as a bounty hunter.

The first day of lessons, Wilson had come in to find both women sitting side by side on the sofa. He'd seen them with their heads down, leaning so close together that their foreheads were almost touching. When he realized what they were doing, he walked right back out again without disturbing the process.

He'd been floored by what he'd seen, but at the same time, touched by Cat's willingness to try something new. He knew from experience that she didn't like to be put in unfamiliar situations and hated to show weakness. Once in a while he would stop and watch her with his Dad or his Mom and wonder where this woman had come from. She was nothing like the bullheaded, do-it-myself female he'd known. If he hadn't known better, he might have thought the real Cat Dupree was in hiding and a body double had taken her place. It wasn't a complaint, but it made him nervous, wondering if this about-face was going to stick, or if she would suddenly switch back to her cantankerous self and nail him to the wall for bringing her here.

The morning had passed quickly, and Cat was lazing in her chair with the yellow afghan over her legs. She was wearing camel-colored pants and a white pullover sweater. Her dark hair was hanging loose, but in deference to the special day, she was wearing a tortoiseshell clip on one side.

Wilson was wearing blue jeans, a denim shirt and an old pair of brown boots. His hair, as usual, needed a cut, and he was still sporting the small gold loop in his ear. Cat was beginning to appreciate the significance of that small rebellious gesture. She, of all people, knew about rebellion.

She had her crochet work in her lap and was adding a new row when Carter suddenly pointed out the window and jumped up.

"Here comes Charlie," Carter said, and headed toward the front door.

Cat looked at Wilson, then took a deep breath. She'd gotten comfortable with his parents, but meeting his brothers and sisters was like starting from scratch. There was a whole new set of people and names to remember. The bruises on her face were fading from dark purple to a paler shade, mixed with a little green and brown. It wasn't a pretty sight, but it was what it was.

Wilson could tell Cat was nervous. He didn't know how to make this any better for her.

"Cat . . ."

Cat rolled her eyes. "Quit fussing," she said. "I'm fine. If I can put up with you, the rest of them will be a breeze."

Wilson felt a kick in the pit of his stomach. "So . . . is that what you've been doing? Putting up with me?"

Cat sighed. From the look on Wilson's face, she'd said something wrong. She just wasn't sure what it was.

"Wilson."

"Yeah?"

"Whatever it was that I said wrong, get over it. You know I don't know how to do this relationship stuff. You can either bear with me or toss me out on my ass and shut up, 'cause I'm doing the best that I can."

Wilson heard the fear in her voice and got up from his chair, and took the yarn out of her hands and set it aside. Regardless of the fact that his brother Charlie, sister-in-law Delia and their three kids were coming through the door, he kissed her square on the mouth, without regard for bumps and bruises. When he pulled back and looked up, Charlie was grinning, while the rest of the family looked a little shell-shocked.

Cat would have been more comfortable taking down a reluctant perp than meeting the rest of Wilson's family. However, if she was going down, she was going down fighting. She stood up, unaware that she'd lifted her chin in a defensive position, and waited to see what came next.

Wilson stood with her, then put his arm around her shoulders. Immediately Cat felt sheltered, as if Wilson was ready to defend her despite what anyone thought. It was a daunting emotion that she didn't know how to take.

"Everyone, this is Catherine," Wilson said. "Catherine, this is Charlie, his wife Delia and their kids."

Then the smallest of Charlie's children, three-year-old Mindy, broke the ice. "Unca Wilson . . . is she you girl fend?"

Everyone laughed, and then Delia dispatched the kids to the swing set out back and her husband to the back porch to keep an eye on them. After that she slipped her hand in the bend of Cat's elbow, eyed the state of her face and frowned at Wilson before turning to Cat.

"I'm assuming Wilson Lee didn't do this to you, honey."

Wilson frowned. "Damn, Delia . . . you just lost your status as favorite sister-in-law."

Cat couldn't help smiling. She was beginning to understand the love beneath the bullshit this family handed out. And she set her place in Wilson's heart forever when she calmly stated that she'd gotten herself into a really dangerous situation and he had saved her life.

Delia's eyes widened. "Seriously?"

"Seriously," Cat said.

Delia kissed Wilson on the cheek. "You know I was teasing . . . but this obviously wasn't a funny subject. Sorry." Then she pointed toward the kitchen. "I think I hear a potato calling my name. Come on, Catherine. I need a drink, and I know where they keep the good stuff."

Cat looked a little startled, which was what Delia was obviously aiming for. "I'm kidding," she said. "How about some of Mom's sweet tea?"

"Sounds good to me," Cat said, gave Wilson a quick look, then let herself be led away.

Soon the rest of the family arrived and the kitchen was filled with the women of the family helping Dorothy finish up the meal. The men came in long enough to snitch bites, taste-test sauces and carry heaping bowls of food to the dining room table.

Cat had slipped out of the kitchen a short while earlier on the pretext of going to the bathroom, but what she really needed was some quiet. The noise level was beyond loud and the number of people overwhelming. She'd gone down the hall toward her room, but her escape ended when she heard a baby fussing in Carter and Dorothy's bedroom.

She knew that Wilson's baby sister, Emily, had a new six-month-old baby, who'd been asleep when they'd arrived, so they'd put her on the bed to keep sleeping. Obviously baby Lynnie had awakened to find herself all alone.

The door was ajar. Cat pushed it the rest of the way open and walked in. The little baby was penned in on the middle of the mattress by pillows that had been propped up all around her to keep her from rolling off the bed. Lynnie's squawking stopped immediately when she saw a friendly face. She broke out into a big smile, and began kicking her legs and waving her arms. It was a "pick me up" plea Cat couldn't ignore.

"Hey, sweet thing," she said softly, and picked up the little girl.

The baby immediately grabbed hold of Cat's hair and pulled.

"Ouch," Cat said, then quickly sat down in the rocking chair so she could get the little fist untangled from her hair.

A few moments later she had the baby's fingers untangled. Careful of her bound ribs, she shifted the baby to her shoulder and began patting her on the back as she rocked. Almost immediately, Lynnie gave a large burp, and after that she began to relax.

Cat kept on patting and rocking, whispering soft little nothings that were strictly between Lynnie and herself. Within a few minutes the baby had fallen back asleep. Cat knew she could have put her back down, but she didn't want to. She liked holding this warm, tiny body against her heart, feeling the softness of hair and skin against her cheek.

She was so focused on the baby that she didn't hear the footsteps coming down the hall.

Wilson was a little uneasy. He hadn't noticed Cat leaving, but once everyone began to gather in the dining room, he realized she was missing. His first instinct was to panic. Someone must have said or done something to send her running. But then he quickly discarded that thought, because the woman he knew didn't run.

Still, her absence was enough to worry him. Her injuries were far from healed. All of this commotion might have been too much and sent her to her bed.

A quick look through the dining room and living room failed to turn her up. Next stop was her bedroom, so he started down the hall. He would have walked right past his parents' bedroom except that the door was open and he thought he could hear someone singing. He stopped in the doorway, then breathed a slow sigh of relief.

He'd found her.

But not in a way he would have believed if he hadn't seen it with his own eyes. His pretty, hard-nosed bounty hunter was rocking a baby and, from what he could tell, doing a damn good job of it.

"Catherine?"

Cat heard Wilson calling her name. She looked up, then put a finger to her lips, begging his silence.

He walked into the room, sat down on the side of the bed and started to speak, then swallowed around the lump in his throat and tried again.

"Once again, Catherine, you surprise me," he said softly.

Cat didn't know what to say, but she knew what she was thinking. *What would it be like to have a baby with this man?*

She slid her hand up the baby's back, rubbing it in a soft, caressing manner as she continued to rock.

"She was fussing when I walked by."

"She looks good in your arms."

Cat leaned her head against the back of

the rocker and for a moment closed her eyes, then kept them closed as she started talking.

"Wilson . . ."

"What, honey?"

"When I was in Mexico . . ."

Wilson's heart suddenly hammered against his ribcage. Something told him that she was about to take her first step toward trusting him, and he didn't want to mess it up.

"Yeah?"

Her voice trembled. "I found a dead woman and a baby in the desert."

Wilson was shocked. For a few seconds it felt as if all the air had been kicked out of his lungs. Suddenly the lack of communication from her began to make sense.

"God, Catherine . . . what a horrible thing. What did you do with . . . the bodies?"

"Oh . . . I didn't say that right. The baby was alive," she said, and then opened her eyes. They were swimming in tears.

"The mother's name was Pilar. She died of a snakebite. She and that baby were in the middle of nowhere, and I kept thinking to myself, why couldn't I have found her sooner? Then I thought of Marsha and wondered why I hadn't been able to find her before it was too late. Why are these women dead and I'm not? I didn't have a baby depending on me. Why did God keep me alive and let them die?"

Wilson sighed. Lord God . . . all this was inside her head and he'd never known it. Guilt? For God's sake, she felt guilt for not dying?

"Catherine . . . Jesus, sweetheart . . . you can't think like that. Ever. Death isn't about being fair, and it isn't about making deals with God. After all that has happened to you in your lifetime, I can't begin to guess why you're still alive." Then his voice began to shake. "I don't know why you've been spared, but I will spend the rest of my life thanking God that you were. You are precious to me, Catherine. I wish you knew how much."

Cat looked at him through a blur of tears, wanting to say what he was beginning to mean to her, but afraid to give life to the words.

"Thank you, Wilson. Thank you for loving me . . . and thank you for bearing with me through this."

Then they heard another set of footsteps coming down the hall.

"They've sent a scout to look for us. Dinner must be ready," he said.

"What about the baby?" she asked. "She

379

was crying before, and no one heard her."

Wilson got up just as his brother Charlie entered.

"Hey, you guys, Mom says dinner is ready." Then he saw the baby in Cat's arms. "Is everything okay?"

Wilson looked at Charlie and grinned. "The baby was crying."

Charlie arched an eyebrow, then grinned back. "She's a natural, isn't she, Will?"

"A natural what?" Cat asked.

"A natural mama," Charlie said.

Cat didn't know how to respond, but the declaration filled her with an odd sort of joy. She'd never thought of herself as any kind of normal female. She didn't fuss with her hair or her nails, or worry about makeup and clothes. She wouldn't ever have believed that she would care about wanting children, but she did. She'd known ever since she'd lifted Maria Elena out of her dead mother's arms and felt her baby breath against her neck that this was something she could do. She'd known what it was like to be without parents, which in her mind made her highly qualified to be a better parent than most.

"Can I bring the baby with me?" she asked.

Wilson rubbed a gentle hand over the sleeping baby's dark hair, then stroked the side of Cat's cheek with a finger. "Absolutely," he said. "Emma will thank you. She's a real mother hen with her kids, and wouldn't be happy knowing the baby was unattended and crying."

"Are you sure?" Cat said.

Charlie backed Wilson up. "Absolutely, honey. Now come on and get yourself a seat at the table before it's too late. You don't want to get stuck in the chow line behind a table full of McKays. You'll go hungry."

With Wilson's help, Cat stood up. Still carrying the sleeping baby, she walked with the men to the dining room. The moment she walked into the room carrying the sleeping baby, the noise level dropped.

Dorothy saw Cat and hurried over to her.

"Bless your heart, darling . . . I'll bet she woke up and we didn't hear her, right?"

Cat nodded.

Emma was fixing plates of food for her two older boys when she looked up and saw her baby in Cat's arms.

"Oh no . . . poor baby. Was she crying?"

"Just a little," Cat said. "She burped when I picked her up, so I rocked her back to sleep."

Emma lifted the baby out of Cat's arms. "Are you all right? You didn't hurt yourself lifting her, did you?"

"I'm fine," Cat said, and tried not to resent the loss of the baby.

"Sit here," Carter said, and pulled out a chair for her.

Wilson sat down beside her, and the meal began. Cat had felt welcomed before, but now, for some reason, she felt *accepted*. It was as if, by caring for one of their own, she'd become a part of the family instead of just a visitor.

She sat rather quietly, letting the sounds of laughter wash over her as she ate. Every now and then Wilson would give her knee a gentle squeeze, or slide his arm across the back of her chair and whisper a bit of explanation as to why the story that had been told was so funny to them.

Once he got up and refilled her glass of iced tea and brought it back to her without comment, then noticed she'd eaten all her broccoli casserole and asked if she wanted some more. And all the while he was seeing to her needs and making her a part of the family, she thought to herself, is this what love feels like? If it was, she liked being loved. And if this was so, then she might also like being in love. It was definitely something to consider.

Wilson and Cat were leaving after breakfast

382

on Tuesday. Cat had been out of the hospital for a week, and she was due to go back and get her stitches removed the next day.

Except for her still-tender ribs, she was almost as good as new. The bruising was nearly gone, except for lingering patches on her face. She was well on her way to finishing her first afghan and had a big bag of homemade cookies to take home, as did Wilson. Dorothy had even packed them some of the leftover baked ham from Sunday dinner, enough so that Cat wouldn't have to worry about shopping for food the moment she got home.

Wilson was still uneasy about what was going on at his office, although no more property had been damaged since the security cameras had gone up, which told him that whoever was messing with them also knew that the cameras had been set up. Either that was deterring him or he was waiting for something else. He tried not to think about what that might be. He had too much to live for to be careless with his life.

He had their suitcases loaded and the only thing left was saying their goodbyes. It had been great spending this much time back at home, and it was going to be a bit of an adjustment to get back into the hectic lifestyle of being a bail bondsman. He wasn't going to think about the guts it would take to step back and let Cat resume her own life, as well, seeing as that life had nearly gotten her killed. He knew she deserved to make her own choices, just as he did, but that didn't mean he had to like them.

He walked back into the house just as his mother came out of her bedroom. She was carrying the pale lavender afghan from Cat's bed.

"Catherine, I want you to have this to remember us by," Dorothy said, as she placed it in Cat's arms.

"Oh, my . . . oh, Dorothy, it's beautiful. Thank you." Cat clasped the afghan to her, then brushed it lightly across her cheek. "It's so soft."

Carter grinned. "Well, you don't know it, missy, but you've just been given Dorothy's whole hearted approval. She doesn't give away her afghans to just anyone."

The emotions Cat was feeling were spreading. She didn't know whether she wanted to laugh or cry.

"You both know I didn't want to come here," Cat said.

Dorothy giggled. "Honey, if Carter had done to me what Wilson Lee did to you, dragging me off to a bunch of strangers when I looked like hell warmed over, I would have wrung his neck. I can't imagine how awkward we made you feel. Still, you need to know that we loved having you, and we look forward to seeing you again."

Cat laughed. Hell warmed over. Yes, that was about how she'd felt. But that was then and this was now, and she knew that when she was completely healed, she would be better than before. The rage she'd carried with her for so long was gone.

"At any rate," Cat said, "I'm so glad Wilson brought me here. Thank you for all the wonderful food and for sharing your home. Oh, and thank you for teaching me to crochet and for my beautiful gift. I wish I could repay the favors."

Carter slid an arm around her shoulders and gave her a gentle hug.

"You don't repay something that was willingly given, Missy. Just don't wait too long to come back and see us, okay?"

"Okay," Cat said, and kissed him on the cheek, then kissed Dorothy, as well.

"Hey," Wilson said, as he came back into the room. "Save some of that for me."

Cat rolled her eyes, which made Carter laugh.

"What?" Wilson asked, as he reached Cat's side. "Are you making fun of me?"

"No way, McKay."

Wilson grinned. He would take all kinds of teasing just to see this look of joy on Cat's face.

"Everything is loaded," he said.

Cat sighed, watching as Wilson said his goodbyes to his parents, who followed them onto the porch, then stood and waved as Cat and Wilson got into his car.

They were still on the porch watching as Cat and Wilson topped the hill above the ranch. Cat thought back to the moment when Wilson had stopped there on their trip down. It had been her first glimpse of where he'd grown up. She'd been so afraid, and it had been for nothing.

It was, for her, proof that change wasn't necessarily a guarantee that everything would be ruined. Sometimes change was what saved a person. Maybe it was going to save her.

EIGHTEEN

Cat was home. Her apartment smelled a little musty, like rooms did when they'd been shut up for too long. Mail had piled up in her mailbox to the point that they'd begun putting the overflow into a sack. She recovered it from the apartment manager on her way up and dumped it on the kitchen counter to be looked at later.

Wilson carried her bags into her bedroom, and took the laundry bag full of her dirty clothes to the small utility room off the kitchen and laid it on top of the washer. From there he made a quick check of her refrigerator.

"Hey, honey, if you'll make a grocery list of what you might need for the next few days, I'll go get it for you."

"You don't need to," she said. "I'll get it myself when —" Then she sighed. "Crap. I don't have a car anymore, do I?"

She moved to the counter, picked up a

pad and pen, and began jotting down the necessities.

Wilson watched her concentrating, studying the way her eyebrow arched when she was thinking and noticing that she chewed on her lower lip as she wrote — taking notes on the woman who'd stolen his heart.

When she looked up and caught him staring, she stopped. For a few moments, they said nothing. Then Cat laid down the pen and walked toward him.

Wilson's heartbeat stuttered. What was she up to?

She touched the side of his face, then the earring, then traced the edge of his lower lip with her thumb. She saw his eyes darken and his nostrils flare as her hand moved to the center of his chest. She could feel the rhythm of his pulse against her palm as she looked up.

"I have something to say to you," she said.

Wilson stilled. *Please, God, don't let her tell me it's over.*

Cat was afraid, as if she was about to lose her sense of self, but she'd learned something this past week. She'd learned that she didn't want to lose this man. He needed to know that she would do whatever it took to keep him.

"Ever since we've met, I've been mean to

you. I know it, because I did it deliberately. I didn't have space inside myself for anything but hate and revenge. I treated you like shit. I didn't fully appreciate the lengths you went to, to help me, and for that, I am sorry."

Wilson cupped her face. "You don't have to say this."

"Yes, I do," she said. "I need to hear the words coming out of my own mouth, and you need to hear them from me."

"Okay . . . so talk to me, honey."

Cat nodded. "I know how you feel about me, because you told me. What I didn't tell you was how scared that made me feel."

Wilson frowned. "Scared? Having someone tell you he loves you scares you?"

"Like nothing I can describe. What you don't know is that I've never — in my whole life — been in love. To me, that meant giving up what I viewed as . . . I guess . . . myself. I've had sex, but none too often, and never with the same man twice. Then you dropped into my life. So all the while I was trying to find Marsha's murderer, and then running to hell and back after Tutuola, I kept thinking of you. Every so often you would pop into my thoughts, and it bothered me. I didn't know what to call it, but I couldn't get you out of my head." She cast

389

a sideways glance at him, then sighed. "Then, after a while, I couldn't get you out of my heart."

Relief swept through Wilson at a rate so fast he felt light-headed. This wasn't the brush-off after all.

Cat started to put her arms around his neck, then winced as the sore muscles shifted over her still-healing ribs.

"Allow me," Wilson said softly, and pulled her close.

Cat laid her cheek against his chest, then wrapped her arms around his waist.

"What I'm trying to say is, don't quit on me, Wilson. I want your love. I want to be what you want me to be. I just have to figure out how to accept what you're giving me without being an ass, and more importantly, I have to learn how to give."

Wilson lifted her chin until they were locked into each other's gaze. He wanted — no, needed — to hear her say the words. Just once.

"Give? Give what, baby?"

Cat froze. For a moment she was acutely aware of the feel of Wilson's breath on her cheek, the tick of the kitchen clock hanging on the wall and a faint sound of sirens from somewhere outside the apartment. Through a trick of the light, she saw her own reflection in his eyes, and for a moment she thought that she'd already lost herself.

Wilson sighed. He'd pushed her too far, too fast. It was time to let her off the hook.

"It's okay, Catherine. You'll say what you want to say when you're ready to say it, and you know —"

Cat put a finger across his lips, silencing him.

"Love, Wilson. I need to be able to give you whole-hearted, unabashed, unadulterated love. And for God's sake, I need to be able to say it without feeling like I'm going to throw up."

Wilson chuckled, then kissed the top of her head.

"Lord, honey . . . I don't want to make you sick. I just want to love you. And if you can't say the words, I don't care. As long as you're a willing participant in the process, I'll be happy."

Cat sighed. "Thank you. Thank you for bearing with me. I can only imagine how stupid all this seems to you, but —"

Wilson's smile disappeared. This time, he was the one interrupting her.

"You're worth whatever it takes, so cut yourself some slack." Then he lowered his head.

Their lips touched.

Wilson groaned.

Cat sighed.

Wilson cupped her face with both hands as he deepened the pressure on her lips. Kissing Catherine was one of his favorite things. That she was still alive for him to be doing this was something he would never take for granted again.

Wilson was the first to stop. "Lady . . . when your ribs get well . . ."

Cat's lips were still tingling. She was smiling as she looked up at him.

"I'll be sure to let you know," she said.

Wilson groaned. "Where's that damned grocery list?"

Cat handed it to him.

"I won't be long," he said.

"I'm not going anywhere," she said. "At least not until tomorrow, at which time I am going shopping for a new car."

"For now, why don't you rest a little? I'll be back soon."

"Maybe I will," Cat said. "But I want to call Art first. Tell him I'm back."

Wilson pointed at her. "But not going back to work until you've been cleared medically. Remember that."

Cat made a face. "I'm not stupid."

"No, but you're sure hardheaded."

"I'll cop to that. As for the shopping, I

don't have much cash here, so I'll have to write you a check for the cost when you come back."

"It's just a couple of sacks of groceries," he said.

"And I can afford to pay for them."

Wilson held up his hands. "Okay. I get the message." He pointed to her bottle of pain pills. "Take one of those and go lie down . . . please."

Cat nodded. "Yes, I think I will."

"I'll let myself out," Wilson said, and winked at Cat as he left.

Cat waited until she heard the front door close, then shook out a pill, downed it with a sip of water and headed for her bedroom. Once inside, she kicked off her shoes, pulled off her pants and sweater, and started to pull back the covers, then turned around and picked up her gift from Dorothy instead. The afghan was soft against her skin as she crawled onto the bed with it. When she pulled it up and over her, the faint scent of lavender from the sachets that Dorothy had put among the folds reminded her of the woman who'd made it. She fell asleep wrapped in the memories and the love with which it had been made.

Jimmy Franks was in jail. He'd been picked

up making a meth buy. Houston was so pissed at him, he wouldn't even come see him in lockup, and Jimmy heard that he'd left town.

Jimmy knew he'd blown it with his brother, but Houston didn't understand. When you had a need like he did, you had to feed it, only things hadn't quite worked out as he'd planned. Not only did he miss the buy, but he was beginning to detox in jail. Things could be worse, but right now, Jimmy couldn't think how. He was awaiting arraignment, but uncertain if bail would be set. He'd been out on bail when he'd been picked up the second time. He didn't know what that meant to his future, but it wasn't looking good, and he blamed Wilson McKay. Wilson had been the reason he'd been arrested the first time, now this.

"Damn you, McKay," Jimmy muttered, then slammed his fist against the wall of his cell. Pain shot up his arm to his shoulder, which only added to his fury. "Payback is a bitch."

"Hey, shorty . . . shut the hell up!" someone yelled.

Jimmy grabbed hold of the bars of his cell and shoved his face up against them.

"Come over here and make me, honey!" he yelled back, then slammed the flat of his hand against the bars before all but throwing himself onto his cot. All he needed was to get out, and then they would see. By God, they'd all see.

Cat had a new SUV — a gray Chevrolet Trailblazer, complete with a GPS tracking system that included a separate phone and a medical alert program. If she should have a wreck or become disabled in any way, her GPS system would be able to locate her whereabouts within twenty feet and dispatch medical or mechanical help if needed. It was a safeguard that made Wilson as happy as it made her.

Her stitches were out, and, according to her doctor, her ribs were healing nicely. Within a week or so, she would be able to go back to work. Art was a little nervous about giving his okay, but Cat was itching to become productive again. In the meantime, she had to satisfy herself with waiting, and the fact that Wilson was coming over after he got off work was something worth waiting for.

She'd promised to feed him. Her culinary skills were next to non-existent, but Joe Bob's Pit Barbeque was only a mile from her apartment, and tonight Joe Bob was cooking.

She'd stopped off there less than an hour ago, and was in the act of putting the food in the refrigerator to be reheated upon Wilson's arrival when her phone rang. She set down a carton of coleslaw and picked up the phone.

"Hello."

"Hey, honey, it's me."

"Me, who?" Cat said.

Wilson chuckled. The fact that she was able to joke with him was a good sign that she was at ease.

"The me who's gonna come over and kiss you senseless," he said.

"Oh. That me. So . . . what's keeping you?"

Wilson growled softly into the phone. "You do know that you're driving me crazy, right?"

"If I'm driving, then that means I'm in charge, and you know how I like that," Cat said.

Wilson laughed out loud, and she grinned. This relationship thing was getting easier by the day. Making Wilson laugh felt good.

He was still chuckling when he finally remembered why he'd called.

"I'm going to be getting out of here a little earlier than I thought. Is it okay to come over?"

"Come whenever," Cat said. "I'm here."

"See you soon, love," Wilson said, and started to hang up.

"Hey, Wilson?"

He put the phone back to his ear. "Yeah, honey?"

Cat wanted to say it. *Love.* It was a four-letter word, and God knew she'd used plenty of those in her lifetime. Why this one wouldn't come out as easily was a mystery to her.

"Uh . . . we're having barbeque."

"Sounds good," he said. "Be there shortly."

The dial tone ended whatever else Cat had been trying to get said.

"Crap," she muttered, and hung up the receiver. "What the hell is wrong with me? It's only three words. I love you. I. Love. You. I love you. I *love* you. I *love* you."

Disgusted with herself, she took the rest of the food from the sacks and stuck them in the fridge. It wasn't quite four o'clock. Even if Wilson got here before five, there was no way he would want to eat so early.

She rubbed her midriff, testing for soreness. Her ribs hardly hurt at all, and for the first time in days she was thinking of more than kissing and cuddling.

John Tiger laid the last of his paperwork on

LaQueen's desk, then glanced outside.

"It's gonna rain," he said.

Wilson looked up from his desk to the gathering clouds outside. "When did that happen?"

John shrugged as he continued to stare out the window.

LaQueen was at the courthouse, but her umbrella was hanging on the coat hook behind her desk. John pointed to it.

"LaQueen is gonna be mad. She doesn't like her hair to get wet."

"No woman wants that," Wilson muttered, and went back to his paperwork.

John stood up, then walked to the plate-glass storefront for a closer look.

"It's really getting dark."

"You already said that," Wilson said.

"No. Before, I said it was going to rain. *Then* I said it was getting dark."

Wilson wadded up a piece of paper and threw it at John's back.

John was grinning as he turned around. "What?"

"I have an idea," Wilson said. "Why don't you take her umbrella to her down at the courthouse? She walked down there, so she'll really get wet if it begins to rain before she gets back."

John grabbed the umbrella and headed

for the back door where he'd parked his truck.

"You are so whipped," Wilson said, as John hurried past.

John paused. "I'm doing exactly what I want to do," he said. "That makes me one lucky dog, not a whipped one."

Before Wilson could comment, they heard the front door rattle, something that always signaled a strong gust of wind.

"Hey, lucky dog, you better hurry. Wind is getting stronger."

John bolted, his long hair flying out behind him as he ran. A few moments later Wilson saw John's pickup come around the corner and head up the street in the direction of the courthouse, a few blocks away.

He glanced at the clock and thought of Cat. As soon as John and LaQueen got back, he was going to leave them to it and go over to her apartment early.

He sat for a few seconds, sorting through the tasks he needed to do tomorrow, then reached for his coffee cup, only to find it empty. When he got up to refill it, he found the pot empty, as well. He couldn't complain. John didn't drink coffee, and LaQueen didn't drink it after three o'clock, which meant he was probably the one who'd emptied the pot.

He dumped the used filter and coffee grounds into the trash, put in a new filter and measured out coffee, then took the carafe to the sink to get water. He was filling it when he heard the front door open.

"Be right with you," he said, as he poured the water into the coffeemaker, then slid the carafe in place and pushed the start button.

He turned around, then froze.

There was a gun pointed straight at him, and the man holding it was unkempt and dirty, fidgeting from one foot to the other. From what Wilson could see, his pupils were blown, and he was nursing a runny nose. Wilson had seen too many junkies not to recognize the symptoms.

He also recognized the man with the gun. He'd filed charges against him only a few weeks ago.

Jimmy Franks.

Suddenly all the vandalism and harassment began to make sense.

"What the hell do you think you're doing?" Wilson asked.

Jimmy giggled and did a little sidestep. "I think I'm gonna shoot your ass."

"You're already in enough trouble, Franks. Just put that gun down, walk out the door and we'll call it quits."

"You're not in charge here!" Jimmy

shouted. "I'm in charge! You messed me up, man! You had my ass thrown in jail for nothing! Nothing, man!"

"You manhandled my secretary, then threatened her, and we both know it."

Jimmy snorted. "Hell, that woman ain't no secretary. She's just a nig—"

"Shut your mouth!" Wilson snapped, unwilling to let the man even utter the word.

Jimmy flinched, then cursed. "You don't tell me what to do! I'm the man. I'm the one with the gun. You don't tell me nothin'!" he yelled.

Wilson's hand was still on the counter, his fingers only inches away from the rapidly filling coffeepot. It was obvious that this conversation was only going to go downhill, so he made his move. He grabbed the half-filled pot of hot coffee and flung it toward Jimmy, then made a dive for his desk, where he kept his gun.

Jimmy saw it coming but was too high to figure out what to do first. He cursed, then moved. It was a mistake. He should have moved first, then cursed, because the contents of the pot, as well as the pot itself, hit him square in the chest. The scalding liquid soaked into his coat and splashed up into his face. In a rage, he began firing.

Wilson was already in the air when the

bullets began flying. His fingers were on the drawer when the first bullet hit his chest, spinning him around and dropping him like a rock. Blood began flowing out of the open wound and pooling beneath his back as another shot hit him in the leg. After that, everything went black.

Jimmy wiped his sleeve across his burning cheeks and then laughed.

"I got you, you son of a bitch, just like I promised I would. Payback, man! You had it coming . . . ain't payback a bitch?"

Then he bolted out of the office and into the street, still carrying the gun. The wind was rising, the sky dark with scurrying clouds. He felt wild — as wild as the oncoming storm.

A passerby had heard the shots and was already hurrying toward the building when he saw a man come running out. He ducked into an alley as Jimmy turned and ran in the other direction. As soon as Jimmy was gone, the passerby ran into the office, found Wilson on the floor and dialed 911.

It was after six. Cat kept telling herself not to worry. Even though Wilson was late, she was sure something had come up to delay him. She knew the business. She was well aware of how crazy it could be. She'd occupied her time by crocheting another four rows onto her growing afghan. Another thirty minutes went by, and then there was a knock on her door.

"Finally," she said, setting the crocheting aside and running for the door.

The warmth in her heart had already spread to a smile. She yanked the door open, then froze.

It was a tall dark-haired man all right, but his hair wasn't short and spiky, it was long and straight, and hung well below his shoulders. And he didn't have a scar on his cheek or an earring in his ear, just a bear-claw necklace around his neck. She frowned.

"What . . . ?"

"You Catherine Dupree?"

Her frown deepened. Any time someone knew her and she didn't know them, she was suspicious.

"Yes."

"My name is John Tiger. I —"

Cat's eyes widened. "You work for Wilson." Cat looked beyond John to the empty hallway. "Where is he?"

John took a deep breath. This was hell, and it wasn't going to get better any time soon.

"Wilson . . . uh, Wilson was —"

Cat's heart dropped. Her gut was already

tying itself into knots when she grabbed his wrist. "What happened to him?"

John Tiger shuddered. The look in her eyes had gone from calm to something he would expect to see in a wild animal.

"He was shot. He —"

She felt the room spinning around her. Shot? God, no! *No!* Not Wilson! Her grip tightened on his wrist. She was afraid to ask, but she had to know.

"Is he alive?"

"Yes, he's at Dallas Memorial. His secretary, LaQueen Baldwin, told me to come tell you and see if you need a ride to the —"

"He's alive. He's alive. Oh, thank you, God." The knot in her stomach eased just a little as she began to take stock of what had to be done.

"No. I don't need help. I'll take myself," Cat said, and grabbed her coat, shoulder bag and car keys from the hall table, and pushed past him on her way out the door.

John felt her intensity in every fiber of his being. He knew the news he'd brought was devastating. He also knew from the way she'd reacted that she had no business driving herself. He shut the door to her apartment, then ran down the hall to catch her. He slid into the elevator with her just as the doors were shutting.

"Miss Dupree, you're upset, and I want you to let me drive you to the hospital. The last thing Wilson would want is for you to be injured again."

Cat punched the button for the lobby, then fixed John with a fiery glare.

"Upset? Hell, yes, I'm upset. That doesn't mean I've lost my damned mind. I appreciate your concern, but I will drive myself."

"Still, I —"

"Do they know who did it?" Cat asked.

John sighed. "Yes, we know who did it. It was caught on the security camera in the office."

"Did they catch him?"

"No, but there's a BOLO out for him now. I'm sure —"

Cat poked a finger in John Tiger's chest. "Here's what you *can* be sure of. You tell the Dallas police department that they'd better find that bastard soon, or I'll do it for them, and when I find him, I'll bring him back in pieces."

The elevator doors opened, and she strode away without looking back.

John was so stunned by the rage in her voice that he forgot to get out of the elevator. The doors were already closing when he came to himself, thrust his arm into the opening and pushed through.

All the way to the car, he kept thinking of Catherine Dupree. He was beginning to understand Wilson's fascination with the woman. John had expected her to be horrified by his news, maybe even hysterical. He would have expected her to cry. He hadn't expected the female warrior who had come to life right in front of him.

By the time he got to the parking lot, she was already gone.

Cat was beyond scared. This couldn't be happening. Not now. Not when she'd finally let herself believe there was such a thing as being happy. She drove through traffic, flying through yellow lights and taking corners on two wheels. Even though the rational part of her mind was telling her this wasn't her fault, she couldn't help but think that she'd somehow jinxed him, too.

Everybody she loved always died. She should have known better. She should have been thinking of someone besides herself.

He'd been fine until she'd come along. She'd tried to tell him right off that she wasn't into love, but he wouldn't listen. He knew her history. She didn't know what she'd done in a former life that was so awful that she had to atone for it now, but for anyone who was listening, she was heartily sorry.

She braked for a red light, and for the first time allowed herself tears. Her vision blurred, and there was an ache in her chest that kept getting bigger and bigger. Her fingers tightened around the steering wheel, and she started to shake.

"God . . . please, please . . . don't let him die."

A horn sounded behind her. She looked up, saw that the light had turned green and took off through the intersection. A short while later she was running through the parking lot and into the hospital.

LaQueen had never met Catherine Dupree, although she had her own opinions about her. Any woman who had caused as much grief to Wilson as *she* had couldn't be all that. She had a mental image of some pretty, pushy female who didn't know what was good for her.

But all that changed when Cat appeared in the surgery waiting room. She took one look around at the people who were waiting, zeroed in on LaQueen and headed straight for her.

LaQueen looked up, saw the tall, leggy woman trending to skinny, and stiffened.

Could this be her? The woman had long black hair, an angular face and a gaze so intense LaQueen felt instantly branded. The closer she came, the more details LaQueen could see. There were fresh scars on her face, as well as the fading remains of bruises. But it was the thick, pink, ropy scar on her throat that shot her first assessment. She didn't know what had happened to this woman, but she wasn't a pretty piece of fluff. This woman had been through fire and lived to tell. LaQueen had some tough times in her past, as well, and recognized a kindred spirit.

She took a deep breath, then stood up.

Cat stopped in front of her, unaware that her eyes were swimming in tears or that her chin was trembling.

"Are you LaQueen?" she asked.

LaQueen nodded. "And you are Catherine."

"Where is he?" Cat asked.

"In surgery. Sit down before you fall down," LaQueen said, and pulled Cat down onto the sofa beside her.

Cat sat, wadded her hands into fists and jammed them into her lap.

"How long has he been in?" Cat asked.

"About two hours."

"Jesus," Cat whispered, and then leaned

back and closed her eyes.

"I already prayed to Him," LaQueen said. "But it won't hurt to add yours to the pot."

Cat shuddered, then looked at LaQueen. "He can't die."

LaQueen sighed. She knew better. People died all the time, whether you liked it or not. "He's in God's hands," she said.

Cat shook her head. "No. You don't understand," she whispered. "He can't die. He can't . . . die."

After that, there was little to be said. A few minutes later, John Tiger entered the waiting room. Cat didn't acknowledge his presence. She couldn't. He was the one who'd brought the bad news. Instead, she watched the clock. Another hour passed before a doctor came in.

"Is the McKay family here?" he asked.

Cat stood up. LaQueen and John followed. "His parents are on their way from Austin," LaQueen said. "Until they get here, we're it."

The doctor nodded to them, then began explaining what procedures had been done.

"The surgery went well, although he lost a lot of blood. We had to transfuse him twice, but the bleeding finally stopped. Both bullets were through and throughs, which was good. They missed the bones. He'll be in recovery for about another hour, then we'll move him to his room. I suggest you all go home and get some rest. For a while, we'll keep him heavily sedated to keep him immobile, so you won't be able to talk to him."

"Is he going to be okay?" Cat asked.

The doctor hesitated, then nodded. "Barring any complications, I would expect him to have a full recovery."

Cat's eyes welled. Tears spilled over, then ran down her cheeks. She took a deep breath, then walked out of the room without looking back. She got all the way to the bathroom before she came undone. At that point, she started to sob.

LaQueen walked in right behind her, took one look at Cat and knew she'd been right to follow. She grabbed Catherine by the shoulders, turned her around, then pulled her into her arms.

"Go ahead and cry, honey girl. Cry it all out, 'cause when you see Wilson, you'll be needing to put a smile on your face for him."

Cat cried until she was sick to her stomach and her head was throbbing to the point of detonation. Then she pulled out of La-Queen's arms and headed for the sink. She sloshed her face with cold water over and over until the swelling in her eyes was beginning to subside.

When she looked up in the mirror, she saw LaQueen standing behind her, watching.

Cat reached for a paper towel and swiped it over her face, then tossed it in the trash.

"Thank you," she said, and started out the door.

"Where you going, girl?"

"To wait. I can't leave. There's something I need to tell Wilson."

"You can tell him tomorrow," LaQueen said.

"No. I've learned a long time ago that, for a lot of people, tomorrow never comes."

NINETEEN

Cat had been there all night. She'd been in the hallway when they'd brought him to his room. She'd sat by his bedside through every shift change, through all the nurses' visits, watching them taking his blood pressure, readjusting drips and injecting pain meds into his IV. Everything that was said about him, or done to him, she was there. Finally, when the hustle of settling in a new patient had subsided, they were alone.

She moved to the bed, then laid her hand on his arm.

"Wilson, it's me, Cat. Somewhere in there, I hope you can hear me, because there's something I need to tell you."

She paused, watching his face. Except for the slight rise and fall of his chest and the steady beep of the heart monitor, she would have thought he was dead. She moved her hand a little farther up his arm, feeling the tone of his muscles, remembering his strength, remembering all the times he'd held her and she'd shoved him away, and she wanted to weep. She leaned down until her lips were only inches away from his ear and then spoke, clearly and distinctly, so there was no danger of misunderstanding.

"I love you, Wilson." Her voice shook, but she kept on talking. "Do you hear me? I love you. You are my heart. You are the reason I wake up happy, and the reason I sleep without nightmares. Rest well, my darling, and know that I am here."

Then she kissed the side of his face and briefly touched her forehead to his before pulling back. She'd said them, the all-powerful, all-terrifying words that now seemed so easy. If only he had been able to hear them.

Along about midnight, Carter and Dorothy arrived. They walked into his room, saw Cat and immediately went to her.

Dorothy's face crumpled as she threw her arms around Cat and wept. "Catherine . . . oh, Catherine . . . how could this happen?"

A muscle jerked in the side of Cat's jaw as she hugged Dorothy back. "It's the business," she muttered. "The miserable business of bailing crooks out of jail."

Carter hugged her; then he and Dorothy moved to Wilson's bedside.

Cat backed away, giving them some space. She kept watching Wilson's face, searching for a sign that he knew they were there, that he was aware of how much he was loved. But just like before, there was no sign that he'd heard.

They'd been there for less than five minutes when she heard a distinct skip in the pattern of his heartbeat.

Breath froze in the back of her throat as she bolted toward the bed and reached for his wrist. His pulse was slow and thready. The beep skipped again, then sounded twice in rapid succession.

Cat reached for the call button just as the monitor flatlined. There was a brief moment when she felt and saw and heard everything around her in slow motion.

The shock on Carter's face.

The shriek from Dorothy's lips.

The immobility of Wilson's body.

The life that was no longer there.

Cat grabbed his wrist, as if holding on to his physical being could keep him with her.

"Wilson!" Her scream was shattering, her body shaking with fear and rage. "Don't you do this!" she cried, as she threw herself across his body, trying to hold his soul to earth. "Don't do this . . . don't do this . . . don't you dare die on me, too!"

She heard herself screaming, but it didn't change a thing.

Wilson's heart had stopped beating. Someone pulled her off the bed and shoved her aside.

She stood against the wall as her own heartbeat began to skip. A doctor was shouting orders faster than the nurses could obey them.

Dorothy was weeping. Carter's face was frozen in a grimace of disbelief. It was a nightmare, but without the relief of an awakening. Everything that was happening was happening now, and too fast for Cat to take in.

The doctor suddenly shouted the word "Clear!" The nurses lifted their hands from the bed just as the doctor slapped two paddles onto Wilson's chest and hit the trigger. Wilson jerked as if the bed had been jostled, but the flat line still registered. "Clear!" the doctor shouted again, and again Wilson's heart was zapped.

Nothing.

Everything within Cat's vision tunneled down to the man lying on the bed. She stared at the flat line on the monitor until her vision blurred, then she screamed, her voice raw and shaking with rage.

"Wilson! Don't you go and die on me,

too, goddamn it! You can't do that! Do you hear me? Don't you dare go and do that to me!"

The doctor was incensed.

"Get her out of here!" he shouted.

Cat was sobbing, deep, ugly sobs that burned the back of her throat, but she knew enough to know that she wasn't being moved anywhere. She glared at the doctor, then grabbed the foot of Wilson's bed.

"I'm not going anywhere, and neither is he!" she sobbed.

Before anyone could move to do his bidding, there was a beep on the heart monitor, then a second, then another, until the heartbeat was registering once again at a normal rhythm.

The doctor's eyes widened as he stared at the monitor, then back at Cat Dupree.

"Well, lady . . . looks like he heard you loud and clear," he muttered, then began a quick assessment of Wilson's vitals.

Once he was satisfied that the crisis had passed, he issued a few new orders to the nurse, then looked at Cat.

"Is he going to be okay?" Cat asked.

"It appears so," he said, then put a hand on her shoulder in what was meant to be a comforting gesture, felt the disapproval in her body at being touched, and left.

Dorothy and Carter moved to stand beside Cat; then, without speaking, both put their arms around her and just held her. Long minutes passed as they stood in silence, watching the steady rhythm of Wilson's heartbeat being registered on the monitor.

Then something began to change. Wilson's eyelids fluttered once. Cat saw them and quickly moved to his side.

"Wilson, I'm here," she said.

Wilson inhaled slowly; then Cat saw him trying to lick his lips. She grabbed a washcloth, wet it at the sink, then went back to his bedside and dabbed it along his mouth.

"Your mother is here, honey, and so is your dad. You're going to be okay. Do you hear me? You're going to be okay."

Wilson's eyelids opened slowly. Cat could see that it was taking him a few moments to focus, but when he saw her face, she knew he recognized her.

"Hey, you," she said softly. "It's me. Cat."

He blinked once, then closed his eyes as the medicine began pulling him back under. He fought the feeling, knowing there was something he'd come back to tell her. He could feel her hands on his face and the nubby texture of the wet washcloth against his lips. He took another breath, willing himself to talk before he passed out again, knowing that she needed to hear what he had to say.

"Catherine."

Cat gasped, then leaned down.

"I'm here, Wilson. I'm here."

"I hur oo."

His voice was so soft, and his speech so tangled from the drugs in his system, that Cat couldn't understand what he'd said.

"What, honey? What did you say?" she asked.

Wilson felt her hand against the curve of his cheek and leaned into it, taking his strength from her, and repeated his words.

"I heard your call," he said. "I came back . . . for you."

The jolt from his words rocked Cat to the core. She leaned down and kissed the side of his face. When she stood up, she staggered.

Carter caught her and promptly sat her down in a chair, with orders to stay there.

Cat nodded without taking her gaze from Wilson's face. He'd come back to her, and, God willing, he would get well and they would live happily ever after, just like in the movies. Of course, that would be right after she saw Jimmy Houston drawn and quartered.

Then they would live happily ever after, but not before.

ABOUT THE AUTHOR

Sharon Sala is a *New York Times* best-selling author who's written over sixty-nine books under her name, as well as her pen name, Dinah McCall. Her emotionally charged stories are about ordinary people whose experiences are often larger than life. During her writing career, her reading audience has expanded to include a large number of men, joining the thousands and thousands of women who've been reading her for years.

We hope you have enjoyed this Large Print book. Other Thorndike, Wheeler, and Chivers Press Large Print books are available at your library or directly from the publishers.

For information about current and upcoming titles, please call or write, without obligation, to:

Publisher
Thorndike Press
295 Kennedy Memorial Drive
Waterville, ME 04901
Tel. (800) 223-1244

or visit our Web site at:

http://gale.cengage.com/thorndike

OR

Chivers Large Print
published by BBC Audiobooks Ltd
St James House, The Square
Lower Bristol Road
Bath BA2 3SB
England
Tel. +44(0) 800 136919
email: bbcaudiobooks@bbc.co.uk
www.bbcaudiobooks.co.uk

All our Large Print titles are designed for easy reading, and all our books are made to last.